The Enigma Variations

Cari Dubiel

DUSKBOUND
BOOKS

For Ed

Author's Note

I wrote this book in 2017-18, when my agent at the time had shopped it to traditional publishers. As such, the story takes place in 2018. The math doesn't work out otherwise.

Trigger warning: the novel contains self-harm and a struggle with addiction. Take care of yourself while reading.

Local Woman Dies in Highway Crash

CHESTERFIELD, Ohio - A local woman is dead after colliding with an oil tanker truck on Route 271.

Hannah Madison, 38, a bartender based in Mayfield Heights, was driving north around 2 a.m. Friday night. According to witnesses, Madison rear-ended the tanker truck before her Ford Focus burst into flames.

Although Madison's remains could not be located, authorities are investigating whether Madison was intoxicated at the time of the accident.

Madison is survived by her mother and her 15-year-old daughter.

Comments (26)

Arthurchester80 I graduated with her. She was always drunk.

Ancillarytruth probably texting

Graylady123 How horrible. That poor little girl.

XxHeavenLyxx what a waste of a human being

Prologue

Once he finished the letters, the game would begin.

He fought to keep the fountain pen steady. His hand shook and ached. But he continued, scratching the tiny figures into the parchment, watching them emerge as he bit his lip in concentration. A bead of blood burst from his cracked skin, and he tasted copper. His stomach turned.

It had been a horrific six months. One moment his life had been easy-breezy. Privileged. He'd moved through the world with a fluid grace, happy even when attending meeting after meeting with distributors and investors. The work never drained him. He had so many assistants, employees to bring him coffee and water and dinner. He had nothing to think about but the work, and the work nourished him every day.

Until he saw the article.

His closest advisers often accused him of dramatics, and if he was being fair, they weren't totally wrong. They seemed to think he thrived on drama, but that wasn't it. His feelings were big, important. Emotions that fired him from the inside, electrifying his core. That passion had given him the strength to create his empire.

But it also fueled him now, as he grieved.

Hannah. How had he forgotten her? She'd faded into the background of his big life as it only got bigger. Reading the comments on the article, seeing what everyone in that foul town thought of her death—it enraged him. No wonder she'd died. She was already a ghost.

These six months, he'd planned this game. To punish them. They deserved to feel the pain he felt.

What would their faces look like when they opened the envelopes? He took a curious delight in controlling them from afar.

He shifted his long legs under the desk, brushed sweat from his bare forehead. Even the icy water in his glass couldn't soothe the pain in his belly. Hunger was a cruel master. But it wouldn't detract him from his task. If he had to stop to rest, he would. His energy wasn't what it used to be. Besides, his four-poster bed, with its luxe sheets and fluffy pillows, sat only a few feet behind him. He loved this room, this house. He'd spent so much time making it perfect, and it served him well.

Just as they would.

The sun had set hours ago, and his room was lit only by candlelight now. The scent of cloves and allspice filled the air. He'd opted for a fall candle to set the mood. Halloween would be here soon, the night of spirits and ghosts. His favorite holiday.

Tonight, though. A crisp October night. He didn't know the day of the week—he'd lost track. To anyone else, the time would pass unnoticed, disappearing in the haze of a television screen or a social media app. He pictured all those glazed eyes out there in the world, the bored furrowing of brows, bottoms sinking into sagging couches. Those erased minds. For those people, this night meant nothing. But for him—and for the players of his game—tonight was a new beginning.

His stomach shifted, and he tried a sip of water. The liquid was cool on his broken lip. He felt the swallow all the way down his throat. He stuck out his tongue and focused on the pen, giving just enough pressure to keep it moving without tearing the parchment.

When he finished, he laid the final sheet aside to dry and closed his eyes. The strains of *The Enigma Variations* came small and tinny from his Bluetooth speaker, but for all the pride he felt, he may as well have been conducting the symphony.

Once the ink was set, he slid the papers into the envelopes he'd pre-addressed. Then, as the music swelled, he reached for his seal and tray. He flicked a lighter and held it to the wax. The small solid piece melted and spread, a crimson pool, the scent mingling with that of the pumpkin spice candle. He crashed the seal into the wax and then onto the envelope. He did this three times.

He admired his handiwork: the final piece he'd set on the board, but the first piece they would uncover.

"This dark saying," he said softly, leaning back, breathing out as his insides settled. "This will begin our game."

Part One

From "The Great Genius of Edward Elgar," a high school paper by Jude Lassiter

Edward Elgar was a British composer, who lived from 1857 until 1934. He is best known for his graduation anthem, Pomp and Circumstance, which is played around the world at ceremonies big and small. However, Elgar's genius was not limited to music. He was a master codemaker. He hid puzzles in his music, in letters, and there is even one code that has never been broken: The Dorabella Cipher. Who was this brilliant man, and why have his mysteries been locked away for so many years? In this paper, I will tell you.

COMMENT BY JUDE'S *English teacher, Mr. Peachtree—Good use of specific examples. Avoid using the first person in a research paper. Try not to overstate the composer's importance. I'm intrigued, but I won't be if the paper continues to use hyperbole as a device.*

1

Dora

I almost didn't find the letter.

Every day, Grandma marched down the driveway to the mailbox. She was vigilant about it, sorting Mom's stuff into a separate pile, then making sure to recycle the ads. She'd sigh, like Mom's memory was weighing her down. All summer, Grandma made phone calls, sent in copies of the death certificate.

But she was out getting her hair done. It was Saturday, and she'd left me home alone. The house felt so empty and quiet as I sat in the kitchen with my salami sandwich, my English paper open on the laptop in front of me. I heard the mail truck trundle down the road, so I went outside to see if there was anything good in the delivery.

The envelope stuck out because it was red. Not that Christmas or Valentine's Day primary color type. This letter was blood-scarlet. It was addressed to me in a spidery handwriting: *Miss Dora Madison.*

My grandmother and I weren't the kind of people who got mysterious messages. We weren't in a secret society. I couldn't even join Key Club because she refused to pick me up from the evening meetings.

"We'll talk when you get your license," she said, and I resigned myself to my pariah status, too lame for the nerd club. I wasn't old enough to get my license, but if I could drive, I would've left Chesterfield long ago.

I slid the envelope from the stack and left the mail in its disorderly state on the end table by the front door. I crept into the kitchen, grabbed a butter knife, and dragged it across the seal.

A piece of parchment fluttered out, folded in half. I opened it, but my fingers felt too awkward for the delicacy of the paper. I smoothed it flat on the kitchen counter, so I could read without damaging it.

But there were no words. A line of figures crossed the page, their stick arms and feet posed in all different directions. Some waved flags, small rectangles drawn where their hands would have been. I turned the sheet over, but I found no other markings. Only the tiny approximations of people.

I picked up the envelope again and examined it. No return address. How would the sender ensure I'd receive it? Did they even care? I gritted my teeth. I didn't like it when people deliberately turned simple things into games. Bullies had messed me up enough in grade school. That was what happened when you had no real dad, your mom was a drunk, and the bus was filled with daily taunts of "Dora the Explorer."

Oh, and now my mom was dead. Didn't change much, though. Not like I ever saw her.

My grandma said I'd get used to the bullying. She said it was part of high school, part of growing up. But I heard it in the halls—a whisper as I passed a locker, the whistling of the show's insufferable theme song echoing from behind me. I was sure when Nickelodeon created that innocent educational cartoon, they never thought it could cause a person so much angst. Oh, well. Those kids would never know how much they hurt me. Once I left Chesterfield, I'd never look back.

I returned to cleaning, determined to ignore the envelope.

2

Patrick

I still paid bills with paper. Checks and pens. Envelopes and stamps.

My wife thought I was crazy. "Wouldn't it be so much easier to set them all up as auto-debit?" she'd scold on the regular. I didn't know why she cared. It shouldn't have mattered to her if she didn't have to think about it—which she didn't.

Once a week, I poured a cup of coffee and retreated into my office. French doors opened from the sunlit master bedroom into the nook, which was lined with shelves and wood paneling. My desk filled one corner. That morning, I pulled the beaded cord attached to the banker's lamp and opened my laptop.

I kept online accounts—I wasn't that much of a Luddite—and I lived by my budgeting spreadsheet. I pulled up all the investments, the regular checking, and my paper ledger, and cross-referenced every-thing. Then I wrote the checks. I loved the smoothness of my pen across the signature lines.

The envelope had appeared sometime during the week, among the bills. But because of my ritual, I didn't notice it until that Saturday morning. Amy had taken Liam to the Little Gym. Aidan was asleep, in the trance of adolescence. He'd had a game the night before, so wouldn't be awake until noon. I'd found a good opportunity for solitude.

The bills fanned before me on the desk, and I plucked out the odd red envelope, used my silver monogrammed letter opener on it. I had to shimmy the fragile sheet out of its enclosure. There was no writing on the message. Not a single clue as to where it might have come from. All I saw was a jumble of line-drawn stick men.

It puzzled me, and I was careful not to spill my coffee on the letter. But I didn't have time to be puzzled. I didn't like the change in my routine. I frowned at the message, set it aside, and continued with my work. Satisfaction filled me as I filled in my spreadsheet and signed my name. *Patrick Reed. Patrick Reed. Patrick Reed.*

3

Caroline

The day the envelope came, I got home just before six, my feet aching. I couldn't wait to ditch the pumps. I kicked them off and set them carefully in the closet, then reached into the mailbox. No bills, thank God. Some ads, which I recycled. I can't stand having junk mail in the house. No real mail besides a red-brown envelope.

It was probably an invitation to one of those home parties. Multi-level marketing stuff. All the women in town invited me to things now. On Facebook, primarily, because most people these days are too lazy to put paper in an envelope and mail it. Anyway, it had gotten to the point where I didn't want to log in to any social networks. All the notifications to sift through. I didn't want a new fancy cleaning product or a dress that looked like a bag. I didn't even want to be back in Ohio.

But maybe I'd go to this person's party, since they'd taken the time to find my new address and send me something. I liked the fancy script that my name was written in, all loops and curves. It looked familiar, though. I didn't know many people who could produce handwriting of this caliber. My stomach knotted.

I held the letter close to my chest, padding in my stocking feet into my new office-slash-reading room. Had the house not been located precisely here, on 25 Rose Lane, in the town where I was born, I would've been pleased with it. I'd decorated it to my exact liking, purchased the overstuffed gray couch and loveseat from Wayfair, and they'd arrived in pristine condition. The walls had already been a muted gray-blue, so I'd installed the crown molding myself and painted it white.

I loved the contrast and simplicity. This was my sanctuary. Kieran and Kyle could trash the rest of the house however they wanted, and although it pained me, I could ignore it as long as my personal space was clean and calm.

I sank into the soft fabric and put my feet up, settling back into the quiet. Kyle was at football practice, and who knew where Kieran was. I didn't care. My husband was a loser, a stoner. I'd known this going into our marriage, even welcomed it—his devil-may-care attitude had seemed so thrilling when were younger. But now I was okay being alone.

I slid my nail under the flap and pried open the seal. The paper was wedged in tight. I unfolded the message, the parchment creasing under my fingers, and saw the dancing men.

The muscles around my mouth twitched. I knew who'd sent this letter.

4

Dora

I hated school. Mostly, I hated the kids at school. I might have liked education more if I wasn't surrounded by jerks, players, and snobs. Grandma said it was the same when my mom went there twenty years ago. I didn't always believe my grandmother, but I believed that. Nothing had changed.

The Monday after I found the letter, I woke to the five a.m. alarm, preparing for the hour-long bus ride. But before I left, I hesitated at the door. Grandma hadn't touched the envelope.

Not really sure what to do with it, I stuck the letter in my backpack. I kept it in my English book, so it wouldn't get ripped.

I also hated the bus because I had my bassoon for band and my trombone for jazz band. I supposed it could've been worse. I could've played the tuba. But as it was, my instruments were awkward. I had to sling one in front of me and the other one behind. And then when I got to school, I never knew whether the music room would be open when the bell rang. Dr. Rhinehart was often late.

That day, like many Mondays, was one of those unfortunate

locked-band-room days, and I bumped through the hall awkwardly. I jiggled my locker open, fumbling with my stuff.

"Hey," came a voice next to me.

I jumped at the sight of Kyle Cannon.

Thankfully, I had the excuse of being surprised. But I couldn't help the shameful speeding of my breath and heart. Or the heat creeping up my spine, headed towards my neck and face.

"Oh, hey," I squeaked, in a brutal effort to be cool, and I lost my grip on the trombone's handle.

"Let me help you." Kyle picked my trombone up off his foot. If I had hurt him, he didn't let on.

"I have to go dump this stuff."

I knew what Kyle wanted, what he always wanted, and what I gave him because I was a stupid, stupid girl.

"I'll go to the band room with you. It's in your bag?" He picked my bookbag off the floor then, too. Kyle didn't seem fazed carrying my cartoony Japanese backpack. Pink and purple wide-eyed characters stared at me from Kyle's back as I followed him down the hall, trailing with my bassoon.

I pulled open the double doors to the band room, and Kyle followed me into the instrument room. My locker was a wide cage with a combination lock. I dialed in the code and sighed as I pushed my cases in. They'd stay there until our next weekend gig, or until I needed to practice.

"Thank you," I said to Kyle.

"No problem." He lifted my bag off his shoulder and handed it to me.

I bobbled it, my knees buckling to the floor. My Norton anthology, the mammoth English book, peeked out. I scrabbled for it.

I was fifteen, but I had always been a little advanced for my age. I liked being smart—I prided myself on it. It was part of my identity. But there was a large part of me that wanted to be mainstream.

If my brain were a pie chart, 64% would imagine myself as a normal girl, a girl who attracted boys, who was alluring by nature—nubile and young, a temptation to any man with testosterone in his cells. That 64% longed to be someone other than myself. I'd sacrifice intelligence, in that moment, for some of that beauty. For the opportunity to be an object of desire.

Here, I was an object of desire for another reason.

16% of the pie chart was devoted to self-flagellating the 64%.

The remaining 20% was hungry.

I pulled out the English text and reached inside the cover. Two clean white papers, typed and neat, fell out. One for me, one for Kyle.

"Thanks, Dora." He grinned and snatched his, which was written in a completely different style from my own, of course. Several planted spelling errors, plus a heftier margin and Courier font, would fool Ms. Krieger.

"You're a-dora-ble. Haha. Has anyone ever told you that?"

"All the time," I muttered, but Kyle Cannon was already gone, the heavy metal doors banging closed behind him.

"Ugh, what are you doing with Kyle?"

I was struggling to get my stuff back together in the hallway when Aidan Reed snuck up on me. Yet another surprise by a cute boy. I'd be in cardiac arrest by the end of the day.

"Oh, nothing." My voice rose to an unnatural pitch. "What's up, Aidan?"

As if this football player would take to me for any reason. Maybe he'd heard that I could write papers for people. Pretty soon I'd be cranking them out for the entire team. In all seriousness, though, if Aidan found out, I could be in big trouble. Kyle and Aidan were the top starters for JV and ultra-competitive. Aidan might have been fishing for information.

"You dropped this." He handed me the red envelope.

Shit. I suppressed a gasp and grabbed it. "I can't lose this. Thanks."

He crooked an eyebrow. Aidan was cute, although not in the same way Kyle was. Kyle was chiseled, floppy-haired, tan. Aidan wore glasses unless he was on the field, and he cut his wiry hair short like a shrub. But he was strong, and he smelled like a forest, a clean cologne.

"What's important about it?"

I paused with my mouth half open, hyper-aware of my boxy stained T-shirt and frayed leggings.

Lunch was almost half over by this point, and my "hungry" pie-chart portion was increasing. But I had to distract him.

I moved over to the block wall and leaned against it, ignoring the rumbling in my gut. Aidan watched as I pulled out the sheet.

He studied the stick figures. "And this is…"

"I don't know. It came in the mail over the weekend." I shrugged. "I think it means something. I just don't know what."

"Weird." Aidan scratched his curls. "Well, I'm glad you didn't lose it."

"Me too. Thanks."

He saluted me and left. I stuck the paper back in my book and hustled towards the cafeteria. Ten minutes left to stuff my face.

AFTER LUNCH, I hurried to English. With no time to return to my locker, I lugged my entire bookbag back to Ms. Krieger's room, avoiding her eyes when she smiled at me. Ms. K was a young teacher, probably in her twenties. She was tall and maybe too lean, her clavicle and wrists bony. And she definitely tried too hard to be friends with the students.

I slid into my seat in the front, flushing as I gathered my bearings. Our desks were a tight fit, and I hoped my huge bag wasn't in someone's way.

"Let's turn in our papers first thing," Krieger said. I didn't look at Kyle, who sat in the back of the room, as he handed his sheet to the kid in front of him. If I pretended this was over, it would be over… at least until the next time.

My best friend, Mallory, sat behind me. She handed her paper up.

"This one sucked," she whispered, rolling her eyes.

I didn't comment.

I collected the papers and handed them to Krieger. She nodded to me and stood up. "Today, we'll be moving on to the early 1900s. One of my favorite time periods. And we'll start with my favorite detective, the icon Sherlock Holmes." She walked in front of her desk. "Can anyone tell me what an icon is?"

I wished I were in the back of the room, that no one could see me. I wanted to morph into a new body, maybe one that matched the color of the floor, or the desk. Because of course, if no one answered, she would call on me. Because she knew I would know.

"Dora?"

I sighed. "It's like, a big thing. Something that means something."

The class laughed. I cast a glance toward the other students, at their snickering faces.

"Can you be more specific?" Ms. Krieger grinned, thin lips stretching around her big teeth. Did she enjoy my pain?

"Sherlock Holmes is an icon because everyone knows him. Like, if someone wears that hat, everyone knows what they're getting at. They're trying to evoke him."

More giggles. Oh, no, I used a big word around the country bumpkins.

But Ms. Krieger loved it. She beamed as she crossed the room to turn off the classroom light. "Exactly. The deerstalker hat."

She aimed her remote at the smartboard, and as it illuminated, Holmes appeared on the screen.

"Sir Arthur Conan Doyle wrote four novels and fifty-six short stories featuring this iconic character." Krieger paced in front of the smartboard, heels clicking on the linoleum. "And there have been countless adaptations of that work. We'll be reading 'A Scandal in Bohemia.' Then each of you will read another story of your choice, and you'll write a paper comparing and contrasting the two."

That meant I would be reading three stories.

"When is that due?" I asked.

Ms. Krieger consulted her smartwatch. "Two weeks from today. It's all on the class website. I'll hand out the assignment, too."

I'd have to go to the library after school. We didn't have Internet at home—too expensive—and Grandma didn't know how to use it anyway. I scribbled in my planner, a poor substitute for a phone, which all my classmates had their noses in. Well, I had a flip phone that could get texts, but besides that, it was a lump of useless plastic.

"Why don't we read the first few pages out loud."

I groaned and suddenly felt less bad for my deception.

I heaved the Norton anthology out of my bag. Some of my classmates stored their books on their phones or tablets, which I would do if Grandma would let me have one. She said a kid my age shouldn't have any electronics other than my school-issued laptop. I'd had to beg her just for the flip phone.

As I adjusted the book on my desk, the red envelope slid out. Mallory and I both reached to the floor to snag the letter as it fluttered down, but Ms. Krieger got there first.

She slid the paper out of the envelope. "What's this?"

I grimaced. I didn't want anyone's grubby hands on it. Maybe I didn't know what it was, but I knew I didn't want it to get damaged.

Then she laughed. "Have you been reading ahead, Dora?"

I wished again for that new body, the one that could disappear on command.

"No," I mumbled. "Why?"

"Then why would you have a Holmes code in your bag?"

I wanted to snatch the red envelope from her, yank it from her annoying bony hands.

Ms. Krieger peered at the letter. "These are the dancing men. From 'The Adventure of the Dancing Men.' You haven't read it?"

I shook my head.

Ms. Krieger handed my envelope and paper back. "Well, then you'd better get reading if you want to know what that letter says."

I tucked it under a thin page, making sure to hold it in place. I would *not* lose it again.

5

Patrick

I left Chesterfield early, driving half an hour to the train, so I could spend another forty-five minutes on the light rail into Cleveland. Not my favorite way to commute, but also not my least favorite, which would involve driving and parking downtown.

Once I arrived at Tower City, I took the elevator up to the fifteenth floor of Terminal Tower. I settled into my leather chair and took in the view. While I preferred working remotely most days, my desk there was majestic and impressive, and signing checks on it was even more satisfying than doing so at home.

And I'd signed many checks at that desk. As an accountant, I worked for a start-up—ForkFlavor—a website where people could order groceries from their local merchants, then use them to make recipes curated by our chefs. We also packed boxes for the premium customers, the ones who couldn't be bothered to cook the meals themselves, but we didn't do that here. This office was where the action happened: the strategy, the planning.

There weren't many of us in this office, but I was glad our CEO had chosen to rent the space. I could always work from home if I needed to, and the location gave us the urban cachet we wouldn't have in the suburbs. Chesterfield was rural enough to be outside Cleveland's suburban ring, but we were lucky we weren't even deeper into the farms and fields of Northeast Ohio. Aidan complained about our town all the time, and when I gave him this rationale, he rolled his eyes.

I didn't waste any time digging into my e-mail, pulling up my work spreadsheets. I always got at least twelve e-mails from Matt Corrigan, our CEO, daily. But the top one in my inbox, with two lone words in bold—*See me*—made my stomach sink.

I was tempted to click through my other work, to check if there were any invoices I needed to pay before I went out into the hall. But I couldn't put off the inevitable confrontation with Matt. I hoped it wasn't bad news. I didn't want to have to tell Amy she would need to start shopping at Save-a-Lot or that she would need to stop buying clothes for the baby. She liked doing that, and I knew she felt bad not bringing any income to the household. I always assured her we had what we needed, even as our credit card balances rose.

As I exited my office, my stomach in knots, I noticed that Holly's desk was empty, her stuff gone. Poof, no more administrative secretary.

I pulled open Matt's door. "Did you let Holly go?"

He swiveled towards me. Dark circles colored the light skin under his eyes. "I had to, yeah."

"Is that what you wanted to see me about?"

Matt wore jeans and a rumpled T-shirt that read *Attempt to Care Loading,* with a red bar half-filled below it. Funny, for a tech guy, but not his usual attire. I looked down at my own chinos and pressed shirt. When investors came in, we wanted to look good. That was why we'd hired Holly in the first place, because she always wore suits and straightened her wild red hair. That was the image we wanted to present, that Cleveland wasn't a mistake on a lake, that we could make money and bring in jobs. ForkFlavor was professional.

Matt sighed. "Well, as you know, the numbers aren't good right now."

I swallowed and nodded. "You thinking about selling?"

That was the risk when you worked for a start-up. We were profitable, if not by much, but maybe he wanted to cut his losses.

"No." Matt was a big guy, six five and lean-muscled. His chair was custom made for him, but his desk was small, and when he leaned over it, he looked like that statue of The Thinker. His voice was low. "You didn't catch the math mistake."

I shook my head.

Matt pulled out a ledger covered with scribbled numbers. I relaxed a little as I leaned over, squinting at the figures. They weren't anywhere close to what was on my spreadsheet. ForkFlavor was in the black. But Matt jabbed at one of the lines.

"This is where we're behind," he said. "There's a gap of nearly twenty thousand."

"That's no big deal." I turned in the direction of my office. "I see some errors there, so I'll e-mail you the correct spreadsheet. You don't need to worry. Call Holly and bring her back. We've got the money."

"Wait, Patrick."

I swiveled.

Matt sat up, then stood, so he was hovering over me like a satellite. "We don't have the money. You want to explain where it is?"

My face and neck cramped as I folded my arms and opened my legs. "Are you accusing me of something, Corrigan?"

Matt couldn't get any closer to me. I could smell the coffee on his breath, which reminded me I hadn't had nearly enough to deal with this bullshit.

"You're the accountant. The money isn't there. There's a mistake somewhere. It's either your mistake or you pocketed the money."

"You don't know anything about my finances." I'd been thinking of taking money out of the Roth, to pay the debt off once and for all. Or a home equity loan. There had to be untapped value in the house. We'd been there since Aidan was little.

"Give me proof."

"The proof's in my spreadsheet." I turned again. "Like I said, I'll send it to you. Only you and I have access to the accounts, and I don't think what you have there is correct."

"I guarantee you wrote a check that was too big. Or several checks that were too big. Maybe not to yourself, but someone isn't talking. What about one of the lenders?"

I fumed. The only way to solve this problem was to get back to work. Puzzle this thing out, call Holly, get back to the way things are every day. Corrigan was often hot, but he usually trusted me. This particular betrayal stung.

"If we overpaid a lender, I'll contact them and get it rectified. I can set it up, so we won't owe payments for the next few months. The books will balance." I spun to leave again. "Let me work. I'll find the problem and deal with it. There was no reason to take extreme action."

Matt turned back to his computer, his voice dark. "You don't want to see extreme action from me."

"You're home early!" Amy called out as I entered the foyer.

I rounded the corner to find her in the kitchen. A ForkFlavor box sat half empty on the counter. I resisted the urge to drop-kick it off the back porch. No use in wasting fresh food, even if it was psychologically tainted.

Amy folded her arms and leaned against the laminate counter. She wore a soft tunic and jeans that skimmed her body in the right places. Even after two kids more than ten years apart, she was still gorgeous, a California dream in the wrong state. I loved to wring my hands in her thick, blonde hair.

Her plump lips twitched. "Did something happen at work?"

"I don't really want to talk about it."

"Liam's asleep. It's a good time to chat. Do you want coffee?"

"Sure, yeah." I went past her into the dining room, where I opened my laptop. I felt out of sorts, the day uneven.

I heard her bustling behind me, putting coffee on. The water burbled and hissed. I accessed my report, scanned the numbers again. Nothing looked out of place. I'd have to download a complete batch and start over—if the raw data didn't match, something was missing.

I tried to log in remotely, but my access was denied.

Amy carried two mugs to the table and set one down in front of me. The liquid inside was black and steaming. "Will we be okay? I mean, until you can find something? I have Aidan's football pay-to-play bill coming."

"Matt didn't let me go," I said sharply. "We're having a... disagreement."

I picked up my coffee, letting the heat of it scald my tongue. I wasn't about to confirm or deny anything. She could believe we were okay. She needed to believe it.

I logged into my e-mail, intent on pinging Matt for my access back, but I had a new message that made me stop.

The subject was "Don't Be Afraid" and it was from a "Hey Me."

I could almost hear the Beatles song echoing in my head. *Hey Jude...*

I took a halting breath. Clicked on it.

Hear you've got some extra time now! Do you need a little hint? I'm anxious for you to get started. Some big money could be coming your way!

A YouTube clip was attached. It wasn't spam. Couldn't be. No spammer knew my history with Jude Lassiter. This message had to be from the one and only, the individual, the man himself.

I clicked the clip. A lone bassoon whined away on "Nimrod," from *The Enigma Variations*. Unaccompanied, the sound was tinny and haunting. I muted it.

My high school best friend—my frenemy, really—was the only other bassoon player in our class. I'd switched to the unwieldy instrument in eighth grade. Dark and resonant, it held a mystery and uniqueness that rows of clarinets and flutes couldn't carry. It wasn't long until Jude Lassiter switched, too, because he couldn't bear the thought of me having something he didn't. And, as with everything, he had to be better than me.

LATER THAT NIGHT, I bent over my desk with my head in my hand. I had gone over the spreadsheets a hundred times, squinting at the columns until my eyes ached.

Hear you've got some extra time. I didn't even know if I'd been truly fired, and yet it seemed Jude had already gotten his hands on that information. And what was that supposed to mean about money? I knew he was some sort of millionaire, maybe even a billionaire, but I didn't want to take money from him. Even if we'd need it more now that I might have lost my job.

Aidan came in then, slumping onto the couch next to my desk, tablet in hand.

"Hey, bud," I greeted him, tearing myself away for a second.

Every day, I was in awe that this beast was my son. He wasn't overly tall but not short either—maybe 5'10". But he was relentless on the weights, and he'd built a rangy yet compact muscular frame, a far cry from my band-geek physique. My son got his looks from Amy's side.

"Hey, Dad."

It pleased me that he still hung out with me, even if it was only for an hour or so before bed. "How was school?"

He shrugged. "The same."

"Learn anything new?"

"If I did, I forgot already."

We chuckled. That was what he used to say as a kindergartener, and it had stuck.

I blew out a breath and smacked my thighs. "Well, I'm not getting anything else done today. Want to watch something on TV?"

The intersection of Jude and Matt tickled at the back of my brain, but I didn't have the brainpower to process it.

Aidan was looking at my desk, at the red envelope shoved to the back with all the mail. He reached for it and pulled it open.

He scanned the delicate paper. "Where did this come from?"

I was thinking of Liam and Amy, upstairs in the bed. Of the crib in Liam's room, which sat empty every night. Of the guest bed, which was now my bed. My little boy's night terrors were getting worse. I missed sleeping with my wife, and not just sex, but the closeness of her, her warm body against mine. I missed her smell.

I betrayed her every night. Not with another woman but with my lies. With the lies that she would be safe with me, that I would provide for her, that we could afford this house. This life.

Maybe I did want Jude's money.

"Oh," I said. "I don't know. Why?"

He tapped the paper. "A girl at school had this same envelope."

"Huh. Weird."

We studied it together. Those little men, dancing across the page.

6

Caroline

Jude was always obsessed with codes.

Back then, we didn't have Internet. Or texting. Kids didn't know how good they had it now, their friends always there at the touch of a button. Not even a button but a screen. Touch-screens. We wouldn't have dreamed of technology like that. That was the stuff of *Star Trek*.

Here's what we had: long, winding phone calls. We huddled in corners, wrapping the cords around our hands. We didn't have cordless phones, and if we did, they were the giant 90s ones, the kind featured on repeats of *Family Matters* and *Full House*. We lolled on window seats, heads hanging off the edges, all the blood rushing to our faces. And our long hair hung down behind us. I had hair like straw that had been left in the sun too long, brown and stick-straight and stiff. When I grew up, I learned to cut it close to my head, to shellac it, whip it into submission with product.

We sat there for hours, listening to each other breathe. We couldn't see each other in person. We didn't have cars, and other than the main drag of town, Chesterfield wasn't walkable. I often wanted to escape the calls, to go watch TV or read a book, but this was how we socialized. We bonded by doing nothing, connected only by the space on the line between us.

I had these calls with Jude. Not so much with Patrick, because by the time we got together, he had his license. But we'd get in trouble sometimes, leading to stern groundings from our parents and furtive whispering in the middle of the night.

We spoke secret words on the phone, the occasional spurt of Pig Latin. But Jude knew that most codes succeeded on paper, and not so much aurally. Even though he was a band nerd, like Patrick, they had their musical messages, I was sure. Codes, however, could be preserved for posterity. They weren't so fleeting. They were open to be broken by anyone with the fortitude and intellectual capacity.

Sherlock Holmes was Jude's entry into the obsession. We read "A Scandal in Bohemia" in school, which prompted him to check out all the other stories. "The Adventures of the Dancing Men" involved these messages, scrawled on the walls in a rich guy's house. The details of the story didn't matter. Jude was lured by the idea of code making, code breaking, communicating in secret. Later, he got into all that stuff with Elgar's codes, but Holmes had been his first love.

Back then, we used to pass notes. Pre-texting!

So, I knew the language of those men and their little flags, their stick arms waving in the air.

I took the parchment paper to my new office, which was still littered with boxes. My desk was a jumble of papers, books, old photos. But I'd already set up my computer, and I found the mouse among the detritus. I pulled up Wikipedia to remind myself what each letter stood for, then inked the new letters onto a page of my own—the back of an old envelope. I wasn't about to mar the original.

I stuck out my lip as the letters emerged.

. . .

XQDHT LDI FQVD XILRQPT

Didn't make sense.

I should've known. Jude was too smart for easy answers. He'd know I could simply Google the story. That I'd remember those little drawings.

Ugh. I pushed the garble of letters aside and typed in "white pages" instead. *Jude Lassiter* or *Jude Harlow Lassiter*. Nothing.

Tried a straight Google search. LinkedIn. Nothing. It was like he'd never existed.

I slapped my hands on the desk and got up from the keyboard. I was so agitated since we'd moved back to Chesterfield. I knew I needed to be here for my mom, but I hated being so far from excitement, from things to do. I missed Fresno, its boutique shops, blazing sun, and fresh Chinese cuisine. People said Fresno was a dump compared to other parts of California, but I loved it, even when my clothes were sticking to my back and we were drinking gallons of water. I hated my new job and the slog of a commute—45 minutes each way, and not even on the freeway.

Kyle seemed to be adjusting, but I couldn't see inside his thick teenager mind. And Kieran was already fading here, deprived of sun and surf.

California felt full of potential, always shiny and different. Here, I couldn't see into the future, couldn't see past the darkness rolling in outside.

I sank back into my seat and stared at the mess of alphabet in front of me.

❧

"Hey." Kieran put a hand on my back, and I jumped. "Aren't you hungry? I made quinoa and tofu with a cranberry slaw."

Kieran drew himself to his full height, proud of his work, and I couldn't help but smile.

"You can take the boy out of California..." I got up and leaned against my chair, pushing it in. It clattered against the desktop. "I'm sorry."

"No worries."

I squeezed my eyes shut and followed him to the kitchen. As usual, no ask—what are you doing? How was your day? My husband followed his own nose through life. It was a wonder I'd managed to pry him from his beloved beach.

When we were young, and I worked hard, I'd loved having him at home. He was great with Kyle, and it was nice not to have to worry about babysitting. Kieran had worked as a barista when our son was born, and coordinating care was such a nightmare that we decided he could quit.

That life was good. I'd get to the office early, put in my billables, sometimes pause for lunch. Working soothed my spirit, gave me a purpose. I felt fulfilled, like I was helping people. As an attorney, I worked with senior citizens who were denied disability or Social Security because they were too young for the threshold, but still couldn't work due to illness or chronic pain. It was gratifying to write those briefs, to see people get the money they needed so desperately. Sure, we had charlatans, fakers who ignited my sense of justice. But I liked what I did, and I got to come home every day to colorful sunsets, a sexy long-haired husband, and a sweet little boy.

Now the sweet little boy was a hulking teen, bent over cereal and his phone at the kitchen table, and we lived in a gray, flat, hopeless expanse.

"You're not eating dinner?" I asked Kyle.

He looked up, brows knit. Surly. "You know I don't eat that stuff."

"And you know you shouldn't talk to me that way." I edged past him, knocking his chair with my hip.

He grunted.

I sighed and filled my bowl. It smelled good, like California. I breathed in the steam, the sweet cranberry mixed with the savory tofu.

"I need meat," Kyle said. "I can't build more bulk with this lack of protein." My son was slim like his father, but he was lifting at school, trying to get bigger for football. Another scourge of the small town.

I snorted. "Like Lucky Charms are protein?"

"You can buy it and learn to cook it," Kieran said mildly, coming to the table with his own food. "It's not what your mother and I want."

I bristled as he spoke for me, but I stayed quiet.

Kyle stared. "What money am I supposed to use?"

"You can get a job."

"Fourteen is too young. And besides, I don't have time to work." He stabbed at the bottom of his bowl, the spoon clanking against the ceramic.

"Then ask your grandmother. My money isn't going to support the meat industry in this country."

My money.

Kieran pulled the elastic out of his hair, ran a hand through the blonde tangles.

Kyle mumbled, "Fucking hippies."

Kieran's head snapped in our son's direction. "What was that?"

"Fucking teenagers." I grabbed Kyle's dish, stalked to the sink, and slammed the dish down among all the others Kieran hadn't handled. Which he'd had all day to do. "Kyle, get out of here. Do something productive."

My son shoved in his chair and elbowed past me. Kieran pushed his hands through his hair and breathed out. I ate my quinoa.

In bed—early, since I had to be up for work the next day—I tossed, the coded letters churning on the backs of my lids. Kieran was up late doing God knew what. Kyle was pasted to his phone in his room.

The new letters had to mean something. It was unlikely they were an anagram—so many Xs and Qs. I had memorized them, tried to rearrange them every possible way. The letters had to stand for other letters. Just like each dancing man had its own associated letter based on its appearance.

Four words. Five, three, four, seven. Almost a haiku. Wait, a haiku was syllables. These were characters. My high school English skills were rusty.

I turned over, buried my head in a pillow. Something smelled. Like a skunk had been in here. Or—more likely—someone had smoked weed. I threw the pillow off the bed and curled in a nest of blankets.

The next thing I knew, Kieran was poking me. His breath was sweet and musty, like dinner and cigarettes. Only Kieran didn't smoke tobacco.

I also knew what he wanted. Now, it was a matter of giving in or holding out. I was tired of both. I was tired of fighting on every front.

"Hey," Kieran sang in my ear, his breath tickling, irritating. "Wake up, sweetheart."

I pushed him back. He stumbled, hitched up on his knees. "Come on, babe. Come on."

"Sorry," I said.

The clock read 1:58 a.m. I grabbed my pillow and stalked downstairs to the couch.

Alone, I settled back and bunched a blanket around me, fighting the late-fall chill. Wishing for the natural warmth of my old house, where we never had to consider turning on heat. I flipped through podcasts on my phone and found one about Sherlock Holmes. Maybe I'd absorb the answer through my sleep.

From "The Great Genius of Edward Elgar," a high school paper by Jude Lassiter

Elgar was born in Worcestershire, the fourth of seven children. His father worked selling music and tuning pianos. Elgar started learning music at an early age. His first instrument was the violin. He also learned the piano, and later, became a bassoonist. He also loved books, and one of his first compositions was a musical play written for his siblings to perform.

Elgar wanted to build his career, but it was hard because he thought he should go to Europe, and he didn't speak German. So, he learned it, and then he went to Europe a few times. That was where his European influence came from. But he mostly stayed in London.

I can see why you are glossing over Elgar's early career—I know you want to focus on his codemaking—but I would like to see more specific examples here, like in the first paragraph.

7

Patrick

Despite my lack of a workplace to go to, I woke up the next morning renewed.

I didn't think Matt was the type of man who kept a secure password. He spent life flying by the seat of his pants: the entrepreneur who dreamed, who dealt in ideas. Idea people rarely cared much for details. But accounting people did. And while I couldn't puzzle out the men on the parchment, I could puzzle out Matt's password.

I'd seen him type it many times. It had letters and numbers, was long, a passphrase. It wouldn't take me long to crack. Sitting at my desk in my office, I closed my eyes and visualized him typing, his fingers on the keyboard.

"I am awesome 4-1-4," I said out loud as ForkFlavor's data populated on my laptop screen.

"What, Dad?" Aidan, dressed for school, peered in at me.

Liam wailed somewhere far away. It was the first I'd registered of my family since waking. The house had been quiet up until now.

"Matt's password." Pride swelled in my chest. I'd be in and out with a full download before my boss—ex-boss?—was even out of bed.

"Nice." Aidan sauntered over and picked up the coded paper. "Now, if we could only figure this out."

I wasn't listening. I was navigating to the export screen, my hands sure on the mouse. I selected my parameters and hit "run."

And my screen went dark.

I swore. I'd have to reboot and log back in. But that would be no trouble. I had access now.

Deep breath, Patrick. This was some bullshit Windows update. Nothing out of the ordinary.

Liam was still bawling.

"Patrick," Amy called. "I need your help."

I clenched my fists. "I'm working."

"I need you." Was it desperation in her voice, or annoyance? Either way, it was imperative. I shoved back my chair and left my study with its gray morning light. I'd return fresh, with more coffee.

Amy's face was bleary with fatigue and lack of makeup. She'd pulled her hair into a rushed ponytail. Still sexy, beautiful, in a stained T-shirt and yoga pants—but she was pissed.

"Liam is losing his mind, Aidan needs to get the bus, and I don't have his lunch packed. We need to discuss the sports issue."

"There's no issue," Aidan grumbled.

First I was hearing of this. I looked between them.

Liam whined. Amy snatched him up and hitched him onto her hip.

"Mom, I'll buy lunch." Aidan shouldered his bookbag. "Dad, you can take me to school."

"We still need to discuss this." She pointed at me, then at Aidan. Liam buried his head in her shoulder. "Why don't we all go. Let's take the van."

Liam let out another massive scream.

"He's teething," Amy said. "I just gave him ibuprofen. He'll fall asleep in the car."

"We don't have time to talk." Aidan dug in his pocket for his phone and glanced at the screen. "I'm gonna be late."

Amy sighed. "Fine. I'll talk to your father when he gets back. Don't sign up for anything until we've discussed it. As a family."

Aidan groaned and turned his back to her. I snagged my coat from the closet and trailed him to the car.

"WHAT WAS THAT ALL ABOUT?" I asked my son as we pulled out of the driveway.

The route to school wasn't long. But there was something to talk about here, and if Aidan could explain, maybe I could shut Amy down.

He shrugged. "She doesn't want me to do wrestling."

"Is that it?"

Football season was wrapping up. They had one more game, on Friday. I remembered the last game of the year from my marching band days. Apart from one year, when it was blessedly 55 in November, it was bitterly cold. Our thick band uniforms could not keep us warm. Our breath stained the air, and our fingers were almost too frozen to play our clarinets. I huddled in the stands against Jude and Caroline, our bodies pressed together.

"Yeah, it's stupid." Aidan grunted. "I built all season. I'm not waiting till next year to compete again."

"She afraid you'll get hurt? You've never wrestled."

I swung the Escape into the front drive, a long semicircle filled front-to-back with parent cars. My school had changed little in seventeen years. The number of parent drivers had, though. I'd always walked to school, but my generation seemed to prefer chauffeuring our children.

Aidan rolled his eyes. "Ask her. She's crazy."

He opened his door and launched into the stream of kids before I could say anything else.

WHEN I GOT HOME, Amy had strapped Liam to her back with one of those crazy wrap things she likes to buy and sell online. My little son's face was pressed into her back, his rosy lips parted. Liam was a marvel, a bucket of energy except when he ran out, and then he was an angel, usually cradled with my wife. We hadn't slept in the same bed since Liam was born, and sex was a series of furtive, hidden moments around the house. Which seemed more like an obligation, a task she performed to keep me from bothering her.

She always said he wouldn't be like this forever. And that was true. I could already feel myself getting older, these days moving like a carousel, a whirling blur of colors and weather and milestones. Aidan in high school. Liam's first words. My boys were far apart, but we'd started early. We were far from old. Our days alone were coming.

It was hard to think that far ahead, though.

Amy grimaced as she rocked from side to side. "He's getting heavy."

"Put him in the crib," I blurted.

I didn't mean to be so sarcastic. Liam had never slept in the crib. Three hundred dollars to replace, as Aidan's had become out of date with its unsafe drop side. Our oldest child had survived to adolescence, but apparently crib manufacturers knew something we didn't.

I filled my coffee mug and wandered toward my study. My nerves were firing at the prospect of opening my spreadsheet, at diving into the data.

Amy followed me. "We need to talk."

"He told me in the car. I don't see any issues." I turned my laptop back on, and the Windows symbol came up, etched in white-on-blue.

She stood framed in the doorway, standing on the steps that led down into my office, shaking her head. "I wanted to talk to you first. I don't want him to do it. I'm tired of the rivalry."

"What rivalry?" I asked. Chesterfield's team never won anything. There were like—God—fifty kids on the team, if that? I hadn't been to any of Aidan's games this year. I felt a twinge of guilt, half-listening as I logged back into my analysis engine.

"Kyle. It's the worst." Amy sighed. "I hate the parents. The mom is one of those Type A helicopters. She's gotta work and micromanage her kid at the same time. The dad stays home, but does he do anything? You should see the drama on the parents' listserv. Actually, you should get on there, or at least join the Facebook group. You need to get more involved. Liam takes a lot of my time..."

Amy's voice was an ocean roaring soundlessly in my ear, because I was typing Matt's password over and over, and nothing was happening.

Locked out.

I turned back to my wife. My stomach rolled. All the blood had drained from my face. I could feel it pooling in my hands.

But she didn't notice. She was still talking on and on.

And I had noticed something else—the red envelope from Jude was gone.

8

Caroline

I dreamed Hannah and I were dragging a mattress up a long staircase.

She looked the same, hadn't changed in eighteen years. She was slight, skinny, with mousy hair. But her face held a peculiar beauty when she smiled. That was a rare event, but I could also catch it when she was sitting in contemplation.

In the dream, she'd been determined. I'd never seen her like that in real life.

"Come on, Caroline," she said. "You can do it."

I stood at the back of the mattress's bulk, heaving behind it with all my might. But it was awkward, oddly shaped, and I didn't have the strength.

"Don't give up!" Hannah called from the other side. "You can do it!"

I looked past the bumpy surface to see that face again, and I realized it wasn't Hannah at all.

I woke up angry.

The place stank. I tripped over piles of filthy man-clothes in the upstairs hall. I thought I caught a whiff of cat urine on the carpet, too. Otis wasn't adapting well to our move. I coughed, my throat clogged with the scent, and ran my hands back through my thick hair.

I'd worked so hard to make my space nice. My little office had perfect furniture and was painted just the right shade. I had hoped that would be enough, but it wasn't. When I went back upstairs to get ready for work, I was confronted with the reality. Even with my own refuge, I still had to live with two disgusting, hairy, complacent men.

"Hey," Kieran drawled as I entered the bedroom.

I jiggled his leg under the blankets. "This place is gross. Are you going to do anything today?"

He shrugged. Having slept off whatever drug he'd been on the night before—likely weed—his eyes were only a little pink. But he needed a shower. His blond hair was mussed, sticking up all over the place, and I could smell his putrid breath.

"Listen. Kieran." I pointed at him. "You have got to clean this place while I'm at work."

"I thought you were working from home today?" He rubbed at his face, yawned.

I usually worked from home one or two days a week, since the drive into downtown Cleveland was brutal, and I wasn't always needed at the office.

But the thought of being around my husband all day made my skin crawl. "I'm going to the coffee shop in town."

"Oh." He lay back down and covered his face with his pillow.

I groaned and grabbed clothes out of the dresser. Time to wash the stink off me.

As the water beat down on my head, my sinuses opened, and I formed a plan. This was me at my best, Productive Caroline. Clean a little, throw in a load of laundry, then leave the house. Bill some hours from the little coffee shop in downtown Chesterfield.

Fucking Jude. The thought came out of nowhere and I swallowed it hard.

Jude had to be the prize at the end of the hunt. He always had to be the center of attention.

I drew in a long breath, letting the shower's steam fill my chest. Jude could die in a fire for all I cared. He'd suggested the *Titanic* party, had pulled out the Ouija board. I blamed him for Hannah's actions that night.

But that was a long time ago. The questions now were different. Why was he doing this? What did he want?

It could be one big "look at me." But I'd also been thinking about how I couldn't find anything about him online. No search results for his name anywhere. Jude had wanted to make a lot of money after college. He had grand ideas. He treasured the limelight. His sudden vanishing had to be part of a bigger trick.

I wasn't that teenager anymore. I had been through a lot, and I had come out stronger for it. Jude must have changed, too. Somehow.

Wrapped in my robe, a towel on my head, I started coffee. My mind wandered into its usual rut of thinking, its working patterns. I pulled up my to-do list on my phone and skimmed over the list of briefs I needed to work on. I could chew on my ideas while I cleaned, and I'd be more productive once I reached the coffee shop.

My head was still down when I sensed movement, heard the grunting of a male animal. Not the cat. Probably Kieran. I didn't move.

"Mom?"

At Kyle's voice, I looked up. *Shit.* I'd forgotten it was a school day. "What are you doing home?"

"I could say the same for you." He wrinkled his nose. "Why do you always have to drink coffee?"

I couldn't help smiling. That was our little joke when he was a kid. He could never understand why I was so dependent on the stuff.

"Really have to wake up this time." I put my phone down. "Seriously, why are you not in school?"

"I didn't wake up in time. Neither did you or Dad. So, I didn't have any way of getting there."

My cheeks flushed. I got up and poured myself a cup of the brew, adding milk. "I'm sorry, honey. Want me to call? Or I can take you for half a day."

"It doesn't matter. As long as I'm there tomorrow, I still get to play Friday."

"But I don't want you to be behind on your work."

He scratched his head. "It's okay, Mom. I'm keeping up."

Sighing, I took another long swallow, the bitter warmth washing down my throat. "That's good. Why don't you go upstairs and work on your homework? Or you can help me with some of the cleaning down here?"

He shrugged. "See ya, Mom."

Then he shuffled out of the room without even getting himself breakfast.

ALTHOUGH IT HAD BEEN through many incarnations, the Chesterfield coffee shop had been around as long as I could remember. This time, the new owners had dubbed it The Daily Grind, its logo complete with a tired-looking cartoon businessman holding out his cup for more. The front bell jingled as I passed through the entry.

I sat and slung my bag onto the table, waving at the barista so she'd know I would buy something in due time. I extracted my laptop and took in the new interior. The place was calm, cozy, and clean. My skin prickled as I thought about the disaster of a house I'd left behind. I'd picked up as much as I could, did the dishes and so on, but who knew what I would come home to. Just once, I wanted to enjoy the peace of being alone in a tranquil space.

Before long, I was in a groove, with a fresh cup of joe and my headphones on. I knocked out brief after brief, emailing them to my boss, and I checked my calendar to verify court dates. When I finished writing, I switched to reading, going over the case material for my next hearing. I bounced along to the music piping from my computer, feeling lighter for the first time in weeks. Maybe The Daily Grind was what I needed for the daily grind. Ha, ha.

The doorbell jingled, and I looked up, my concentration broken for a second. The barista and I were alone in the shop, so another human presence was something to note.

A man walked in and began to peruse the coffee menu. He wore chinos with a blue shirt, tucked in. His hair a chocolate brown, his head turned, his profile long and angular.

I sucked in my breath. I recognized him.

He turned, seeing me as if I'd been a ghost just making myself visible. "Caroline?"

9

Patrick - Earlier

Late morning. We were sitting in the kitchen, after I'd been locked out of the ForkFlavor accounts. Liam happily pounded on pots and pans in the middle of the floor. The coffee was strong, and good, but Amy looked exhausted.

"Liam up last night?" I hadn't heard any crying. I'd slept long and deep, though, in the other room, and she was always near him.

She rubbed at her eyes. "Couldn't sleep."

"Any reason why not?"

Liam handed her a white plastic spoon. She smiled, accepted it, handed it back. This was the game they played.

Lines formed around her jaw. My wife wasn't the college cheerleader she'd been. Shades of an older woman moved across her face—a woman with problems, worries, fears. Not the carefree girl I had married.

"Amy?"

"I'm scared."

I sipped my coffee and thought of the letter. Did she think it was a threat? That I was part of some elaborate government cover-up? That we were being stalked? My wife was afraid. She should have told me, but instead, she feared that I brought danger to the family.

"You're supposed to ask me why." She was all scrunched up, hunched over her coffee mug.

I moved toward her and put my hands on her birdlike shoulders. I kneaded the skin of her back, expecting her to yield, to sigh. Expecting that I could reassure her, could make things better.

But she blew out a long breath and stepped away from me.

Liam said, "Mama!" Amy bent to scoop him into her arms.

"Don't worry," I said. "We're not a target. I'm sure that letter was some weird scam."

I didn't want to tell her about Jude. She knew who he was, but she didn't know he had something to do with this, and she didn't need to. It would be better for him to remain a memory in this house, a shard of my past, something not to be spoken of.

Amy stared back at me, blank. "Letter?"

"A high school prank, probably," I said.

Amy buried her fingers in her hair and slowed her voice down as if I couldn't understand her otherwise. "I am not talking about a letter. I am talking about the house."

I frowned. The house was in perfect order, had been ever since we moved in. I always kept the back garden landscaped and made sure that the sump pump was working. We had a new water heater and a fresh paint job in Aidan's room.

"Your job. How are we paying our bills? Are we going to lose the house?"

Good question. I went through the mental inventory, the monthly ledger of checks I wrote. Credit card payments. Utilities. The loan we'd taken out to make improvements to the house.

"I'm still on the payroll. Matt hasn't fired me, and we don't have any evidence that he did it behind my back." *Other than my being locked out of access to everything.*

I couldn't help thinking that Jude's money would help me quite a bit right now.

Liam crowed. Amy handed him to me. He smelled like apples and milk.

~

I took my laptop to the coffee shop in downtown Chesterfield. When I worked remotely, I liked to spend time there. It was comfortable—lots of seating, handy outlets—and it was a change of scenery.

Amy's stress was stressing me out. She was all worried about Aidan's sports crap. Then she forgot about that to get worked up about my job. As long as I had a way to bring in income, it didn't matter what I did for a living. I made a note to check in with my son about the wrestling situation.

There was an itch in the back of my head, a tiny thought, that Jude and his game would not go away. But I pushed it back. High school was over. I had real-life responsibilities, fortysomething goals. To make amends with Matt if possible and then look for another job. End things amicably. I'd enjoyed my time at ForkFlavor, but I was done there.

The little bell jingled as I pushed through the front door. I wasn't sure what to order, since I'd already been sufficiently caffeinated, but I wanted to buy something to support the business. I scrutinized the menu. An Americano wouldn't hurt. It'd be a nice pick-me-up for a sleepy afternoon.

I heard a hiss of breath behind me and turned toward the sound.

A woman sat behind a laptop screen of her own, her face illuminated by the glow. The sky outside was darkening—a thunderstorm was coming—and she looked pale in the light. I knew her instantly.

"Caroline?"

"Patrick." She jumped from her seat and rushed to embrace me. "How are you?"

"What are you doing here?"

Seventeen years unwound like a ribbon. Her body was the same, compact like always, fit. I almost touched her hair, out of instinct, but let go of her quickly.

"We just moved back. I'm working from home today."

"Me too." My hand twitched with the lie. Sort-of lie. "Well, I didn't just move back. We've been here for a while. But I'm on the clock today. We should camp out together, catch up. Want a coffee?"

"I've got one, thanks." Caroline stepped back, smiled. "But camping out, sure. I'd like that. I've been... kind of lonely."

It wasn't exactly like old times, but it was nice.

We were both older. I noticed it in her hands, not as nimble, lined like Amy's. I wondered what Caroline saw in me that was different. She told me about a husband, a son, and part of me diminished when she said that.

After some time, Caroline lapsed into silence, focusing back on her computer. "I have to make sure I bill these hours today."

"No worries." I fired up my laptop.

What did I expect? I wasn't sure. She was a surprise, a little delight, and my brain was all over the place. Should I try to log back into Fork-Flavor? No reason to bother. I pulled up Indeed instead. Time to send out resumes. But when I opened my Word document, I realized I hadn't even updated it, not since before ForkFlavor. I sighed.

"What's wrong?"

I hesitated. "I'm pretty sure I lost my job."

Caroline set down her coffee.

"Really? Oh, Patrick, I'm sorry." She touched my shoulder. "That sucks."

I thought back to Jude's little message. *Hear you've got some extra time now!*

"Jude may have had something to do with it," I told Caroline. It was the first time I had admitted it.

She didn't say anything. But her eyes were darting around, in that way I remembered, the way they did when she got nervous. Then she shut her laptop and leaned closer to me. "Did you get that letter?"

10

Patrick beside me at the coffee shop was an alien invasion. An alternate universe. The playing out of a scenario I had imagined as a girl so many times. In that other world, the one where we stayed together, we sat as a couple, working in comfortable silence, rings on our fingers.

There were still rings on our fingers, but they belonged to other people. At least until I figured out what to do about my marriage.

I tried to focus on my case material, but I read the same sentence over and over, unable to make any notes. I could smell him—that clean, physical scent. It hadn't changed.

And he'd gotten the letter too. He'd been in contact with Jude. Both of us needed to get back to work, needed to be productive, but that was impossible now.

I closed my laptop, unable to stop my running thoughts. "I should get back."

"You don't want to stay and talk?" Patrick looked up from his screen. "You just got here."

55

I twisted an elbow toward the clock as I loaded my computer bag. "It's been two hours. And Kyle's at home."

"Kyle?" Patrick snapped his cover shut.

"My son."

He clucked his tongue. "That's what I was afraid of."

"What?" Maybe I could stay as mad as I had been long ago. I could summon the anger from the past, draw it up like magma bubbling to a volcanic surface. "You know my son?"

Patrick smiled. "He's only my son's greatest rival."

My stomach dropped.

"My wife is freaking out because Aidan wants to do wrestling, but she doesn't want to deal with another season of Kyle."

I blew out a breath. "God forbid your wife freak out."

Patrick put up a hand. "Hey now."

"Nice to see you. Hope my son isn't too much of an inconvenience." I hoisted my bag on my shoulder and headed for the door.

"Wait." He was on his feet, his hand sparking on my shoulder.

I jumped.

"I'm sorry. Why don't we do something about this code thing? Let's work together."

I took a breath. I didn't want to go home, but I couldn't be sure I could trust my old flame. "Do you know something I don't?"

"I don't know. I got a hint in my e-mail—a YouTube video. He said there would be a great reward for whoever finishes the quest first."

I shivered as Patrick's voice crawled up my spine. *A reward.* I didn't even know what that meant.

"You want to know what he's up to. So do I," Patrick said.

Jude's unspoken name crawled in my thoughts like a spider. I closed my eyes. My bag dug into my shoulder. Patrick's hand splayed over the strap.

"Then let's do it," I said. "Not talk. Not even mention our families. Just... find Jude. That's what he wants, isn't it?"

I met Patrick's eye, and I thought I saw him flinch.

11

Patrick

Caroline walked me to my car, but I didn't want to go home. I sat in the driver's seat and stretched out my legs, leaning back as far as the thing would recline.

I imagined myself as a very comfortable homeless person, taking up space in the coffee shop parking lot. Eventually, the head honcho might offer me a job as a barista. I'd learn the ropes quick and, with my financial knowhow, I'd move up the ranks to manager in no time. I could upgrade to a BMW, trade up to finer sleeping conditions.

"Fame and fortune," I muttered.

Maybe I shouldn't have told Caroline about Jude's money. We needed it too badly.

Like a portent of doom, my phone whistled with the particular sound engine for Matt's number. I was tempted to chuck the thing out the window, when I would then crunch it with a tire, but I couldn't afford a new phone. So I opened the text.

Hey, buddy! Give me a call.

Perhaps this was a spam message? The generic language had me wondering if Matt had been hacked. Maybe that was why all the financials were off.

The phone whistled again. *Come on, you piece of crap.*

Now that was more Matt's speed. I dialed him.

"Pat!" I hate being called that, but Matt loved rhyming our names, especially when he was in one of his manic good moods. "Man! I got a call from an investor today, and boy are things looking up!"

"Go on," I said, neutral. Best not to increase hope just yet.

"Paddy boy, it's your lucky day. Luck of the Irish, must be. This guy knows you, and he wants to give us money. Loads of it. Buckets of it. Pots of gold! More than enough to make up for your accounting errors." He said this blithely, but a muscle jumped in my eye. "I'm even willing to put our pasts aside. Just say you'll stay, because old Jude is delivering. And so is ForkFlavor. Now, we can expand even farther into the boonies!"

I threw my head back against the headrest. My stomach, parallel to the floor, tied itself over and over again like the Gordian knot. "So, my access is back, then?"

"Back and better than ever. New passwords. You'll have to come downtown tomorrow. We have lots to discuss."

Behind my eyelids, images jumped. Amy, the way she flinched from my touch. Caroline, this new face of hers, worn by time, age, and stress. And Jude, perennially seventeen, lips curling around a bassoon reed he'd shaved himself. That man could do anything, almost anything.

I walked my way back through the logic. My Quicken log of transactions hadn't matched Matt's own records scribbled onto paper. He thought I had stolen money. Matt was wrong, but there was nothing I could do to convince him of that fact. Until Jude showed up, bringing the big bucks. Jude, rescuing me from somewhere on high, after he may have manipulated Matt to begin with.

Always putting me on the emotional roller coaster.

I cleared my throat. "I'll see you soon."

Matt remained effusive. "Yeah, man! Stay warm. It's supposed to snow."

I PARKED the car in the garage and wiped my feet on the doormat. The kitchen smelled of sage and garlic.

"Liam!" came a screech from inside. "Don't touch! It's hot!"

My giggling son careened towards me, chubby arms reaching for my calves. I lifted him, scratched his soft skin against my incoming beard. He laughed and laughed.

Amy sagged next to the island, holding the red spatula. I thought of all the bills in my desk, my spreadsheets, and how there would be money now, at least until the next time Matt fired me. I reached for her waist, spinning her, and she emitted an indignant squeak, so I slowed down.

We could have slow-danced, except she wormed away to attack the meat browning on the stove. "You found a job that quickly?"

"Nah. Matt took me back."

She snorted. "It's like an abusive relationship."

"But at least it's one where we get paid."

"There's that." She put down the spatula.

Liam, intent on one of his toy trains, murmured at our feet. Amy let me kiss her, long and deep, and I warmed to her touch.

Later that night, after we'd made love, I thought of Jude. His face, his body, swam through my consciousness—unbidden, unannounced.

12

Caroline

After work, I stopped at Bright Flower. Kyle was at football practice, and the thought of being alone with Kieran prickled my skin. I might have to actually talk to him.

Seeing Patrick had knocked something loose in me. I crackled with new energy, alive, part of something bigger. I'd figured a return to Chesterfield was a detour, but now I wondered if it was the destination.

My mother lay in bed as dusk fell. She didn't look sixty-eight, really. Didn't even look sick. But my father had wrestled with cancer and died at sixty-two, and it was the same then. Bright Flower was my mother's first choice for the last days of her life.

"It's so calm here," she'd said when she moved in. "Peaceful."

"Because everyone here is dying," I'd replied, matter-of-fact, practical. A realist.

"Death is part of life," she'd said. "And I'm in that stage. I need that vibe."

Now, she had a stack of books at her bedside—*When Breath*

Becomes Air on top, *Advice for Future Corpses* below. I sat on her bed, picked up each book, and flicked through the pages. "Mom. This is so morbid."

"We're all going to die, honey. Might as well learn about what's coming." She rose from the bed to hug me. Her scent had changed—less gentle, more institutional. Her shoulders were bonier, her torso losing muscle. Ribs protruding. Maybe I was in denial.

My mother slid delicately onto the couch across from her bed. "What's the good word?"

"Are you sure you don't want to move in with me?"

She clucked. Her long hair was dry, graying-white, and she ran her hands through it as she loosened her ropy braid. "Do you hate your family that much?"

"You're my family."

Mom laughed. "Dinner's coming. There will be tea and soup. Want to stay?"

"Of course." I leaned against her headboard. My back cramped if I sat unsupported for too long. "I could use the company."

We'd always had a chill relationship. Even when I was a teen, I was fairly straitlaced: good grades, only ever straying into bad behavior with Patrick. Even that wasn't truly bad. Possibly irresponsible, tactless. I cringed at the memory of places where we'd been inappropriate. Anyway, my mother wasn't my friend—she held that boundary—but she was a confidante.

Come to think of it, maybe that boundary was why she didn't want to move in. Either that or she didn't like my new family.

But I always wanted her approval, always absorbed her advice like gospel. She was an anomaly in this hick town of gun people and racist jerks. She brought her Zen and light everywhere. And that was why I couldn't lose her.

"I saw Patrick yesterday," I told her as we ate. The green tea soothed my throat. Snow fell softly outside. "Ran into him in town."

"Yes, he lives here," my mother said. "He has a lovely family."

"You know his wife?" I couldn't help being curious about her, this woman he'd chosen.

My mother raised her teacup to her lips.

"Only by sight. I remember the baby was so cute." She studied me across our trays. "Reminded me of you as a child. You were like sunshine."

Part of the reason I'd gone to California was because my mother had been born there. She ended up with my dad when she came to Ohio to attend school at Case Western Reserve University, and they'd both worked in Cleveland chemistry labs throughout my childhood. She loved her work, but I could tell she missed home. After she retired, she'd visited with us in Fresno for weeks at a time, especially after my father passed. I'd thought for sure she'd join us permanently.

I was so confused when she'd chosen to stay in Chesterfield. I reasoned that Bright Flower held the memory of my father. It kept her connected to him. My mother was her own series of mysteries. She was so easy to read on the surface, so easy to be with. But I knew she was like an iceberg, hiding so much. I also knew all her secrets were benevolent—not scandals, but knowledge, the inner workings of the universe.

I wondered if I should say anything about Jude, about the codes. But instead I asked, "What about Hannah?"

My mother put her cup down. "That was the thin, little girl you used to drive around."

"Her mom wouldn't let her get her license."

My mother nodded. "I haven't seen her. I wondered what happened to her."

I opened my mouth but paused. "Yeah. I wonder."

When I left the building, I pulled out my phone. It had been some time since I'd looked at it, what with work and seeing Mom. Plus, I'm not one to be tethered to technology. Lawyer life in the age of the

BlackBerry made me want to chuck my smartphone before I even bought one.

And my notifications had exploded with texts. Not from my family. I could be in a hole under Route 271 and they wouldn't know it till the next day. No. The texts were all from Patrick. I read through them right there in the parking lot.

13

Caroline

After visiting my mother, I still didn't want to go back to the house.

I kept thinking about Kieran, how I'd fallen for him: that golden surfer boy, not beholden to anything, following his own whims through life. It had seemed so romantic back then. And still, there were days when I saw the best parts of him, like when he'd made that delicious bowl of quinoa and tofu. I loved when the house smelled good, when it felt like somewhere I wanted to be. It wasn't fair that he had changed so much. I kicked myself for not realizing it until we came back here. I could have, should have, left him in Fresno. Maybe I'd let the sun blind me to the truth.

Patrick was different. He was organized, put together. And as we texted in the parking lot, I lost track of time. The sun went down. One minute I was sitting up straight, fingers flying across my phone screen. Then I was lying back, feet thrown up on the dashboard, eyes burning but still fastened on the text chain.

Me: *What do you think "great reward" means?*

Patrick: *Money. Don't you think? He's a freaking millionaire.*

Me: *What?*

Patrick: *Did you not know this?*

Me: *I have no clue what you're talking about.*

Patrick: *Google it. Jude's Panic Room. Then come back and tell me what you think. ;-)*

I'd heard of Panic Room. They were an escape room company, with franchises all over the country, and there were apps you could buy too. I'd seen the board games in Target, but I'd never thought to look more closely at them.

Of course he hadn't vanished. He'd become someone else.

I should have known. He'd always wanted to make games—all those codes—all those games he played with us. Manipulating our feelings as if they were the pieces.

I started the car. But I didn't go home.

My coffee cup was empty again.

The server swung around my table, tired but kind. She filled my cup.

"Thank you," I said, my voice hoarse.

The sun was rising, darts of light shooting through the east-facing window.

The night had passed in a caffeine-infused haze as I worked the letters, over and over and over. I tried so many combinations, starting with that three-letter word. It wasn't "the" or "cat" or "had" or any other Scrabble word I could think of. The phrase still looked like gibberish.

I texted my boss to let her know I wouldn't be in. I had to get home and sleep.

It was too bad Kieran never left the house... I dreamed of a day to myself, a day where I could sleep until noon, then take a warm bubble bath while reading a good book. But that wasn't possible. Inevitably,

Kieran would be there bothering me, wanting me for anything and everything.

How much longer could I work on the code? I could wait to go home, at least until Kyle went to school. If he remembered to get up. I hated the sarcasm in my mind—it sounded harsh and felt harsher, especially when I thought about his child-face, the boy in the pictures on my phone. But that child was gone. Fourteen was new territory.

The server came back around. "Ma'am, I'm so sorry to bother you, but the breakfast rush will be in soon. Were you planning to stay any longer?"

"Oh, I've been here a while, haven't I?" I gathered my things. "I'll get out of your way."

She softened. "No, no, you don't have to. I just refilled your coffee."

She was my age, maybe a little older. Faded grayish hair tied in a neat bun.

"You look familiar," she said. "Did you grow up here?"

I nodded.

"Caroline, right? Caroline Cross?"

"The very same." I looked up, smiled. "Remind me of your name?"

"Beth Lawson." She didn't meet my eyes. "Or, at least that's what it was. Before the marriage, and then the divorce."

She grimaced.

"That's why I kept my name."

"You divorced, too?"

I hesitated. *Not yet.* I didn't say anything. Let her think what she wanted.

"It's rough." She slid into the booth beside me. "I hate working nights, but I have to stay in town. Ray works at HarborTop. You know, the granite factory. I have to be close for our son. He's just little."

"Aww. I miss little ones." Sitting, I reached for my coffee while Beth peered at my work. Just because she said she went to school with me didn't mean we were automatic besties. But I was so tired, my guard was down.

"What's this now?" she asked.

"Just a code, a message." I waved a hand. "You remember Jude Lassiter?"

Maybe she'd know what had happened to him.

Beth laughed.

"Jude. Such a riot. You guys were always so tight. I remember wanting to be in with your group. But it would never happen." She picked up my pen, twirled it in her fingers. "This is from him?"

"He was into codes. I got it in the mail. I mean, I haven't seen him since school. But he sent this to me." I felt stupid saying it out loud, admitting it. "These letters stand for something. I haven't been able to work out the substitution."

"Hmmm."

The dawn light strengthened, and I felt the glow of exhaustion. I swallowed more coffee. I was about to faceplant on the skeezy diner table.

"Why don't you try each letter of the alphabet? Like, write the alphabet out a bunch of different times and then find the letters that seem the closest?"

I showed her my scribblings. "Yeah. But it's all over the place. It's because I'm so tired."

"Lucky for you I've been doing these night shifts for a while. I'm used to it." Beth winked. She skimmed my paper, then pointed to one scrawl. "The first and the last word both end in the same letter. Maybe it's S? Like, if they're plural nouns?"

I had one iteration where I'd substituted in the S. I leaned over her shoulder, squinting at my work. "That doesn't help me with the rest of the letters."

"Try writing out the alphabet."

The T equaled S. Maybe each letter was off by one place?

I was getting closer.

∾

I was still there when the lunch rush arrived. Beth had moved me to the bar, and then she left, needing sleep. I vowed to dust off my yearbook and find her photo when I got home.

I was so close. The alphabet was off by one place in some spots, but in others, the substitutions made no sense. If I had to guess, I'd say the message read *Words are your weapons*, with X standing in for W and P oh-so-close to R...

But this meant nothing.

I spent an hour anagramming the phrase, searching for the meaning hidden in yet one more layer.

The bar stool position set up a deep ache in my lower back. I stretched, bent, hunched, drank more coffee. I ordered and wolfed down a turkey sandwich.

I closed my eyes and drifted. A memory surfaced, playing in my subconscious. Little Kyle, his chubby hands around an alphabet block, watching Sesame Street and humming along with the song. I saw the letters, dancing across the screen. Saw my son, the way I wanted him to stay forever.

Then I was falling, hitting the ground hard.

The bar stool plunged out from under me and fell on the tile with a metallic clunk. Diners turned and stared. I blinked, shook my head.

"I'm fine!" I called out, ignoring the sting in my shoulder where I'd collided with the floor.

I was fine. I knew what to do next.

"Caroline Cross. As I live and breathe."

As I walked into the Chesterfield Library, I felt as if I had stepped back in time twenty years. The smell was the same, that aged-book aroma, except in the new section, where the magazines called out with their shiny prints and alluring celebrities.

Lena Caldwell, it seemed, was now Chesterfield's librarian. She stood behind a giant fort of a desk, a tall auburn monolith that obscured most of her body. A sign screaming REFERENCE sat in front of her chest, so all I could see was her tiny head sticking out. I always thought it was funny that someone with such a giant ego could have such a small head.

In high school, Lena and I were deadlocked in a race for valedictorian, almost from the get-go freshman year. She was sneaky, always trying to sabotage me. Like when she kept talking about how great the art teacher was. I'd been tempted to sign up for that elective, but I had to stop myself, because if Lena took all accelerated coursework and I didn't, she'd pull ahead. I could never trust her after that. In the end, the point was moot, because the school crowned us both. And I hadn't thought of it since.

When I wrote out the alphabet, substituting the new text, I found that the beginning of the coded alphabet spelled "LIBRAY"— without the extra R, because one R can't stand for two letters. *Words are your weapons.* But what was I fighting for? Or against...

Lena came around the corner of the desk and folded her arms. She was still petite, scrawny even, her brown hair long and tipped with pink ends. She was going against the stereotype. That was for sure. But I had to laugh a little, that she'd ended up here. She was so pissed when I'd been voted the girl Most Likely to Succeed. And I had, hadn't I?

I was dizzy with my victory. I swayed, waiting for her to say something.

"Caroline, are you okay?"

Could a person become drunk with lack of sleep? Could this bitchy girl have become a woman with some compassion, some concern reflected in her voice? Or was she worried that I would pass out in her library, her territory?

That was the last thing I remembered.

14

Dora

On Wednesday, I headed to the library after school. No band practice, since the game was Friday, and we'd do a dry run beforehand. A few measures of pregame, a few measures of halftime. We knew our stuff, though.

Grandma said she'd pick me up after I worked on my paper for a little while. I had found the Conan Doyle books, and I was leafing through them when the lady fainted.

At first, I heard the thump, then Mrs. Caldwell's yelp. I darted out of the aisle to find the librarian bent over the prone woman. I couldn't say anything. I stared.

I felt overwhelmed by the sensation of it all. What else could I do besides watch it happen? No fifteen-year-old girl takes on the responsibility of calling for help when a grown woman passes out.

Except I had. I'd done that many times.

No, I was frozen because I'd never seen this woman before, but she looked familiar.

She groaned, stirring on the floor. Wiggled her hips. Mrs. Caldwell caught me watching, and I would have gone if she—the woman on the floor, I mean—hadn't spoken.

"Hannah?"

I swallowed. "Is she okay?"

"She thinks you're your mom."

As if I didn't get that, Mrs. Obvious. "Who is she?"

It was getting dark early, although it wouldn't be past daylight savings until the weekend, after the last game. Streetlights warmed to life outside the library's large picture window.

"Her name's Caroline," Mrs. Caldwell said. "She went to school with us. Me and your mom."

Yeah, like everyone else in this town. I turned to go.

Curled in an armchair next to the library's fireplace, I read through the Holmes story backwards and forwards, combing through it for the code. The answer was there. I could feel it in my fingertips as I turned the pages.

I pulled the parchment from my bookbag and compared it to the men of the story. But the letters were a jumbled mess.

I sighed, pushed the book away.

The lights flickered. The library would close soon. I wasn't looking forward to walking home, with the air getting colder and the sky growing darker. I heaved my bookbag over my shoulder and headed to the desk, but then I changed my mind and left the books on the table. Maybe this search wasn't worth anything.

I stopped short at the door, where Mrs. Caldwell and the fainting woman—Caroline—stood facing each other.

"I told you, it's not for checkout." Mrs. Caldwell locked her arms across her chest.

"I need it, though." Caroline clutched the book. The woman looked as if she might pass out any moment. Again. The skin under her eyes was purple, translucent. "You can't stop me from taking it."

"Yes, I can. It's called a reference book." Caldwell extended one hand, although not far enough to open herself to a threat.

"I'm not an idiot. You don't keep classic fiction on closed reserve."

"Unless I'm specifically requested to by a teacher."

Caroline sniffed. "No high school reads Thomas Hardy. Certainly not in Chesterfield."

"We're closing." Caldwell cleared her throat. "I'll call the police if I need to."

I couldn't help clearing my own throat. A mirror reaction, I supposed. We learned about that in Psych 101, how our bodies respond to others' in the same ways. But also, they were blocking the door.

Each woman turned to me. I suspected Caldwell only wanted to go home, but the look on Caroline's face was of muted wonder.

"It's you again." She stepped towards me.

Mrs. Caldwell snatched the book and dipped past us, through the double doors. The lights dimmed.

$\sim$

"I'm not sure you should drive," I said.

I may be only fifteen, but I can tell when people are not working at 100%. This woman swayed when she walked, and her already-pale skin glowed ghostly under the parking lot lights.

It was cold. The dropping temperatures made me worry about the last football game. I could already feel the chill in my feet. They'd be stuffed into my ugly off-white band shoes with no room for an extra pair of socks.

"Mrs. Cross?"

She sniffed. "It's Ms. If I were a Mrs. I'd have a different last name."

"You passed out in there." I pulled my coat more tightly around myself, stamped my feet. Tiny dots of chilly rain snuck down my neck. "Come on. Let's at least get in your car."

"Right." She shook her head and dug through her purse. Another minute and I was about to start walking. I heard the thunk of locks engaging, and a Hyundai Tucson lit up. I scuttled to it, clambered into the passenger side, and blew on my fingers.

Caroline dumped her phone into the center console and twisted her key. I prayed. Well, I didn't go to church, so I didn't know if I was doing it right. I wondered if I'd get a critique from God... I hoped not through a form of retribution. I wanted to at least make it to my high school graduation. Beyond that, my future was an indistinct blur—but I knew I wanted one.

"Tell me where you live." Caroline's voice was almost mechanical. How long had it been since she'd slept? Did I need to call an ambulance?

I grabbed her phone. "I'll put it in your GPS. What's the password?"

"Like I'm telling you anything." She snorted and took the phone back, wobbling a little. She stabbed in some numbers, and the background picture bloomed in full color.

I froze. "Are you Kyle's mom?"

He looked a little younger on her wallpaper, fuller-faced, smiling in a way I'd never seen. Not cocky or sullen. I almost felt good that I was helping him. Then I shook my head and banished that thought.

Caroline sighed. "For my sins. Yes. Kyle belongs to me."

She handed the phone to me, presumably happy with its continued security. Heat blasted from the vents, and I bathed in it for a moment, forgetting why I was there. Then I recovered and plugged our address into her maps app. I could do this. I could grab the wheel if I needed to. It was only a mile to my house.

It wasn't long before she found it, and I breathed out, sagging against the leather.

"Thank you, Ms. Cross." I reached for the door handle, about to jump out, but I had a feeling she wanted to say something. I waited.

"This was her house." She stared past the windshield. "You haven't moved? Ever?"

"I live here. With my grandma."

Kyle was from California, I remembered. It was so unfair. He was more popular than anyone. New kids were supposed to be losers. The joke was on him now that he was stuck in Chesterfield.

Caroline nodded. "So, Hannah—I mean, your mother. She's here? In Chesterfield?"

I shook my head. Didn't seem like the right time to spill my whole sob story. If this woman really cared about my mother, she'd find out about her death soon enough. Besides, I didn't like talking about it. At all.

Caroline drummed on the wheel, tapping her long fingers. It seemed like she was about to say something else, but she stopped herself. Then she sighed. "Well, honey—what's your name?"

"Dora."

It was hard to tell in the dim light, but it looked like her eyes widened a smidgen.

"Not like the explorer," I said.

"Oh, I know." Her voice was low, quiet. "I know."

From "The Great Genius of Edward Elgar," a high school paper by Jude Lassiter

Elgar's first interest in code may have come from the influence of Robert Schumann. Schumann used a cipher-wheel to encode his wife's name into music. Schumann also wrote letters to her in code. Elgar did that too. He started writing codes into music when he was a violin teacher in England. He wrote music for his students that included their names as part of the theme. Because the first seven letters of the alphabet represent notes of the scale, and the students' last name was Gedge, Elgar could easily write a theme that used those letters.

15

Dora

Since I didn't have to worry about my instruments, I arrived at Ms. Krieger's room long before the after-lunch bell on Thursday. Mallory looked like she would burst if she didn't speak immediately.

"I'm having a board game party tomorrow!" She sounded so excited that I could almost ignore the whispers from the rest of the class. Poor Mallory was oblivious to all of it. She just liked board games. "You should come. All the cool people will be at the football game, but we don't need them."

"I have band, remember?" I loved Mal—I'd grown up with her, after all—but sometimes I wondered if she ever thought of anyone besides herself. I mean, forgetting that one's best friend needs to be at every Friday game is pretty self-centered.

She winced. "Come over after."

"Maybe. If I can get a ride." Another detail she'd forgotten: Grandma hated picking me up and dropping me off.

"You can spend the night." She grinned and leaned forward.

I moved back. Her perfume or body wash or whatever clung to her, too floral for someone our age. She smelled like someone's grandma. Probably hers.

"I checked out a bunch of new games. The library has them now. Pretty fun."

"I'll think about it."

The bell cut through the conversation, and I was silently grateful. Mallory faced forward, her frizzy curls bouncing, and Ms. Krieger strode to the front of the room. The class behind me settled.

"Okay, everyone. Clarifying due dates. The Holmes essay is due in two weeks, and we'll move on to William Carlos Williams today. Has everyone done the reading? Of course, you haven't. I don't even know why I ask." Ms. K slapped her forehead.

I laughed, but I was the only one. The kids behind me faded into a sea of judgment. They didn't get her humor.

She looked at me. "At least I can always count on Dora. What were your thoughts?"

Ughhhh. I suppressed my groan. Ms. K sounded warm, collegial even, but she probably didn't realize how embarrassing she was being. I gave my interpretation of "The Red Wheelbarrow" with as neutral of a tone as I could muster.

When class ended, I headed for the door with everyone else, but I felt a soft tap on my shoulder. Mallory exited with the crowd. I took a breath and turned back to face Ms. K.

"Miss Madison. Are you going to let Kyle know about the new assignment?"

"Huh?" I had no idea what she was talking about. Fear stirred in my belly. "Wasn't he here today?"

"I thought you'd know. You seem pretty close lately." She folded her arms, leaned back against her desk.

I stood, holding my stuff, shifting my weight back and forth.

"Don't worry. I'll give you a pass to class."

I still said nothing. If I said nothing, I couldn't lie.

She sighed. Ms. K was an adult, but I saw a girl in her. A girl with knobby knees and braces, a girl who liked books and kept to herself.

"I'm worried, Dora. You're so young. You remind me of myself."

I'd known that was coming.

"At your age, I was always wishing guys would notice me. I would have done anything." Her face went pink.

I needed to run this carefully. Either she suspected what was going on, or she thought there was something else going on. Either way, she knew Kyle and I were connected.

Sometimes it paid to be a music geek. I controlled my shaky breath and stilled my trembling fingers as I pretended I was on stage. "Well... you know that code from the other day?"

Ms. K straightened, then nodded.

"Kyle's mom is working on it too."

She relaxed a little, and so did I.

"Why? What is it?"

"Not sure. We all got these letters in the mail. That's why I was asking you about the Holmes story." The letter was now in my locker. I hadn't gotten any further with it. But my heart slowed as I sank into my reasoning, which wasn't a lie at all.

Ms. K nodded again, as if contemplating this idea, touching a finger to her chin. That knobby-kneed girl was interested. "So, you don't know why you got the letter?"

I shook my head. Classes were changing now, and a new group of students straggled into the room, slumping into their seats. It felt odd to be in front of them all, like another teacher. "And I don't know Kyle or his mom all that well. They're new in town. But I guess she grew up here."

Ms. K tsked. "I grew up in a small town like this. Gotta say, there's a reason I commute from Cleveland Heights now."

She sighed, and I could tell there was something else she wanted to say, but time was up. The bell clanged. She turned around, dug in her desk drawer for a hall pass, and scrawled on it. "Please tell me if anything else is going on, okay?"

"Okay." I raced out of the room and into the empty hall.

For a moment, I considered escape. The day was gray and cloudy, but the thought of freedom was seductive.

I didn't belong here. Even though I was born here, and Mom too, I was never truly part of this place. Mallory was my only friend, and I was sure that if I left, she wouldn't miss me. I gritted my teeth as I headed back to my bright yellow locker. *Just a few more years.*

As I stashed my stuff and extracted my book for geometry, the coded letter fluttered to the floor. I bent to pick it up, and a crash sounded in my ear.

"Hey!"

I straightened, expecting to see that some asshole jock had slammed my locker, and nearly fell over at the sight of Aidan Reed. *Great.* Another avenging angel here to protect me from Kyle. I hadn't even seen the dude today, yet he was driving the bus from the back seat.

Aidan held out a piece of paper. "Can I see that code again?"

"How'd you get out of class?" I took it and saw the same dancing men symbols, the same parchment. "Where'd you get this?"

"Guidance aide this period. I saw you leave Ms. K's room." Aidan scuffed his sneaker against the floor. "My dad had it. I just... borrowed it."

I handed him my letter. We looked at them both, side by side, not saying anything.

"Kyle's mom got one too," I said.

"Well." Aidan cleared his throat. "I guess we'll have to solve it before she does."

16

Patrick

Caroline and I had texted until late Tuesday night. Then, nothing. Radio silence. I'd told her to Google Jude's Panic Room and then tell me what she found. But she never did.

So, I kept reaching for Amy.

In the kitchen, while we were cooking. In the living room, while she watched some inane show and Liam threw toys into every corner. In bed, when I sneaked into our room to give her a kiss goodnight. And every time, she turned away, presenting her back or tending to Liam. Once she shrank from me to hug Aidan, and my son shrank back himself, caught between crosshairs.

I breathed rejection. Screamed it. Amy kept turning away, and I didn't stop asking. Despite being rebuffed, my need grew.

Then, like a sudden thunderstorm, Caroline appeared.

On the train downtown, Friday morning, in a series of texts: *I met Hannah's daughter. I think she's doing the codes too. She's one step ahead of us. That's so like Hannah.*

I'd never thought of Hannah as anything but a victim, a sad

shadow. After the whole incident with the movie night and the Ouija board, she'd retreated into herself, not interested in hanging out with us anymore. I'd been a selfish kid, thinking about graduation and college, and I didn't reach out to her, even though she could have used a friend. The last time I'd seen her was at OSU, when I was there, and Jude was at Denison. Hannah stayed with me for a few months while Amy was studying abroad, but then she moved back home. I guessed she couldn't handle her classes and the fast pace of the school. She slunk back into my life and then out again just as quickly.

I couldn't believe she'd stayed in town all these years. Maybe I'd even seen her in the grocery store or the post office, but if I had, I hadn't recognized her. She faded, became part of the background. An afterthought. When I read online that she had passed away, it wasn't much of a surprise. Sure, I felt bad. But then, I always had.

When I returned to work, it was as if the past few days had never happened. Holly was back at her computer, her glossy hair shining, her soul mostly intact. Each of us carried at least a few mental bruises.

"Hello, Patrick! TGIF, right?" Holly asked. As if we'd been in every day this week. As if we'd experienced the workaday slog of Tuesday, Wednesday, and Thursday instead of the crippling anxiety of not having a job.

"Yeah." I elbowed my office door open. Apparently, Matt hadn't taken the time to change the locks or the art on the walls. I dumped my briefcase on my computer chair, went to the window, and looked out for a moment.

As I predicted, Matt tumbled in, a burst of sound and energy. "Hols! How you been, babe?"

I focused on a window in the building across from ours. A man in a gray suit crossed the expanse of his office. From so far away, he looked tiny, like a doll in a dollhouse. Did his office not celebrate Casual Friday? I was wearing a pink ForkFlavor polo. *Salmon,* Amy would say.

"Pat! You in there? Come out and meet Duncan!"

I suppressed a groan. The gray suit guy approached his copy machine.

Then I turned from the window to my door and exchanged a glance with Holly. She closed a window on her screen.

Matt stood with a tall kid who looked no older than my son. Duncan's face was peppered with acne spots. I touched my bristly cheek, reflexively. I'd been a lucky teenager. This kid would have scars. His sandy hair fell into his eyes.

Matt was trying to save money, no doubt. We'd had a parade of interns over the years, lasting from a few days to a couple of weeks—however long they could stand the abuse.

I extended a hand. "Patrick Reed."

"It's something about our new investor. I have the resources to hire more employees. We could even expand our office space, depending on our growth trajectory." Matt darted about the front office, draping his leather coat over the leather reception couch. The guy liked quality, liked to throw his cash around. I'd looked at the errant numbers again, now that I had restored access to the accounts. Back in the saddle, I was quite sure that the accounting errors had resulted from Matt's indolent spending, transactions I was unaware of and so couldn't record in Quicken. It all made me want to install myself in front of my spreadsheets at my desk at home, writing paper checks with a smooth-inked pen. And also, to take Matt's credit card.

"So, Duncan, maybe Matt will hire you on." I winked at the kid.

"One step ahead, bro." Matt flitted to Duncan's side and thwacked him on the back. He didn't flinch. "Duncan, here, has got the finest mind in Cleveland. He's a programmer, but he's also got marketing experience. New grad. All the companies in town have him on their watch lists, and we snagged him first."

I raised an eyebrow. "I'll need to update payroll, then."

"More than that. You've got funds to review. Paperwork to sign. Office space to scout out. You're gonna be busy. ForkFlavor is growing, and it starts with our wunderkind here."

"Okay, so the eleven a.m. meeting is a go?" I checked my watch.

"Sorry, man, you're not invited today. After what you did, I'll need you to stay locked on logistics. We'll be brainstorming, me and Duncan." Matt grinned.

I frowned. Holly opened Word. She was definitely updating her resume.

Duncan tossed his head, flipping a lock of hair out of his face.

I looked at Matt. "Does he speak?"

"No, he requires a translator computer. Like that Stephen Hawking guy. Whadya think?" Matt ushered the kid into his office and shut the door. Crashing and yelling ensued. Matt needed to rearrange his furniture periodically, or he "couldn't think."

I returned to my office, shut the door, and basked in silence.

I opened the file for new employee paperwork and printed off the packet. But then I hesitated. Duncan might be gone by lunch. I minimized the PDF window and opened my e-mail instead.

A new one from Amy: *Why aren't you checking your phone? I've been texting you all morning. Will you be home in time for the game? It's Aidan's last one and he's starting. Kyle's benched. You've got to come.*

Then another one pinged in. *Patrick, come on. I can throw Liam on my back, but that's not sustainable for the entire night. I need to know if you'll be there.*

Nothing had changed.

I considered a leap from the window. I walked up to it, tapped the clear surface with my knuckle. Some kind of baked glass, sturdy, meant to prevent suicides. I'd need a sledgehammer to break it. Did they sell those at Tower City?

I sighed and clicked back to my inbox.

No new messages. Nothing new from Caroline.

17

Dora

Just make it through the day. It's the last game.

I was always so tired on game days. I'd wake up before the sun to get on the bus, then be up until at least ten while I waited for someone to pick me up from the high school. Some Fridays, it was even later. Once, the custodian took pity on me and let me into the lobby. I was still there when she left, dozing, my head on top of my trombone case, until my grandma came to pick me up. FYI, a trombone case does not make a great pillow.

"You sure you don't want to come?" Mallory wheedled in the cafeteria at lunch.

I slumped over my sandwich. "I need to conserve my energy."

"I've been chatting with this guy online, and he says he'll be there." She twined a bit of curly hair around her index finger and giggled. "College guy. He's totally into board games."

"And he'll still be into you when he finds out you're fourteen?"

"I'm not trying to get with him, Dora. I mean, come on." Mallory looked away, her full cheeks pinking behind her freckles. "It's just, like, cool to be noticed."

I followed Mallory's gaze across the cafeteria. Aidan sat surrounded by cheerleaders and teammates. I could trace a line in the air to where Kyle sat opposite him with a similar cohort.

"Like Jets versus Sharks," I mumbled.

"Huh?"

"Nothing." We'd played a selection from *West Side Story* earlier in the season, but Mallory wouldn't know because she'd never been to one of my games.

I had to get Aidan's attention. Hard to do at school where no one wanted to be seen with a nerd like me. I tried to tell myself he'd wanted to protect me from Kyle. I could use that, somehow.

KRIEGER PULLED me aside after class. She'd graded our last essay. I was on my way to Busted Town.

"You're not gonna give me a hall pass this time, are you?" I mumbled.

"Honey, I went to plagiarism school," she said—not unkindly, but not gently, either. "I know it when I see it."

"I didn't copy anything." I was proud of my work, actually. I hadn't left any identifying marks in my fabricated prose. I'd even thrown in those wider margins and the bigger font to disguise my less-than-awesome writing as Kyle's.

Krieger folded her arms, and I felt the echo of our last encounter as my stomach dropped through my body onto the floor. "I know."

"I'm sorry," I said.

"You should be. But being sorry isn't enough." She stared past me into the middle distance, chewing on her lip.

I held my books against my chest, waiting.

Grandma was a force to be reckoned with when she was pissed, but this might not matter to her. She'd be more upset that I had messed up my social standing at school, that I might look bad to the community. Ughhh. The rest of me could join my stomach on the floor any minute. Perhaps we could seep through and disappear into the earth's molten core.

"You need to stop enabling him," Krieger said as the next class filtered in. "I'm not going to change your grades now. But if you don't stop this, I will. You need to tell him no."

I shifted my weight. I would be late to my next class if I didn't leave. And he would ask... when? Did my phone already have a text?

Sweat beaded on the back of my neck.

She jutted her chin. "Better light a fire to those Converse."

It didn't make sense for me to go home after school. With only two hours before I had to report back for practice, getting home and back was more of an annoyance than anything. Grandma hated driving back and forth to pick me up.

As the halls cleared, I searched for Aidan. He'd be in the same boat as me, but his more attentive parents might pick him up, take him home for a nice, fueling meal before the game.

"Dora!" When he found me, he was waving the letter, the one that was identical to mine. The one his father had gotten. I'd thought I would have to flag him down, coerce him into helping me.

Something I wasn't used to. Being wanted, being sought out. My face flushed as I rushed to greet him. "Hey, I was looking for you."

"I figured it out." He kept waving the paper, and I thought the delicate parchment might break with the force of his hand. "I figured out the code."

"Seriously?" The dancing men letters had only yielded gibberish to me. "How?"

"Once you translate the man symbols to letters, then it's another code. Like, each letter stands for a different one. It says *Words are your weapons.*" He grinned and scrubbed a hand through his short, curly hair. "I don't know what that means, though."

We stood in the rapidly clearing hallway. I ignored the looks from other kids passing us by, probably wondering what a popular kid was doing talking to a loser like me. I chewed on my fingernail, thinking about words, thinking about how the other kids used them to hurt me. Aidan could be my shield.

Where could I find new words? Words I could use for my own weapons.

Then I had it.

"Aidan," I said. "Do you have to go home before the game?"

"I still don't understand why she didn't just copy the page she needed," I mumbled as Aidan and I passed through the library's automatic doors.

"Maybe it's not one page. Maybe the whole book is the key."

I frowned. Was he seriously trying to mansplain my own project to me? Just because his dad got the code too didn't mean he knew everything.

Okay, so he'd helped me solve the rest of the gibberish code, which cemented our trip to the library, and I already had confirmation that the book Caroline had wanted was significant. We only had to figure out why.

"I know why," Aidan said as we neared the librarian's desk.

"Why we need the book?"

"No, why she wanted to take it." Aidan's jaw was tight. "She didn't want anyone else to have it. I'd expect nothing less from Kyle's mom."

Mrs. Caldwell raised an eyebrow. "I assume you're looking for *Jude the Obscure* on closed reserve."

The air suddenly felt hot, and I shed my coat. When I'd encountered Caroline in the library before, I hadn't seen the book's title. *Jude the Obscure*—this was our answer. I still had no idea who this guy was, but he had to be the one behind all of it. My chest tightened.

The librarian's expression didn't change. She reached into a drawer and removed the book. "This is tagged. If you try to leave with it, the alarm will go off."

"We've got more integrity than that." Aidan took the book, and we found a study table near the librarian's desk.

If Mrs. Caldwell would be watching us anyway, might as well stay close. Besides, I knew she'd gone to school with them, and she might offer us some new information. I sensed some serious jealousy vibes—not unlike those from Ms. K. It felt strange. I was used to envying others, not the other way around.

Aidan wasn't aware of my interior monologue, and he probably didn't have the feels I was experiencing. *Oh, to be that simple.* He leafed through the pages. Life with male privilege and limited emotion seemed good.

Finally, he sighed and pushed the book my way. "Dead end."

I ran my finger along the cover. It was an old edition, a boring red binding, no flashy images on the cover. A basic old book, the kind you could find at any antique store or flea market. I flipped open the inside. "It's got a pocket in the back."

"That was how they checked out books before computers," Mrs. Caldwell said.

I ignored her and lifted the card from inside the pocket. A number was scrawled in red ink, inside: 54.

"That's my jersey number." Aidan's face went pink. Maybe he was experiencing some emotion.

I grinned. "It's also a page number."

Sure enough, starting on page 54, tiny dots sat atop letters, like little hats. I swung my bookbag on my shoulder and scrabbled through it for my math notebook. As I took down the letters, a website address emerged. Craigslist first, followed by a series of gibberish letters.

"Don't tell me I have to figure out another code key word." I groaned.

The only reason Aidan and I had thought to try "library" was because we knew that was where Kyle's mom had been when she cracked it.

Behind me, a customer approached the reference desk, talking with Mrs. Caldwell in low tones.

"It's a website." Aidan whipped out his phone and typed in the letters. "Yeah. It's a Craigslist post. GPS coordinates."

He let out a low whistle.

"What?" I craned my neck, trying to see his screen.

He turned it around to face me. I saw the bold text in stark relief against his screen: **The person who finds me will win one million dollars.**

My whole body started to tingle. A million dollars could put me through a very good college. A million dollars could get me far away from Chesterfield, could put me on the right track to a premium college. Visions of Harvard and Stanford and Brown danced across my mind, twirling like slides in fast motion.

I looked from the book, to the paper, to Aidan. "Let's go."

He glanced down at his phone, thumbed in a response to some text, some other person wanting something from him. "Can't. Practice. And tomorrow's the game."

"Shit, Aidan, a million dollars?" I fought to swallow the burning bile rising in my throat.

He shoved his phone into his pocket. I followed the turn of his head toward the librarian's empty desk. Mrs. Caldwell had taken the other customer to the stacks.

He grabbed the book, shoved it in his own bookbag, and raced to the back of the building.

"Shit," I said again, gathering my stuff and rushing to keep up with him.

His back vanished behind a closed door, so I wrenched it open and slid through. I emerged into a dark but playfully colored room. Happy letters on the walls, a rug imprinted with the Dewey Decimal system.

He paused midstride. "Didn't you ever come to story time here?"

I hadn't. Hannah had never thought to do that. Grandma might have brought me, if she had known about it. Too late now for any of that.

Aidan slipped through a metal door with a garish orange EXIT sign glowing above it. I braced for an alarm, but none came. We found ourselves in the huge field behind the library, a fall chill numbing the air. I shivered with adrenaline.

"Let's meet after the game. Or Saturday." He tapped his bookbag. "We've got all the time in the world now."

18

Caroline

I returned to the library with Patrick in tow.

Today, Lena wasn't her usual smug self. She looked rattled and pissed. "You people are impossible."

"Well, that's rather rude." I didn't even bother to remove my coat. This time, I'd find what I needed and move along. I didn't need her crap. "The book, please."

"It's not here." That troubled look crossed her face. "I never should have agreed to this. But he's leaving us a sizeable donation."

"He is." Then I paused. "What do you mean?"

Lena scowled. "Jude Lassiter? You all were so tight in high school."

I exchanged glances with Patrick. My hands balled into fists. "Why isn't the book here? You stalked me to make sure I didn't take it out of the building. Who got it past you?"

"A couple of kids."

Hannah's daughter. God. Was this the time to explain it all to Patrick? I looked back to see him staring at the ceiling tiles. Not even listening.

"Okay. New plan." I wasn't about to thank her, not after what she'd said to me. I was done with being dicked around. Jude Lassiter would come out of the shadows even if I had to pry him out with a crowbar.

I stalked to the car, Patrick beside me. We got in, and I whipped out my phone, started Googling. Last known address. Wikipedia page. Social media. All I could find was Jude's company page, and a bunch of game threads on Reddit.

"I don't think searching for him is going to help." Patrick craned his neck to view my phone. "He's notoriously private. If there's any personal information online, it's coded like all the stuff he sent us."

"Ugh." I grunted and tossed my phone into the center console, then rubbed my hands together, blew on them. "I give up. I'm done. Time to go back to my piece of shit life."

"Hold up." Patrick's hand covered mine.

I willed myself not to tremble out of anger, afraid he might think I wanted something else from him.

"What's wrong with your life? Why'd you come home? I haven't seen you in so long."

I removed my hand from under Patrick's and put my head into my hands, worrying the grooves in my forehead with my fingers. "Mom's sick. She's at Bright Flower."

"Oh." He paused. "How long does she have?"

"It's Stage 4. Terminal. But the kind she has... Liver. Her doctor says she might hang on for a while. Maybe even a few years." I blew out a breath. The car faced a curb, another parking lot adjoining the library. I stared at the gray, cold pavement, scrutinized the yellow lines carved against cement. "We wanted to be here. Well, I wanted to... so Kyle could get to know his grandmother."

He whistled. "That must be expensive."

It wasn't cheap. Most people who went to Bright Flower only left for the morgue. I wondered if my mom truly would hang on in that environment, or if the constant shadow of death would lead her to an early grave. But I wasn't about to risk losing that time with her by staying in California.

"I was tired of it," I heard myself saying, as I drummed my fingers on the steering wheel. "All the pretending out there."

"In a hospice?"

"No, no. At the beach."

The people there weren't so bad. They lived their California lives, those crazy day-to-day freewheeling hours, practicing their commune with the surf. I'd liked that sun-drenched life so much that I pretended I was okay with my husband's slacking and my constant work. Yes, okay, I was a workaholic. I'd admit that. But I supposed I'd hoped my husband might absorb some of my corn-fed work ethic from the Midwest. So far, no luck on that front.

"Oh," Patrick said.

Silence again. So many years gone by, so much to catch up on, and nothing between us we could say.

I plucked my phone from the center console. The search for Jude's name still blinked on the screen. "I'll drive you back to your car. It's getting late."

"Yeah. I have to get to the game."

If Kieran wondered anything, it was how long he could go without a shower. Or whether he could conjure cheese puffs from thin air simply by thinking of them.

I started the car, but Patrick snapped his fingers and dropped a hand on my knee. It rested there for a hot second before twitching away, and I jumped like I'd been hit with a live wire.

He sat up, rustling in his pocket.

"When Jude e-mailed me about the reward." He swallowed. "It said... *do you need a little hint?*"

"We do need a hint."

I leaned over my shifter, and he held his phone so I could see. He played the YouTube video attached to Jude's message: a haunting, lone bassoon.

"That has to be something," I said when the melody finished. "It's him, playing."

"I bet he has a Heckel now," Patrick said.

A Heckel was the most expensive bassoon a person could own. I knew that from dating Patrick. He and Jude were the only two people in the school, possibly in the county, who played the instrument. And they were stupidly competitive. Not unlike my son and Patrick's.

"He wouldn't send you a message without a code." My mind ratcheted into gear, back on the quest. "Maybe it's in the email's metadata. Can you forward that to me?"

"Um, sure."

He tapped the phone, and I recited my email address.

"Well, good. Now you have it, and we can stay in touch."

I shifted and drew my seat belt across my lap, and he did the same. Then I reversed and pointed my car toward the road.

"You'll let me know if you find anything?" I asked. "And I will, too."

"Right away."

Before I turned, I followed his gaze to the green space beyond the library. The long expanse was empty, save for a single figure in the distance.

19

Dora

The night was cold and black, but senior night was a riot of color on the field, a victory for the lucky ones getting out. I shivered in my band uniform and envied them.

Nights like this, I felt the loneliest. Frozen all the way to my toes in my stupid flimsy band shoes. My fingers stiff and sore even with gloves on. My mouthpiece stuck to my face. I dreaded the possibility of braces, which Grandma had been warning me about all summer. I pulled my blanket, printed with colorful fish, close to my shoulders, and it snagged over my faux-epaulets.

I didn't want to go to Mallory's party. I wanted to go with Aidan to the coordinates we'd found.

I'd looked it up after I got back to the school, sitting in the band room waiting for everyone else to get there. I couldn't wait for Aidan. I had to know. Maybe he was privileged enough to put aside the promise of a million dollars, but I certainly wasn't.

It was one of those storage places, the kind you see on TV, where they auction the abandoned contents and teams of trash-pickers fight for the good stuff. That was all I could figure out from looking at Google Maps. I wanted to get there to find out what we needed to do next.

After halftime, I went to concessions to buy some Skittles. Snow fell, thick flakes coating me and my blanket, and I wished for a poncho. I would be so cold when I got home. I could already feel the chill down to my marrow.

I sucked on a red Skittle and ducked under the stands to shield myself, at least until fourth quarter when the band was required to report back.

"Hey."

The greeting was almost a grunt, and I jumped, catching my breath. *Kyle.*

I didn't turn around, just put my hand on the cold structure to steady myself, then regretted it as an arrow of ice shot down my arm.

"Dora." The person hulked into my field of vision, a shadow cloaked in a football uniform. Padded up by his gear, Aidan seemed taller, more powerful.

I breathed out. The confrontation with Kyle would wait, at least until I checked my phone after the game.

"Hey," Aidan said again.

"Aren't you supposed to be playing?" I held out my Skittle bag.

He took it and shook a few into his palm. "They put Kyle in."

"Is that good?"

Aidan shrugged, handed the bag back. "He's pissed that I started. But whatever."

I shoved the remainder of the Skittles in my mouth and crumpled the wrapper in my pocket.

"What's up? You want to hit up that storage unit this weekend?" I tried to sound cool, but in the very act, I felt desperate. Awkward. Nothing was cool about an abandoned storage unit.

"Yeah. I'll text you. But..." He kicked a cleat against the ground. "I'm not even supposed to be here. Off the field, I mean. But I wanted to warn you."

I felt my face slacken. "Huh?"

"Kyle's people are planning to crash your friend's party tonight. I thought you might want to let her know. It's mean." Aidan could barely get the words out. His lips shivered a little. "I'll go with you, if you want."

I resisted the urge to roll my eyes. "So the college guy is really Kyle."

"Yeah."

The buzzer for the quarter went off. We both had to go back. And I wanted to find that storage unit, but instead, we had to rescue Mallory.

"Okay," I sighed, ducking under the bleachers behind him. "Meet me in the band room after the game."

<h1 style="text-align:center">20</h1>

Patrick

Back in my car, I scrolled through my inbox and found the e-mail from Jude. Clicked the link to the video again, closing my eyes. I had stopped playing the bassoon when I finished college. I couldn't afford the expensive instrument, and over time, I'd forgotten the fervor I once had for it. Jude had the means to continue, and he was as talented as he ever was. I assumed he was playing this melody, since the video portion of the track was blank.

I remembered how he buried codes in everything, and I wondered if the link had metadata buried in it, as Caroline had suggested. Or it could be in the music itself. Elgar—Jude talked about him constantly. It was weird for a high school kid to be obsessed with a dead British composer, but I did learn a lot from Jude's obsession. I was well beyond analyzing chords and note patterns, though. Way too old to find any message within a score.

The "Nimrod" theme ended. I started the video over. This time, I watched the screen. There was only dark, no image. For a moment, I wanted to see him, see how he'd changed over the years. See if his androgynous beauty had held into his thirties.

I squinted, tried to see through the screen.

And that was when I saw the link. Dark blue text on a dark blue background. Unreadable letters—but when I clicked, it took me to a Craigslist page, which harbored a GPS coordinate. Below that, the text, the clear truth: **The person who finds me will win one million dollars.**

I scrambled for my phone, cleared Amy's zillion notifications, and called Caroline.

21

Caroline

By the time I met Patrick in the storage unit parking lot, the night was black, the air filled with pouring snow. It clung to my hair and the fur on the hood of my coat.

"I don't know what we'll find at this hour," I murmured, half to myself.

Patrick pointed. A lone light burned in the rental office.

"It just looks late. Getting dark earlier. We'll still be able to get to the game before it's over."

We trudged through the thickening snow to the light. Behind the glass, a man sat shuffling through paper. Old and weathered, he seemed part of the landscape. The office looked stuck in a time warp. No computer, and a yellowing fax machine perched atop a dusty filing cabinet. I supposed the storage industry hadn't changed much in the past thirty years.

The man came to the window, flashing dingy teeth Under a grizzled mustache. "You all looking to rent? I'm about to close."

Patrick unfolded his printout from the website with the GPS coordinates. "Know anything about this?"

The man's expression changed. He continued smiling, but now it reached his eyes, laugh lines creasing at his temples. "Sure I do."

He grabbed a key ring hanging on the wall and rounded through a door. When he joined us, I thought I smelled the musty scent of his office on his Carhartt jacket. Either that or time had preserved him, like an object in one of these lockers.

The man led us out of the office and back into the lot. We walked all the way down to the rear fence, finding a long row of larger units. These had big garage-style doors. Instead of pressing a remote to open one, though, he keyed a password into a coded lock, then wrested the bottom upward.

"Good Lord," Patrick said.

My heart fluttered, and my hands tingled with adrenaline. I looked at Patrick for help, but he was already stepping inside.

The room was set up exactly like Jude's childhood bedroom. Granted, I hadn't visited his house as often as Patrick had, but I remembered it all the same. Twin bed piled with blankets. A small wooden desk covered with trinkets, a pull-chain lamp at the corner of the writing surface. Boxes and board games lined a tall shelf in the corner. Despite the dank air and lack of walls for *Star Trek* posters, I was transported.

A crash sounded behind us.

When I turned to identify the source of the noise, I saw the bottom of the door hit the ground.

"What are you doing?" I rushed to the door and tugged the small metal handle sticking out of the combo lock, but it stayed put. *Shit.*

"You said you were leaving!" Patrick roared.

Past the heavy barrier between us, a muffled response. "Ayup."

"Please don't go!" I screamed.

"Why?" Patrick yelled.

"Guy's paying me good money to keep you in here." The man's

voice faded into the distance, sounding farther and farther away. "Hope it don't get too cold."

IN THE COMMOTION, we hadn't realized how dark the unit was. The only light filtered in from a glass-block window near the ceiling. Patrick felt his way towards the desk and pulled the chain on the lamp. "There's a space heater over here."

I blew on my fingers. My toes were already freezing, one by one. I hadn't changed out of my work clothes, obviously not thinking something like this would happen. Could happen. I grabbed a blanket from the bed and wrapped it around myself. Patrick fumbled under the desk, and I heard the little heater click on. At least we had electricity.

"Fucking Jude," Patrick mumbled, like he had rocks in his mouth.

I set my purse down and extracted my phone. No signal. "There has to be a way out of here."

"It's his game," Patrick said, his voice gaining strength. "This is all a jacked-up game. The same stuff he used to pull, but on steroids."

"He studied game design in college..." Or at least, that had been his plan. Whatever he had done, it had worked in his favor.

"Most Likely to Succeed, my ass." Patrick slumped, defeated, in the rolling chair. I huddled in my blanket, blew on my hands again. The snow on my hair had melted into ice water.

"Don't talk like that. You're plenty successful." The class always elected one girl and one boy with that title, and he'd been the boy standing alongside me in our yearbook picture.

He snorted. "Everything was always a damn competition with him. I'll never have what he has. I'm gonna die unhappy."

Something unlocked inside me. I thought of all the years, all this bizarre stuff, entire lives lived in between then and now. But here he was, talking to me like he would have back then, like no time had passed. Would we have talked ever again, if Jude hadn't brought us back together? And now we were here, doing this strange dance.

"You won't," I said. "You might need some therapy. Happiness isn't fixed. You don't achieve it. It's permeable. Comes and goes."

"Lawyer. Psychology expert. Super mom. Is there nothing Caroline Cross can't be?" He spun in the chair.

Was my ex becoming—dare I say—slightly unhinged?

I shivered. I had to focus. Especially if I was the only one capable of doing so.

22

Patrick

Caroline paced the unit like a trapped animal. The blanket wrapped around her shoulders billowed like a cape.

I took my phone out, even though I knew it was a futile gesture. The time read 7:57. The game would be nearing halftime. I could only imagine how many frantic messages I'd have when I had signal again.

I moved from the desk to the long twin bed, made up as if Jude slept here. Kicked off my shoes, dove underneath the covers.

Caroline looked at me like I'd stripped naked. "What are you doing?"

"It's cold!" It was. I could see our breath.

She wrinkled her nose. The comforter—I remembered it, covered in Yodas and Lukes from the re-release of *Empire* in the theaters. It wasn't fresh as a daisy, but it didn't smell bad. No worse than that dude from the storage office had.

I scooted over, leaving a spot for her to wedge herself in, and raised my eyebrows at her.

109

"Ugh." She folded herself forward, reaching for her ankles to unfasten her boots. When she got in beside me, her socked feet against my legs were ice blocks.

I whistled. "Damn, girl."

"Shush."

It wasn't as cold now. Our bodies heated the space between us. Part of me felt like this was natural, a return to tradition. Like finding your old letter jacket and realizing it still fits. The other part of me thrummed with anticipation, as if we were beginning something.

Maybe we were.

I reached for her hand, twirled the ring on her third finger. "So, what's this about?"

"Really?" Caroline sat up against the headboard.

"What else are we doing?"

"Something is wrong with you, Patrick Reed."

Absurd laughter bubbled inside me. The situation was absurd. *Just like Jude.* I pictured him on any given night. Cavorting in the cold, a deranged leprechaun, his joint dangling from his lips. Even in band, the random challenges he'd come up with, taunting me, daring me to take first chair from him. Never happened. I was doomed to second bassoon for eternity.

Caroline crossed her arms. "Okay. If you insist."

I'd almost forgotten I'd asked her about it.

"He was a surfer." She sighed, dramatically.

I didn't remember her sighing any other way, so this was reassuring. Back to the old letter jacket.

"I moved out there to get away from... you know... everything. Kieran was a glamorous departure. I never knew a person like him could be attracted to someone like me." She flushed. "Not that... you weren't..."

I held up a hand. "I get it. I'm stodgy."

"No, it's not even that."

I could tell she was struggling to recover. Our close quarters stirred me, too, and I felt my ears heat with the awkwardness.

"Everything in California was new and shiny. An adventure. Nothing could touch us."

"And then something did."

She didn't reply.

"Amy is always frustrated with me because I don't help enough around the house," I said.

Caroline snorted.

"Not only does Kieran not help—he makes the mess." She looked at her hands, which were tangled up in each other. "If I could do it again…"

She couldn't have stayed. Not after our epic breakup, not after I'd shocked her silly with it. Guilt flooded my chest. We'd tried to maintain a long-distance relationship in college, but it hadn't worked. Besides, Caroline didn't know what had happened when Hannah came to OSU, and I didn't plan to tell her now, or ever.

"It's done," I said. "And you have your son."

"Yeah. He's not exactly a chip off the old block." She turned to me. "Are you happy with your wife? Amy, you said?"

I don't like answering loaded questions. So, I looked down at my phone. I couldn't access new messages, but I could get into my stored items. I pulled up a photo and displayed it. Not Amy, but Liam, his light-up smile puncturing the gloom of the unit.

She sucked in a breath. "Oh, Patrick. You started over."

"We're not that old. And we'd always wanted another child." Well… Amy did.

"He's beautiful." Caroline stopped, put her face in her hands.

I adjusted the blanket on my shoulders, huddling down deep.

A long silence stretched between us, even though we stayed close.

I wondered what it would be like to touch her again. I'm a red-blooded American man, after all. My need wasn't as fervent as usual, since Amy and I had slept together the night before—that might have been enough to keep me in check tonight. That, and Liam's picture.

But my imagination conjured other possibilities. Maybe we'd be locked in here until we starved. We'd have to come together in one last-ditch effort to truly live. One last human experience to savor before we said goodbye to the cruel world.

I was thinking about the money, too. She was here, tempting me with her body and her attention. She'd suggested we work together to split the cash, but how did I know she wasn't going to dash away at the last minute and take it all? How did I know she wasn't using me?

Then Caroline jumped up. She clambered out of the bed, fumbling for her boots. "The rental guy used a code to get in here."

I stayed under the blanket. "Yeah?"

"So there must be a code to get out." She raced to the big door, tracing her fingers along the metal handle to the keypad. I got up and shone my flashlight on it. "I should have watched him type it in."

"It's not like you knew we would be stuck here." We stared at the little box with its offending numbers. "Maybe this is, like, Jude's real-life panic room."

She whirled, snapped her fingers. "Oh my God, yes!"

I arched an eyebrow. "Careful. People will think something's going on in here."

Caroline poked my shoulder. "Come on. Let's tear this room apart."

23

Dora

Aidan talked a senior into driving us to Mallory's. I climbed out of the back seat, grateful for my warm socks and tennis shoes. Even with those on, plus my Arctic ensemble of puffy coat and hoodie, I shivered on the stoop. Aidan pressed the bell.

Mallory's mom hovered behind the heavy door. "Oh, come in, Dora!"

She stepped out of the way for us to pass. Mallory's mom was a little chubby and had fair, flushed skin, like her daughter. They shared the same curly hair, too. But Mallory's face was more hawkish, like her father's. Mallory's mom always looked surprised: a frizzy-haired porcelain doll.

Their house had always smelled the same, a fresh linen scent I assumed was their detergent of choice. Their place was clean but cluttered, full to bursting with books, cards, trinkets. My grandmother liked to turn her nose up in judgment when she picked me up. I came to visit nonetheless, but something about the place set me on edge. Maybe it was the fact that they were a real family—something I'd never experienced.

"The girls are downstairs. They'll be up in a minute for cake, though." Mallory's mom beamed. "I'll tell her you're here."

Aidan shifted. I could smell his anxiety, or maybe it was the aroma of unshowered boy. Not one I was familiar with. It was funny that I was comfortable around him. I barely had experience interacting with males, let alone teenage ones.

The girls tittered, coming up the stairs like marching troops.

Board games were everywhere: on the table, on the bookshelves installed in the living room. My wandering gaze lit on one called Jude's Panic Room. Like a magnet, it drew me. I floated to the wall and removed the game, studied its packaging.

Jude is known around the world for his innovative games. He's designed a doozy this time. Can you get out?

There was a photo. My fingers traveled across the smooth cardboard. He was slim, tall, leaning against a surface just beyond the image. Feathery hair framed his face, but it wasn't too long. He was leonine, staring through the box with a smug, hungry look. *I dare you.*

"I thought you weren't coming." Mallory was in front of her gaggle of girls, her arms crossed, looking down her short nose at me.

I wondered if I could get away with having no friends at school. Two more years and I'd qualify for the post-secondary option. Then college... not a moment too soon.

"Aidan found us a ride. What's going on? Your mom said it was cake time."

Mallory uncrossed herself, untangling from her angry position. She sneaked a look at her phone. "Yeah. Cade should be here soon."

"Actually..." Aidan stepped forward, ran a hand over his cropped curls. "We need to talk to you about that."

"Hey. Whadya call a mansplainer's water source? Well, actually..." Mallory hurled the words, practically spitting, and her friends giggled nervously. "Who invited you?"

"I just thought..." Aidan glanced at me, expecting me to save him.

I shrugged. This was not my thing.

"I heard in the locker room..." he tried again.

"You don't know my life." Mallory sniffed. "I hope you have a ride home."

I put up a hand. "Chill. Let's eat some cake and play games. That's what we're here for."

Aidan's shoulders slumped. He leaned against the wall, stepping back from the gaggle of girls.

Mallory put up her hands, mirroring me. "Whatever. You want to play the panic room game?"

Jude... That name was so familiar. Where had I heard it recently?

"Here's the cake!" Mallory's mom crowed.

I smelled it before I saw it, a tower of frosting and cloying sugar. My classmates descended. I stood back, out of the way, until a hand grabbed my arm and tugged me deftly outside.

"WHAT ARE YOU DOING?" I braced myself against the frigid wind. "If you want to go home, I can call an Uber or something."

"Shhh." Aidan pressed a finger to his lips, then pointed.

I followed an invisible line to the curb, where a quiet, lightless car hummed.

We skittered off the steps to the flower bed beside the house, then crouched in the lifeless dirt. Snow coated the grass—enough to be annoying, not piling up yet. I bounced on my heels, holding the cold metal rain gutter to keep me upright.

"Shit," Aidan muttered.

A figure hunkered through the black, emerging under the porch light. He left a parcel in his wake.

Aidan rushed forward, tackling him, and I gasped as they hit the ground and rolled. I stayed locked in place, peering around the side of the house to see what was happening.

"What the fuck, man!"

Aidan let him go, and they faced each other on the driveway. Kyle's beady eyes glittered under the shadow of his hoodie.

"It's not fair to tease this girl. Just. Stop." Aidan spread his stance, settling into fight mode. "This is worthless."

"Who died and put you in charge?" Kyle sneered. "We're having a little fun, is all."

I peeked around the gutter, and Kyle caught my eye. I shrank back, but it was too late. He stalked past the corner of the house, smiling, feral and smug. "Oh, so this is about our band nerd here. You have a crush on her?"

"No," Aidan said, defensively.

Part of me withered. But I held tight to my spot. My shoes squished in the snowy, wet grass.

Kyle jogged back to the driveway, blew me a kiss. "I got you, sweetie. I texted you. Let's catch up later."

My blood didn't boil. It was liquid fire. I forgot how cold I was and charged towards them. "You think I helped you because I like you? You dragged me into this stupid mess. And I'm not doing it anymore."

"We'll see about that." Kyle's eyes narrowed. "Well, I suppose this evening is a bust, my prank getting fucked up and all. Calling it, boys!" he yelled at the car. "She'll have to keep talking to Cade until I can come up with something better." He rolled his eyes. "You nerds keep getting in my way."

Aidan stood with his fists balled. Kyle turned, heading back to his cronies.

I knelt to pick up the package. It reeked. When I lifted the lid, the stench of gross old meat hit my nose, even with the cold air neutralizing my senses. A card inside read: *New Game: Is this still good to eat? You tell me, smart girl. Love, Cade*

I dropped it like I'd catch on fire if I kept holding it.

Aidan was on Kyle's back again, pummeling him. They wrestled under the streetlight. Lazy snow swirled in its halo. I heard their grunting, punching, the meaty sounds of fists meeting faces.

I sighed, kicked away the nasty package, and wrenched the front door open. Yelled for Mallory's mom. Wished I was anywhere but there, but mostly, wished I was in that abandoned storage unit, searching for Jude's clues.

Interlude

Hannah couldn't go home.

It was almost Christmas. They'd gone to see *Titanic,* and Jude kept insisting he was king of the world. They all knew he was. But right now, he was gone, slipped into the night, out smoking a joint in the snow. Hannah sat on the couch eating Taco Bell.

She loved the sharp air of winter. She'd never been colder than she was at the moment, so thin that dewy hair covered her limbs. But she'd started to enjoy pain, in its many forms, and she wondered if she should join Jude.

He'd invited her that night, and she was hesitant at first. Caroline Cross didn't exactly like Hannah, and it wasn't a secret. That girl always had her witch-straight nose turned up, as if she were smelling something disgusting. Hannah had never done anything to upset Caroline, at least not to her knowledge. But Caroline talked about her behind her back, spread rumors about her.

Hannah didn't understand why her friend Jude hung out with Caroline at all. "She's not so bad when you get to know her," he'd said, hanging from his locker one afternoon after marching band. "Come on, Hannah. I want all my friends to like each other."

And so, she embraced that potential: more pain. More discomfort. But she was used to it by now. And being here was better than being at home with her terrible mother.

Patrick and Caroline were playing *Tetris Attack* on the Super Nintendo. They stopped to make out after every match. Hannah could pretend it bothered her, but she didn't care. Here, she could look away, could disengage. Could lose herself in the feel of tacos in her mouth, so crisp and crumbly and spicy. She reveled in the freedom, though she knew she'd pay for it later. Her stomach would hurt, and her mother would be angry.

Outside, Jude hooted.

Caroline rolled her eyes and tossed her controller. Patrick reached for her, wrapping her in his long arms, but she addressed Hannah. "You have curfew?"

Hannah hesitated, cheese trailing from her lip. "Technically."

Caroline's mouth quirked.

Patrick pressed his face into Caroline's neck. "What are you thinking?"

How pissed she'll be when I don't come home. How I'm not sure if I care. Hannah shrugged.

"No comment?" Caroline got up, pulling Patrick with her. "You better not try to pin this one on me."

But there would be no pinning for Caroline, whose parents didn't care. They probably gave her a medal when she lost her virginity. They were hippie deities, children of a generation that railed against war. Hannah's mother never left here, never tasted that revolt. Hannah was trapped under her eyes, a cell below a microscope.

Patrick and Caroline were growing bored—she could tell. There was only so far they could go in front of her. Hannah wanted time to stretch, to give, but it had to break. She couldn't keep hiding here.

She sighed, got up, stretched her back. "It's late."

Jude slid the door open with a creak and slipped inside. He smelled of sweet pot and cold winter in his hair. Hannah breathed in. She couldn't escape his scent. He pulled her back to the couch, and his wrists tangled with hers. Patrick's arms, around Caroline, went still.

"We were about to leave," Caroline said stiffly. "Hannah needs to get home."

"It's okay," Hannah said, soft.

"Good." Jude wrestled her to him, landing his palm on her head. "We have things to do."

HANNAH WILLED herself not to check the clock, trying not to imagine her mother waiting at home.

They went upstairs to Patrick's room. His parents weren't home, so Patrick had taken the opportunity to liberate a bottle of vodka from their liquor cabinet. He pressed a small glass into Hannah's hand.

She sat on the floor, legs curled up under her, and sniffed it. She'd never had a drink before. It smelled like rocket fuel.

"Come on," Caroline said. "Are you chicken or something?"

She elbowed Patrick, although Hannah could feel the blow in her own ribs.

Hannah didn't reply. Just downed the glass. It burned through her system into her gut.

Jude was laying out a spread of bizarre trappings. Pages of gibberish, tarot cards, candles. A Ouija board in the center.

"Messages from the beyond," he said, back almost to his daytime running speed—even pot couldn't slow him down for long. "Look, this is a message from our ghost friend."

He pointed to a page, ripped from some book Hannah couldn't identify. Random letters in the text were highlighted in manic green.

"Steganography," he explained. "It means that our directions are hidden in plain sight. Look only at the highlighted letters."

Patrick and Caroline exchanged a look. Hannah floated alone, wondering if all this was worth it. The glamour of the situation was fading fast. She plummeted down a long, interior tunnel, falling and falling, waiting for the thump, the crack of her bones against dirt.

"What, exactly, are we doing?" Caroline pronounced each word carefully, as if talking to the three-year-old she babysat in the summer. "And why?"

"We need to ask her." Jude indicated the Ouija board.

"Her?" This from Patrick.

"Dorabella." Jude stuck out his tongue. "You know. Edward Elgar wrote her that letter no one can read. If she tells us how, I can crack the code."

None of them moved. Hannah turned to Caroline, ready to ask to leave again. Jude could stay here, sleep on the couch. Caroline could drive Hannah home, get her away before this got weirder. Caroline had a car, had the freedom to make out with her boyfriend later.

But before Hannah could say anything, Jude grabbed her hand, squeezing. She couldn't help blushing, and her lifeless, dry hair fell in her face. Even with zero fat on her body, there was oil on her skin, and a painful zit was erupting on her left cheek. She had never felt so real, so part of the world, and she still wanted to disappear.

"And why does that matter?" Patrick's baritone cut the silence.

"Communing with the spirit world not enough for you?" Jude pulled himself up like a puppet drawn with a string. "The satisfaction of finding an answer, for one. But there could be money—cash prizes. The Elgar Society might bring me to England."

"Talk them into changing our part for 'Pomp and Circumstance,'" Patrick muttered. "I thought my face might fall off after last year's graduation."

Jude leapt his rubber-band dancer's body toward the light switches. They plunged into darkness, a total, consuming black. Jude fumbled with his lighter. Hannah heard her own breathing, and the image of her mother flew into her head: perched on their flowered couch, waiting like a raven.

The candles warmed to life with light and a vanilla scent. Jude stood like a seer behind the dancing flames. He had no actual magic, no powers, but Hannah couldn't help moving her fingers to the planchette. The rough plastic dragged across her skin.

"Do you honestly think we can call spirits using something you bought at the drugstore?" Caroline asked.

"Let's ask Dora." Jude's long, meaty fingers joined Hannah's. "Miss Penny, can you hear us?"

Hannah blinked. The planchette yanked towards YES and circled it.

"That was you," Caroline said.

"Was not."

As her fingers brushed Jude's, Hannah wondered why she was friends with these people. She knew why she first associated herself with them. She didn't have a choice. They were the nerds, band kids, eschewed by the traditional population. Hannah could have joined the Christian Club, but religion wasn't her style.

But they were seniors now, and Hannah could taste her freedom like the chocolate her mother hid—sweet and forbidden and bound to corrupt her. Chesterfield was a cage. She read magazines at the library that talked of this thing called the Internet, America Online. Miss Norris said the library would be getting computers—any day now. Hannah liked the idea of being anyone, of disguising herself in a chat room. A new world full of friends waited for her—if she could only find them.

Caroline's hands were heavy on the planchette. Hannah smelled her strawberry lotion from Victoria's Secret. The planchette traveled up and down the board, never resting in any one place. Patrick wore a goofy, faraway expression. Jude was half in shadow, candlelight flickering on his face.

Hannah swallowed. They were her friends. She would accept this until the fact changed.

"It's way past curfew." Caroline removed her hand and dug in her pocket for a piece of gum.

Jude and Hannah directed the planchette, and Hannah's forearms ached.

"C'mon. I'll give you all a ride." With this, she winked at Patrick, and Hannah's stomach churned.

"No way. I need to keep talking to Dora. You freaks go upstairs and get it on." Jude drew himself up. "Five more minutes. Hannah, you can stay with me."

"Whatever." Caroline leaned back and folded her arms. "I don't know why you two hang out, anyway. Hannah, like, do you even speak?"

Patrick inched closer to her, looping an arm around Caroline's shoulder, but he stared at Jude.

Hannah hated this. She wanted to fly, to escape, to land anywhere but in this smelly basement. Her head pounded. All the different smells—the candle, Caroline's lotion, Jude's sprayed-on Cool Water to conceal the weed stink—everything was mixing and encroaching, and she actually hated herself more than anything. Tacos and vodka rolled in her belly. She swallowed again.

Jude crowed, and Hannah startled. They faced each other, legs crossed, hands traveling the letters like a map.

"She's talking to us. One of you losers get a piece of paper." Jude waved a hand, and Patrick scrambled over to his father's desk, returning with a notepad and pen.

Was Hannah moving it? She couldn't tell, because she was sweating, sick, angry. Her fingers were glued down, the planchette violent. Jude shouted out letters, and Hannah's stomach squeezed, and Caroline was sullen as Patrick scribbled the words.

When it was over, Jude slumped back.

"It's gibberish." Caroline peeked over Patrick's shoulder.

"It's a code," Jude squawked.

And Hannah heaved all over the Ouija board.

24

"It's not fair," Mallory said, as the parade of tired and pissed adults marched through to whisk away her friends. "It's my birthday and I didn't do anything wrong."

"Them's the breaks, kid," Mallory's father grunted. He looked annoyed, as if he had better things to do with his time.

I certainly did.

"It's easier, honey." Mallory's mother traveled the path between the kitchen, dining room, living room—a well-worn route.

I was the only errant teen left. Kyle and I had lingered for a long, awkward twenty minutes. Aidan's mother had been first to arrive, toting a squawking toddler.

"This is the worst," Aidan's mom said. "I should be at home. Both you kids in bed. Your dad—no idea where he is. He should be here. What the hell did you do, Aidan?"

She was still talking as they exited.

Alone with Kyle, I was too scared to say anything, even in the relative safety of Mallory's house. She glared at him, arms crossed, a sullen, unyielding stare.

When his father finally showed—reeking of pot, and I wondered if it would be safer for underage Kyle to drive himself home—Kyle left without a look back at either of us.

"And stay out!" Mallory grumbled. "I'm going to bed."

Mallory's mom rested her hand on my shoulder. "Does your mom still work nights, dear? I'll drive you home."

I'd called Grandma, but she didn't pick up. She was probably asleep in a beauty mask, listening to Delilah on the radio.

Maybe Mallory's mom didn't know about the accident. Maybe she didn't remember. Clearly, it hadn't meant enough to Mallory for her to mention it. I didn't bother to correct her.

When we arrived, Mallory's mom said to me, "It wasn't your fault."

I didn't know what exactly she was referring to. What had happened that evening? I knew that wasn't. She should have been saying that to her daughter. I had not ruined the party. Circumstance had done that. Also, Kyle was a jerk.

Maybe she had remembered my mother's death. Maybe she felt dumb for not remembering. Whatever. I just shook my head and climbed out of the car.

I drifted inside. *So tired*, my body said.

The house was quiet. Grandma was asleep, just as I'd thought. I didn't bother peeking into her room. The distance between my mother and me had been the same as the distance between her and her mother. A series of disrupted connections from mother to daughter to mother. Maybe if they'd loved each other more, I'd feel more loved too.

I'd become accustomed to the independence, to my freedom to do what I needed to do most of the time. Grandma grumbled about my looks and hated picking me up, but she wasn't abusive. Just... absent. My mother, too—she lived here with us, before the crash, but she was never around. Sleeping at guys' houses or hanging out late at bars. They made sure I had food and clothes and, I'm assuming, clean diapers when I was a baby. That was about it. I'd pretty much raised myself, disappearing into books or playing quietly in corners, careful not to disrupt either one of their lives. I didn't even wonder about my father. He was just one nameless man among the rest of them.

I hadn't been in my mother's room since the accident. Now, I slipped through the door. Wanting some sort of connection to her, wherever I could find it.

It smelled musty. Abandoned. And it hadn't been, not really. Grandma was in here from time to time, sorting through my mother's things, giving away clothes and trinkets. But the dresser was still covered in a mess. Grandma must not have gotten to it yet. It was the only place in the room that still reminded me of her. Hannah, I mean— my mother. Grandma was the neat, organized one. Hannah was sloppy, all over the place. Like she didn't care what happened to any of her stuff.

A squat lamp with a stained-glass shade sat on the bureau, and I flipped it on, giving myself a little more light. I trailed my hand over her things, as if I could summon her ghost from them. Mostly costume jewelry, piles of it. A lot of receipts and stray documents, which I was surprised my grandmother hadn't eliminated yet. Maybe Grandma thought she'd need them for bills. A framed picture covered in dust.

Blowing the dust away, I sneezed. The night felt so late, the ache deep in my bones.

The shot didn't even have my mother in it. Three teenagers, smiling big, wearing caps and gowns. The picture was old, from a film camera. I studied it, thinking the subjects looked familiar. But I wasn't sure who they were.

It was only after I'd laid down in my mother's bed, curled up in the new sheets Grandma had covered it with, that I realized the teenagers were Kyle's mom, Aidan's dad, and Jude from the game box.

25

Patrick

I'd never played one of Jude's games—at least, not one of his board games.

Caroline sifted through the boxes, pulling them off the wire shelf and reading the back covers. "The whole scenario is that you're trapped in a room and you need to get out. You solve puzzles, and there are secret envelopes."

She opened a game box and lifted out the contents to show me.

"I've heard of these in real life. Escape rooms. He makes those, too."

She nodded. "Maybe we're his test subjects."

We always were.

As Caroline dug through the games, I went to the desk. I pulled my parka tighter around me and opened the drawers, my hands numb and shaking. The space heater blew stale air on my shoes.

"There's a radio in here," I said. "With a tape deck and tapes. Cassette tapes."

"That could be something." Caroline shook her head. "I don't see anything here, except the codes in the games. That would take forever to go through."

I tried to think like Jude. The task felt impossible, my head muddled with shades of the past. With him, things always seemed more complicated than they actually were. Or he tried to make them complicated. One time, he'd written a note asking me to put together a duet for Solo and Ensemble Contest, hiding a simple message in a forest full of fake letters. Took me three days to figure out what he was getting at, and by then, the deadline for signing up had passed. Why was he so obsessed with hiding? Did he have secrets we didn't know?

I gripped the back of the desk chair, clenching my hands. My legs twitched. I thought of Amy, her earthy lavender scent, her sunny blond hair.

I cast a glance at Caroline, who sifted through envelopes, long fingers flying. She was tall, graceful, her pageboy hair cut close to her face. Did people even use that term anymore? I remembered it from the Hardy Boys books I'd loved in the eighties—the preferred descriptor for the popular cut. I supposed most people called it a bob now. Amy would know. Caroline's hair was sleek and dark, confident, professional. Not the mess of stringy length it had been once.

Caroline sighed. "I'll come back to these. Let's see if we can find anything else."

I set the cassette deck on the desk. These were Jude's mix tapes, dubbed from the radio when his favorites came on. He'd unfold himself —he was all long limbs, like Caroline—and race across the room to capture a song, the blank cassette already pre-loaded. Those tapes were so expensive, but he saved up for them, secreting away cash from his allowance money.

"They never play this one anymore!" he'd announce, as if trapping a rare animal.

I picked a tape and slid it into the slot. "Lightning Crashes" by Live filled the room.

Caroline was on the floor now, crouching, peering under the bed.

"Anything marked on the tapes? There might be a code written on the labels. The audio could be a red herring."

I paused the song. "No, I don't think so."

"No symbols or anything?"

I flipped the cassettes over on the desk, sifting through them. "Nope. Doesn't look like it."

"Maybe it's the number of tapes. That could be one of the numbers on the keypad." Now Caroline was rummaging in a cardboard box. "This sucks."

I was tired and hungry. Sleep pricked at the corners of my eyes. I'd been up since before six to catch my train downtown. I didn't know what time it was, but the football game was for sure over, and the storage unit guy had left long ago.

Yawning, I rubbed my hand over my face. "Maybe we better call it a night. Dude could come back in the AM and let us out."

Caroline looked up. Her eyes flared. "Are you kidding? I don't care if there's a bed. I don't want to sleep here. I want to figure this out. We find the code, and we get out."

"And then what?" I drew myself up. "We get the next clue? We get money? Or when we get out, are we just going back to our old lives?"

Caroline huffed. "We're getting the money. Like we've already discussed. Each of us gets half. So we have to finish this and move on."

"He might be lying about it." *Or you could be baiting me.* I was too tired to even entertain thoughts of her betrayal.

She got up and stalked to the desk to look at the tapes I'd unearthed. I returned to the bed and pulled the blanket over me. When I stretched out my legs, I kicked the game boxes strewn across the top.

"Jesus, Patrick. What a mess."

"I'm sorry. I need to sleep." Shapes and colors already drifted on my closed lids.

"Did you see this one?" She waved one of the tapes in front of me, but I couldn't open my eyes. I was already half-conscious.

The Enigma Variations came on. In high school, I fell asleep every night to the tape Jude had mixed for me: in addition to the variations, he'd included P.D.Q. Bach, Jupiter from *The Planets*, Bela Bartok's duos for strings. Jude interspersed each variation with the non-Elgar tracks, so I'd always fade away before I heard them all.

Then Jude's voice drifted out from nowhere.

At first, I was dreaming it. I saw him there, speaking to me. With that roguish smile. And a column of hate filled me from top to bottom, because I wanted to hit him, to stop all this stringing along. *Tell us why you're doing this. Tell us what you want from us. Stop making me work so damn hard. I'm exhausted.*

But then Caroline shrieked, and it shocked me back to the storage unit, to the dim light radiating from the desk lamp.

"Hey," Jude said, speaking on the tape. "It's been a while, hasn't it? And you got this far all on your own. Unless the librarian or storage guy dropped some hints—although, I couldn't fault them if they did. They have no idea what this is all about. All they can see is my money, which I give gladly. Got nothing else to do with it, really."

The voice was tinny, I realized, as I came back to the waking world. It was no real person. How had I thought it was? I blinked. Caroline sat on the desk chair and leaned in.

"Not sure which of you has gotten here first, but good for you! I won't speculate, of course. And maybe you're not even first, right now. You might not even know. Anyway, I never intended to cause conflict. I just want to reward you. For all your good friendship over the years."

At that, I glanced at Caroline, and she rolled her eyes.

"So, I assume you want answers, and you'll get them in due time. But for now, this most pressing of issues, you only need to know that the answer lies in my games." He chuckled. "I'll see you all soon."

The hum of the static behind his voice dissolved back into the orchestra, segueing into the mystery variation—the one for which Elgar had never revealed the inspiration.

26

Caroline

Past 1 a.m.

Patrick's snoring grated against my brain as I tried to think. I let the tape play until it ran out, hoping for another secret message. I flipped the tape and listened to more classical music. I'd been in band for a time—it was how we all met—but I didn't keep up with the music stuff after school ended. All I knew was that I was listening to an orchestra, and the song probably had some kind of code in it, because Jude was obsessed.

The answer lies in my games.

I'd taken them all apart, sifted through the contents. I couldn't fathom solving all those puzzles. No. I needed to remember Occam's razor. This was a simple thing, thus it should have a simple answer. The code on the lock had four numbers. I remembered the four beeps as the locker man pressed it into the keypad.

Maybe the lock itself held a clue. I grabbed Patrick's phone—mine had died already—but when I lit the screen, I saw there was a passcode there too. A picture of his little son covered the background.

I frowned. Didn't want to wake him. I took the phone over, hoping the ambient light might be enough to light the lock panel so I could see. But no matter how hard I squinted, the anemic glow from Patrick's phone screen wasn't enough. And whatever light from the parking lot that had come in through the glass-block window had turned off long ago. I needed the flashlight app.

I sighed and went back to Patrick, shook his shoulder. He snorted.

"What's your phone code?"

He blinked. "You know it."

"I do not. Tell me."

"C'mon, Amy." He rolled over and snuffled.

God. How could he sleep right now? If I'd married him, nothing would be different. Maybe he was more motivated than Kieran. Maybe we'd have more money. I thought of cruises, long weekends. But there would still be snoring. I supposed midlife came with a series of universal challenges.

Most people weren't stuck in a locked storage unit in the middle of the night. Most people weren't following the demented instructions of a crazy game maker from the past. And yet, many people lay awake next to snoring spouses.

I laid his phone back on the desk and sat on the edge of the bed. My whole body was numb. The fatigue had settled deep. I wanted nothing else but to block the world out, to fall into a place of oblivion. I was tired of all this.

I shoved Patrick this time—not a hard shove, or a violent one, but with enough force to wake him.

"What?" He sat up, dazed.

I envied him the ability to escape. "Your phone password."

"It's my birthday. 0118."

I snatched the device with new purpose, entered the code, and switched on the flashlight app. I stalked to the keypad and aimed the light at its face, like I was interrogating it. It was a regular keypad, the kind you would use to open a garage. A faint red glow lit the keys from behind.

"What are you doing?"

I heard Patrick but didn't look back. I'd thought he'd go right back to sleep.

"Checking out the lock." I peered at it, examining the sides of each button. Someone had taken a pen and inked the sides of four numbers. 8, 7, 2, and 5.

Okay, I could work with it. Only so many combinations of those numbers existed, and I would try them all. I stabbed the keys over and over, holding my breath. But nothing happened. All I heard was beeping as I failed each time.

"Is there something on there?"

"Pen marks on some numbers. Maybe it's nothing." I stepped away.

Those locks could be reprogrammed. Maybe the previous renter had marked the numbers in case they got locked in. But really—who locks a storage unit from the inside? This place was rigged like this. These numbers meant something.

My stomach roared. If we got out of here, I was going straight to the all-night diner.

I strode back to the games. I'd hastily re-organized their contents and moved the boxes so Patrick could stretch his legs. Now I stacked them on the desk, scanning the pile from top to bottom.

Jude hadn't said the answer was in only one game. He said it was in the games, as a group. I needed to look at things holistically.

His games were numbered, the spines showing the order in which they were issued. A player could choose a single game, but playing them in order would yield additional secrets. Jude was smart. He knew people liked secrets, liked being privy to knowledge that no one else had. Liked finding those secrets when they were hidden.

As soon as I'd learned Jude's new identity, I'd Googled him extensively, even though Patrick had said it wouldn't help us. There were entire subreddits devoted to the Easter eggs in Jude's games. That was how he'd become so rich. People couldn't get enough of the connections between the games. They always wanted more. I couldn't believe I had missed him, hiding in plain sight.

I stacked the boxes in numerical order, 1 to 12.

The spines of the games, lined up together, revealed inked lines. Just like the keypad. I couldn't see a pattern to them, only random marks drawn in Sharpie. But they had to mean something.

These lines were drawn here, for me. For us.

27

Patrick

I woke to a rumbling, a sound I couldn't quite place.

Bracing wind swirled across my cheeks. I sat up and blinked. The storage unit door yawned wide, and Caroline stood in front of it. With the streetlamps off, there was little outside light, but I knew her face was aglow with triumph.

"What time is it?" I slid my feet into my shoes. My parka was stuck to my body.

She consulted her phone. Actually, it was my phone. I vaguely remembered her asking me about the password. "4 a.m."

I rubbed my hand across my face. "Jesus."

"I'm starving." Caroline picked her way out of the storage unit, tiptoeing in her heeled boots.

I hurried to catch up. "You're not even going to close the door? All that stuff is in there."

"You close it." Caroline called to me from around the corner. She had already reached her car and was swiping at her windshield with a long brush. "I'll drive around."

I sighed and turned. While it was no longer snowing, the wind swiped at me from all sides. I couldn't remember where the keypad was. I felt around on the door, searching for a button.

But then I stopped and looked inside again.

Now that we were outside, seeing the room felt different. Like we'd gone back in time. All the covers on the bed messed up and the tapes spread haphazardly across the desk—this mess was closer to what Jude's room had really been like. He was too free-spirited to prioritize organization or order. He saved that brainpower for cracking his codes and letting his creative side dance about.

Hearing his voice had made me ache, even half-asleep as I was. If we saw him again, what would that be like? I'd spent so much time fantasizing about punching him in the face that I hadn't considered any other possibilities.

Where would we start, now? Or would we be ending something that should have ended a long time ago?

Caroline pulled up behind me, her car's engine humming. My fingers crawled the unit's inside wall until they found the keypad, and I pressed the down arrow. I didn't need to put in the code to close up the place. The past disappeared behind the groaning door.

I INTENDED to say goodbye to Caroline, but she motioned for me to jump into her passenger seat. She hit the gas, lurching forward out of the parking lot. "What are we doing?" I asked.

"We're going to the diner." Caroline accelerated into the early-morning-slash-night. "I'm starving."

I checked in with my stomach.

"Yeah, I guess," I said absently, focusing all my energy on staying awake. "I want to go back to sleep."

"I'm running on adrenaline." Caroline turned into another parking lot, and we exited into the diner. "It took me all night to solve that last one."

"You're our saint," I said. "Our hero."

The waitress came over, a hint of recognition playing over her face. "You're back! I didn't know lawyers worked night shift."

"Another code." Caroline's eyes sparkled. She was clearly proud of herself, and hell, I was proud of her too. "But we solved it. And it's a good thing it's Saturday."

"Damn, girl. I know what you need." The waitress was slim, blonde, the picture of a midnight-diner denizen. Beautiful in a hard-time kind of way, lines around her eyes. We'd gone to school with her, but I didn't remember her name. She darted behind the counter and emerged with two empty red mugs, then set them in front of us and sloshed steaming coffee from her carafe into them.

Caroline took to the coffee like it was a draught of power. She sat back, the mug to her lips, and closed her eyes. "Yes."

The waitress winked and turned away. I swallowed a few big gulps and waited for the caffeine to saturate my body. I could feel it relax into my face, then into the muscles of my shoulders.

"She knows about the letters?" I asked.

"Yeah, I came here to work on the first code. The one that came in the mail."

Right. The one I hadn't solved. I felt a twinge of failure. Had I solved any of the direct clues? Only the one in my e-mail, the one Jude had meant for me. He knew I wouldn't be as driven as Caroline, would need an extra hint. He was still making me feel bad about myself so many years later. But, to be fair, thoughts of the codes had barely touched my radar, as I'd been worried about the Matt situation. Jude had to push me, to tease me with the promise of sharing his riches.

I buried my head in the menu. Greasy bacon sounded good. And pancakes. Many carbs. I would fall right back asleep as soon as I found my way home. If Amy would let me.

"Aren't you going to ask me how I got the door open?"

I peered over the top of the menu. Caroline grinned with an easy satisfaction. She'd already drained her mug, and the waitress circled around to pour more coffee.

"How did you get the door open, Caroline?"

"You asshole." She reached across the table to punch my arm. "You don't even care."

"I care." I folded the menu, choice made. "Thank you for working all night to save us."

"You're welcome. That's the kind of gratitude I expect." She leaned on the Formica, her elbow crooked on its surface. "I looked at the games. Remember, he said the answer would lie with them. I found little inked lines on the spines."

"And they formed the code?"

"Yeah. They were numbers. But there were also numbers on the keypad. I had to look at the keypad and put the games in the order of the inked numbers there, too." She ticked them off on her fingers. "8, 7, 2, and 5. I put them in numerical order, based on when the games came out. And then the spines formed the lines. The actual code was 5, 3, 1, 1."

"Interesting," I said, like I'd understood any of it.

Our waitress returned, and we ordered our food. The sun wouldn't be up for a while, but the sky was lightening, that early-morning ambience I remembered from many days awake with my children in the wee hours.

"So, what now?" Caroline asked, her leg bouncing under the table. "We got out, but this can't be over yet. We haven't found him."

I nodded. "He said he would see us soon."

"God." She ran a hand back through her hair. "Where is that pot of gold at the end of the rainbow?"

I shrugged.

She looked at the ceiling.

I slipped through the front door at 5:45, into a silent house. I peeked into Aidan's room. He lay sprawled on his queen bed, body twisted, arms stretched out in two directions. His sheets were bunched beneath him, and his mouth was open. *That's how a son should sleep*, I thought. I tiptoed into our bedroom, where Liam curled up against his mother.

I was about to sneak out to my place in the guest room when Amy sat up.

"I'm so sorry," I said. I hadn't thought about how I would explain this to her, and I wasn't sure I could.

"Where the hell were you?" she yell-whispered.

I couldn't help myself. I snickered.

"Patrick!"

My body was giving out. I fell on the bed beside her. "It's a long story."

Amy looked at me for a moment with her eyes wide, then inexplicably began to grin. "It better be a good one."

"It is." The euphoria of her forgiveness filled me. I curled on the other side of her, so she and Liam were both tucked under my arm. "It is."

28

Dora

Saturday came, and then Sunday. I worked on my Holmes paper. The snow cleared up, although there was still plenty on the ground. My neighbors didn't seem to care. They'd had a bonfire Saturday night. Even through the windows, the smell of burned wood seeped into my room and onto my sheets.

I worried about what Kyle would do when I saw him. Besides being pissed about what happened at Mallory's, he was about to flip when I told him I couldn't write papers for him anymore. The weekend did make me forget a little, but when I woke Monday morning, the raw outdoor woodsmoke still clinging to my clothes, the fear returned threefold. As my alarm blared, I hunched below the covers.

It would be so easy to skip school, to miss seeing Kyle. The football season was done, and I had nothing to look forward to in class. I had already e-mailed my Holmes assignment to Ms. Krieger, early, proof that I had kept my eyes on my own paper. I'd put extra work into it to make up for all that had gone before, walking to the library and accessing their digital databases, including extra citations.

Maybe Kyle would forget I existed after a week or two. Could I pretend I had pneumonia? Or mono. That would do the trick. Mono made you sick forever.

I couldn't do that, though. If I hid forever, I wouldn't make it to that storage unit.

That thought had itched inside my brain all weekend too—a nagging feeling, something I needed to address but couldn't figure out how to. Something had been promised to me in that code with the tiny dancing men. I didn't know what I was looking for or what I would find when I got there, but I wanted it.

But I couldn't get there. I had no car, and the storage park was too far to walk from the house, especially in this cold. Either I had to convince someone to drive me there, or I had to get close enough so that I could walk to the park from somewhere else. I did a Google Map search on the computer, and there was a seedy little diner around the corner from the place. Maybe I could talk someone into driving me there, under the pretense of meeting my grandma or even my father. What a tale I could weave around that lie.

School was the only way I could encounter anyone besides my grandmother, whom I'd never be able to con into taking me to a random place like that.

Kyle didn't show up to English or chemistry, and I breathed a sigh of freedom. Aidan was in English, but he wasn't answering my texts. He looked like he'd been awake all weekend, his head on the desk whenever Krieger wasn't watching, his eyes creased with sleep lines. Maybe he'd been working on his paper late.

I scrawled a note and slipped it to him. *You okay? I'm going to the unit after school. You in?*

He wrote back, one word. *Grounded.*

I'd forgotten that I was the only teenager in the world who didn't get in trouble for a single thing I did, unless you counted my grandmother's constant disapproval of my appearance. I wrote an expression of condolence while sticking out my lower lip, but he wasn't looking at me. *At least your mother cares enough to punish you.* If Kyle faced a similar fate, maybe he wouldn't show up at all that day.

But I got overconfident.

As I unpacked my bookbag to prepare for lunch and my second wave of classes, I felt an ominous presence over my shoulder.

It was like a movie, that moment when the villain first gets within reach of the innocent victim. When I shut my locker, Kyle loomed over me, a lock of blondish hair falling into his stormy face. He wasn't there to walk me to the band room today.

"Hi, Dora."

"Hi," I squeaked. "You weren't in class."

"I was seeing a therapist." He glowered. "I don't appreciate what happened the other night."

As if it were my fault.

"Sorry." I glanced around for backup. Teacher... large football player that I might be able to bribe later... Nope, we were alone in the hall. Most everyone else had already gone to the multipurpose room for lunch.

"My mom won't let me do wrestling now. My grades are down the shitter."

"Sorry," I said again.

Kyle took a step closer, his T-shirt an inch from my face. "What are you going to do to make this up to me?"

"Um." I screamed internally. *Not your circus! Not your elephant!*

"You owe me." He leaned down, blowing his sour breath in my face. "Start thinking about it. I gave Krieger some excuse, since you didn't text me this weekend, but you've only got a couple more days before she catches on."

She's already caught on. "Okay, Kyle."

He stepped away and pointed his finger in a gun shape at me. "You better be listening."

I waited until the buses left and crouched in the girls' room, my feet up on the toilet so no one would see I was in there.

When I emerged, the halls were empty. I tiptoed to my locker. After-school activities were still going on, in the multipurpose room and in the gym, so I would blend in. No law prevented me from being in the school after the last bell, but I felt like I didn't belong there.

I spun the combination and reached inside for my bookbag, lost in thought. I still didn't know how I'd get to that storage unit place. I really did not want to walk.

Someone cleared her throat, and I jumped, as if reliving the moment with Kyle from earlier. But the throat-clearing wasn't nearly as threatening as before. Ms. Krieger stood behind me this time. She had a dark purple wool coat on, and a green knit hat capped her red hair. "Miss the bus?"

"Something like that," I mumbled.

"Do you need a ride?"

As a matter of fact... I demurred, mostly for show. "My grandma was going to pick me up later. She knew I was planning to stay late today..." I was a terrible liar, and it showed.

Krieger chuckled. "Where do you need to go, Dora?"

I pulled on my coat and looped my Fourth Doctor scarf around my neck, then followed her out to the staff parking lot. The teachers didn't need many spots, and Krieger's little Ford hatchback was one of the only cars left. I told her about the diner, and when she said she wasn't sure where it was, I recited the address so she could plug it into her maps app.

"I'll call Grandma and tell her to meet me there," I said.

"Does this have something to do with the dancing men?" Krieger kept her eyes on the asphalt as she inched out of the lot, but I knew her brain was working triple time. "Or Kyle again? Is he bothering you?"

Krieger's memory was like a genetically engineered elephant's. I didn't reply.

She sighed. "I know, it's weird, I shouldn't have so much interest in a student."

I counted the moments, the road spinning past beneath her tires.

"I mean, I don't have interest in you, not in an inappropriate way. I mean..." The phone calmly asked her to turn, and she followed it. "I worry."

"I get it," I said softly. I looked at my hands, twisting the fingers in my lap. I was tired of not having any allies. Maybe it was time I leaned on the few people I had, turned them into my team. "Yeah, he said something to me today."

"I thought so, since he said he needed a few more days to finish the paper. I told him he'd lose a letter grade for every day it was late." Krieger twisted the car onto the main drag of town, out past the school and toward the diner. "I think we need to talk. Me, you, and Kyle."

If I hadn't been sitting in my teacher's car, heat blasting onto my knees, I might have fallen over. "I'm not sure that's a good idea."

"Why not? Let's clear the air. Make sure he knows I'm protecting you."

Well, I liked the idea of being protected.

"There was... kind of a problem Friday night." Why was I telling her? The words fell out of my mouth. "With him and Aidan. At Mallory's house... They got into a fight."

Krieger huffed. We sailed over a hill, and the GPS instructed her to slow down.

"I'll talk to the principal. Don't worry, Dora. You'll be okay. I won't let anyone hurt you. Especially not a cheating jerk." She pulled into the diner, and her hand flew to her mouth. "Sorry, not sorry. Don't tell. We're not supposed to have favorites."

I smiled. "I got you."

Then I hustled out of the car.

AFTER MY TEACHER's little blue car zipped out of sight, I rushed onto the hill behind the diner and into the backyard of the storage place, tromping through dirt and slush. I reached the crest of the hill, my breath coming in fits and starts.

I wasn't sure where I needed to go, so I headed toward the light in an office near the back of the complex. Daylight Savings Time was over now, the weekend past us, and night crawled up fast. I peeked inside an open glass window. An old man was picking his teeth with... ew... was that wood? A stick?

He noticed me and got up. "Help you, young lady?"

"I hope so." Adrenaline tingled in my hands, and my legs shook. "I was instructed to come here, to this unit?"

I showed him the address on my phone.

The man scrutinized me, looked me up and down, and for a minute, I wished I hadn't let Ms. Krieger leave. I felt suddenly, cosmically, alone.

Then, he laughed. I saw his yellow teeth inside the maw of his open mouth.

"You, girl?" he asked. "Damn. He ain't paying me enough for this."

29

Caroline

The weekend had passed with little fanfare. Kieran hardly noticed when I came home after dawn for the second time in a week. They told me about the fight at the girl's house. I hated that my son could be so terrible to someone so vulnerable. And Patrick's son, the avenging angel—it all nauseated me. Patrick's wife would love me even more now.

I told Kyle we didn't need to spend the money on wrestling this year, not after his behavior. And it chilled me that he'd been teasing that poor girl while I'd been out gallivanting.

I kept myself busy, cleaning everything until it shone, reading, making an effort to stay distracted. Naturally, none of those things worked. I kept thinking about Patrick, Jude, that damn storage unit. The money. Thousands of dollars couldn't fix my son, but they could pay for therapy. Which I signed Kyle up for immediately.

Monday had gone by easy at work, followed by a collapse into a chair, an ordering of pizza, a nap on the couch.

But Tuesday morning—that was a big day.

I was ready now, after my night with Patrick. It sounded more sala-cious than it had been. Patrick hadn't done a thing. I'd been forced to rely on myself to escape. Men seemed so useless in my new reality.

I'd asked Elaine at the firm to draw up a draft of the documents I required to dissolve my marriage to Kieran. My specialty wasn't family law, but she'd worked in that field before switching to Social Security. She'd e-mailed it to me, and the file burned a hole in my inbox.

It could be worse. I could have simply forwarded it to him, waited until he saw it. Let him figure it out for himself, take bets on how long I'd be gone before he realized he'd been stuck with the mortgage. But no, that wasn't the way to go either. I needed to stay in Chesterfield for my mother. Kieran could return to the land of endless surf. The only put-out person would be Kyle, and well, it was about time he learned maturity.

Once Kyle caught the bus, I called my boss and told her I'd be working from home. I didn't detect much annoyance in her voice, but I suspected that time was coming. *This is important. Once she knows all the details, she'll understand.*

While I waited for Kieran to wake up, I made a cup of coffee and practiced yoga as the sun rose. The screened-in, heated porch was nice for this. It wasn't California, but it would do. When I finished my stretching, I went back inside to nuke the coffee and then returned to the porch. The sun glowed against the white ground.

I wandered back into the bedroom, fiddling with the pearl studs on my ears. Kieran lazed in the bed, long legs twisting atop each other. The weed-funk was stale and strong. I drew a breath.

"I think I'm going to get a job," he said.

I stopped, short-circuited.

"It's time. Kyle can stay home by himself after school. The neighbor lady can make sure he doesn't get into any shenanigans." Kieran yawned and sat up straight. "Be nice to have extra spending money."

My mouth made an O shape. *Extra money. Just think of what you'll blow it on.*

I had to get the divorce done before I got Jude's money.

Kieran smiled until he realized I wasn't. So fucking clueless. I got ready to tell him again, about the papers, the big news that was most definitely not about my high school boyfriend.

My husband's expression softened. He reached for my hand, and I let him take it. Passive, too tired of fighting.

"I know I haven't been doing right lately," he said.

I nodded, swiping at tears.

"It's hard. New place, shit weather."

He looked past me through the window. In true Northeast Ohio fashion, the sun had turned to rain, which pelted the windows with fresh aggression.

"I won't lie to you. I hate it here."

My throat was scratchy. "Do you think it's been easy for me?"

"It's never easy for you."

I was silent.

"Doing hard stuff is how we grow," I said finally. "We have to stretch ourselves."

I thought of the file in my e-mail, of the Very Hard Thing I now couldn't bring myself to do.

"And that, my dear, is why I'm seeking a job." He hugged me, and I let him. "I'll find a challenge and make some money doing it."

"One more thing," I said.

He paused, mid-jump-out-of-bed-to-seize-the-day.

"You have to stop smoking."

Kieran's turn to keep quiet. Could he be weighing the costs and benefits, deciding if he needed to act? I wasn't sure if he was capable of that kind of critical thinking.

"It's not negotiable." Now I'd found my lawyer voice. "You can't pass a random drug test. That's standard in most companies now."

"So, we gotta move to Colorado, babe."

The joke fell flat. I waited for an actual answer.

Kieran sighed and walked into the bathroom. The shower started, water drumming on the tub.

"I'll work on it," he called.

EVEN A FEW DAYS LATER, I was still so tired. I yawned and apologized my way through client meetings. November, that nomad time between Halloween and Thanksgiving, when we tried to cram everything in before the holidays while simultaneously not wanting to.

Elaine asked me about the papers, and I sent her money through PayPal, figuring it was a hint. She stopped by my desk later with a pumpkin spice latte.

"You don't owe me anything," she said.

I wondered if she was trying to make friends.

I was never good at forging friendships. Sure, I had the requisite number of mommy contacts on social media, the people who threw us a going-away party in California, the ones who said they'd miss us, then promptly carried on with their fabulous lives. I wasn't close with any of them, though, and I couldn't think of a friend I'd been close enough to confide in. My mother, maybe. Patrick.

Well, I'd basically told Patrick about Kieran. I didn't give Patrick all the particulars, but I'd unloaded enough of my woes.

And at first, I'd only told Elaine because I needed her. She was a means to an end. But after lunch, when she carried that extra coffee, I wondered if things could be different.

The hot spices from the latte clung to my tongue as I fought fatigue, and my heavy head was grateful for the distraction. Elaine and I sat at my desk beside my flickering computer. As we talked, my screen went dark, conserving energy. *This could be what it's like to have a friend.*

What was all of this? Jude's games. Kieran's reversal. A sudden friend. And Patrick, oh, Patrick. I only came back to Ohio to be with my mother, but so much else had happened.

I realized I'd been monologuing. Elaine sat, listening, patiently.

Oh God. I've fucked it up. I licked my lips. "Um, so, how are you?"

She laughed. "Next time I check on you, leave your bank account alone."

A vibration from my desk—the phone.

She pointed. "That's my cue."

I grabbed the offending device and pressed it to my ear.

"Hello, this is Caroline." Breathless, brisk.

"Mrs. Cannon?"

"It's Ms. Cross. Yes, this is she."

"Kyle Cannon's mother?"

As if my child and I couldn't possibly possess two different surnames. As if this fact were so ludicrous that she needed to confirm a second time. Had to be the school. I blew out a breath. "Yes. What's the matter?"

"We need you here now." This tinny voice. I couldn't take it seriously.

I glanced at the clock. "My husband's home. He doesn't work. You could call him."

"Kyle needs his mother."

Perhaps I could punch this woman. Perhaps a helpful lunch aide could station her at the front door so I could deliver the blow efficiently on my way in.

"His mother has a legal brief to finish," I said.

Silence on the other end. I felt the guilt surging across the telephone lines. Except we didn't have those now, did we? We only had cell phone towers. 4G waves of guilt, electromagnetic, pulsing through the air.

I sighed. "Give me an hour."

30

Patrick - Earlier

I began Tuesday morning by staring at the computer screen.

I was working from home. It was the one thing I could do to exert control over my situation. On Sunday, I'd logged into my bank account to see the balance. At the sight of the number, my chest filled with fear, and I had to squeeze my eyes tight to banish it. A payroll error... but how could it be when I was the one who had done payroll?

I'd opened the VPN and pulled up ForkFlavor's accounting software. Sure enough, Matt had accessed the system after I left. I swallowed, and my dry throat ached as I texted him.

The response came moments later: *Had to adjust the salaries to bring on our boy Duncan. You understand. I'm still dealing with all the fallout from your crap anyway.*

I'd frowned at the phone. We had money in our savings account that I could transfer... We'd have to, to keep up with all the credit card payments. I logged back into the bank account, clicked into the savings, and moved the funds. Then I'd slammed the laptop shut.

Now, Amy came downstairs in her plaid flannel pajamas. I was about to close the door to my study, but she crept in, light on her bare feet. She must have been cold. I gave her a nod and kept working.

"I don't know what you were thinking," she said.

The ForkFlavor accounts spread out on my screen. I struggled to divide my attention between my wife and the spreadsheet.

"You stayed out all night. Like a teenager. Without telling me what you were doing. You missed the game, and you weren't there to back me up with the fight."

She was baffling me. Despite our unexpected laughter Saturday morning, we spent most of the weekend in silence, as she fumed over something I didn't entirely understand. Now she was talking when I needed to concentrate.

"Are you even listening?"

I looked at her. "You could have given me this lecture on Saturday and spared me the days frozen out."

"Don't act like this isn't your fault."

"It's not like I murdered someone."

"For all I knew, you had gotten murdered." Amy took a step back. "I think I'm finally ready for you to tell me where you were."

I'd been waiting for the question, so I was prepared. "Matt dragged me into an event. I didn't have a choice. And there was no signal at the venue, so I couldn't call you."

Yes, I lied. If she'd asked me Saturday morning, I might not have done so, but after a few days, I'd realized it wasn't worth telling her about the puzzle. She wouldn't understand, and she'd be pissed about Caroline. It would be easier to lie and let the subject drop. She'd change her tune after I deposited that cash.

"So that bastard means more to you than your own son?" Amy shook her head. "I haven't had enough coffee to deal with you."

She walked away. The words pricked at my thoughts, but I pushed them back. I didn't love this resolution, but it was still easier than explaining everything. Besides, I hadn't thought Aidan's fight was that big of a deal. Our son was a hero—at least the way he told it to me. He had gone there to help that girl Kyle was tormenting online, to put a stop to it.

Everything would be okay. Caroline and I would find Jude, and I would get five hundred thousand dollars. I'd have to look into the laws on gift taxes, but that would be enough to get us caught up. Enough to pay off the house, even.

In the meantime, maybe I could start a freelance business. I picked up a pen and chewed on the end of it. Small businesses were always looking for accountants. I could use the income to supplement the main job, and when I got Jude's money, I could quit ForkFlavor. Even if it meant going for health insurance on our own, the extra hassle would be worth it to ditch Matt. I clicked over to Google and typed in "freelance accountants."

Amy and Liam were playing upstairs, and I was filling out financials for my monthly report to the investors, when I heard her get up and answer the phone. "Hello? Oh, yes, Mrs. Jackson, is Aidan okay? Sure, okay. We'll be there. Yes, my husband too."

My stomach ached. I pushed away from the computer and trudged upstairs, where she was hanging up.

"Well, you'll have another chance to parent responsibly," Amy said. "We have a meeting at the school today."

31

Caroline

The sky clouded over again as I drove back to Chesterfield from downtown. At least in the middle of the day, I didn't have to contend with rush-hour traffic. I cruised along under the gray umbrella of the world, moving fast.

My boss wouldn't keep putting up with this drama. I hadn't worked a full week since returning to Ohio. Sure, I had a long, robust work history, and I'd interned for the office in high school. But my life was in such upheaval right now.

In a few more years, Kyle would be off to college. As much as I hated to think about it, my mother would be gone. I'd be past the separation—the divorce—and I'd be stronger.

I just had to keep my job.

I was hungry, so I stopped for a cheeseburger and inhaled it while pulling into the school parking lot. Then I stuffed my fast-food bag in a trash can outside the front door and stalked inside. The high school felt wrong, alien, an interloping building where our old hallways used to be. A renovation had changed everything around, and I couldn't find my way. I didn't want to talk to any of those harpies in the office, so I texted Kyle.

No response.

I stood outside the main office and tapped my heel on the hard floor. The sound rang out through the empty halls.

Then a door opened, and a woman with red hair and freckles came out. "Kyle isn't supposed to be using his phone now."

"Not even to communicate for legitimate purposes? I'm his mother. Not his buddy."

"We don't know that, Mrs. Cannon."

I glared. "It's Ms. Cross."

She led me into the room. Kyle was seated at a long wooden table next to another boy. The other teen was shorter than him but just as sullen, his eyes cast down. He looked familiar, but I couldn't place him.

"Have a seat, Ms. Cross," the teacher said, delicately emphasizing my actual name, the one I was born with. "The others will be here shortly."

"You mind telling me what this is about?" I glanced at my son, but he seemed more interested in the whorls and swirls of the tabletop. Such a nice piece of furniture in such an institutional room. Donated by some bigwig, no doubt.

The teacher raised an eyebrow. "You don't know?"

Kyle didn't look up.

"No," I said, clipped. "I don't."

The door swung open, and Hannah crept in. Shoulders hunched, so small. I caught my breath. No, that was her daughter, the one I'd driven home. Her doppelganger. The one who stole the book.

I sat back in the stiff folding chair—so incongruous with this table—and watched her take a place. What else was happening here? I averted my gaze as my stomach dropped. It was a ridiculous notion, but was this about Jude? Did my son know about the game we were playing?

32

Dora

Tuesday, all day, I sat in class, but I heard nothing. My mind wandered, totally gone.

The sequence of events had unfolded thusly. At the storage place, things were bonkers. The man with the yellow teeth took me to the unit listed in the Craigslist clue. He told me that someone was paying him to lock people in as they arrived, but he wasn't about to do that to a minor. And I didn't want to be locked in a storage unit, even if I had the tools to get out.

"He told me people would find their way out," the storage guy said. "Crackers, I tell you. Girl, you don't know what you're getting into."

Generally, I don't like it when old men tell me about my life. But this time, I agreed.

I asked him if I could at least look. When he keyed in the code and the door chugged open, I saw a room—a bed, a desk, a lamp. It was messy, like someone had already been there. *Kyle's mom?* I shoved back the distraction. I had to focus.

The storage guy leaned against the wall with his arms crossed as I searched the place. There had to be another code here, something to lead me to the next clue. I found one of those old tape players, but I wasn't sure how it worked. The storage guy would have to help me, and that would be way awkward.

I hit the jackpot when I came across a stack of Jude's games. They had to be important. "Can I take these?"

He shrugged. "Don't see why not. All youse are through here now, and I don't think this dude is coming back for his stuff."

"Why not?"

The storage guy got quiet, looked at the floor. A bad feeling rose in my chest.

"Alright then," I'd said. "Do you have a bag?"

I filled a plastic bag with the games and lugged it down the hill toward the diner. After finding myself a table, I spent several hours sifting through the pieces, looking at the side panels, trying to figure out how everything fit together. I wished Aidan was there—the extra brainpower would have been helpful—but I resolved to write him a note the next day to fill him in on the new situation.

I didn't have money, but the server took pity on me and brought me ice water, and I downed it. Darkness fell, and eventually, I gave up and called my grandmother to get me.

But then, this morning, as I dressed blearily for school, I tripped over the pile of games. I'd forgotten they were there, and yet again, it was dark. I had to get up ass-early to catch the bus. Fumbling, I reached for the pile to re-straighten it, and my hands found purchase on the top cover of a box.

My fingers traveled the smooth surface until I felt little bumps. I stopped, then ran my hand over the top again.

My heart sped up. I had to hurry, or I'd be late. I raced for my bookbag and shoved the game box into it. I couldn't wait to figure out exactly what this Braille said.

～

I planned to walk to the library after school, but Krieger stopped me in the hall. "Dora, can you wait a minute?"

I wanted to tell her no, but I didn't think I had that freedom.

"Sure," I said lightly. "What's up?"

Kyle had been at school all day, which scared the shit out of me. But at least in Krieger's class, she had my back. He hadn't spoken to me, but I could feel him watching. I scrawled a note to Aidan and explained what I had done at the storage unit, but he seemed to have lost interest. He didn't write me back, and when I tried to catch his eye, he just looked away.

It was okay. I didn't need him. I had started this on my own, and I would finish it that way.

"I've arranged a meeting," Krieger said. "Kyle's family is here, and so is Aidan's. I'm sorry I couldn't get in touch with your grandmother, but we need to discuss this and come to a solution. Work this out once and for all."

My stomach dropped. "Work what out?"

"The cheating. The fighting. It's not sustainable."

"But the fight happened at Mallory's house."

"It doesn't matter. The conflict is in the school. The boys are unable to work together in sports, and if we don't smooth this out, it'll be bad for all of you." Krieger laid a thin-fingered hand on my shoulder, and I flinched. She flinched back, as if she didn't expect that, and dropped her hand to her side. "Clearly, you're involved with them both, and I don't want you to get hurt."

"I'm not involved with either of them." I frowned. Did she think we were a thing? Gross. "Aidan's my friend. We've been working on a project together."

"I think he befriended you because of the situation between you and Kyle." Krieger raised her hand again, then thought better of it. "Come on. Before I speculate any more, let's go to the conference room."

I followed her through a teacher door into a long, airy hallway. The white institutional walls were covered with plaques and recognition certificates. Probably participation awards for all the teachers so they could feel good about themselves. We ended at another door, a swinging one this time, and slid inside to find both boys sitting, staring at an oak table. Neither looked up at me.

But Kyle's mom did. From her spot at the conference table, she targeted me with an icy eye.

33

Patrick

I didn't understand why we had to go to this meeting. Amy had resolved everything with the police and with the girl's parents. Any other issues between those boys could be sorted out without parental or school involvement. But I went along, like the good little puppy husband.

Amy got a neighbor to watch Liam. Thank God. I couldn't imagine doing this with him running around and getting into everything. I followed her as she wound her way through the halls of the high school, a woman who knew where she was going.

She stopped at the office, an open, windowed room with a few women sitting inside. I averted my eyes. If I assumed anything about their roles, I'd be another clueless man. Amy zeroed in on the woman behind the largest desk, and then that woman—maybe a secretary, maybe a principal, what do I know—led us inside, then past a metal door.

We entered a musty-smelling room with matte white walls. At the oak table sat two boys. One, my son, and another I didn't recognize.

Well, I recognized him in the swoop of his jaw and the point of his nose. Caroline's son.

She sat beside him.

Sitting alone was a young, slim girl, and if I blinked, she brought Hannah back to me.

I swallowed and took a long deep breath to keep myself upright.

The teacher—I didn't know her. She looked familiar, though, like everyone in this room did.

34

Caroline

Patrick blew through the door, and I coughed, my chair clattering as I fought to hide my surprise. The teacher frowned and reached into a fridge behind her. She handed me a cold bottle of water, and I took it, pressing it to my face before drinking. My skin was on fire.

Patrick looked dopey and confused, but his wife was pissed. "Will someone tell me exactly what is going on here?" she asked.

I snorted. "I asked the same thing."

"I didn't ask for your opinion."

Okay, then. This wasn't Jude's game. This was the good old mommy war, a fight I had plenty of experience in. I folded my arms tight across my chest.

The teacher put out both of her hands, palms down. "Let's start, so everyone's on the same page. I'm Ms. Krieger—Rebecca Krieger. I'm the English teacher."

"Okay," I said.

No one else moved.

"We have several issues going on here," Krieger said. "One, a growing animosity between Aidan and Kyle."

So this was Patrick's son. The boys played football together, I remembered dimly. They were rivals. In another life, they might have been the same child. I thought of that child sometimes, the one who had never lived, my son and Patrick's. He'd have my sharp nose and Patrick's big brown eyes.

Instead, my surfer-blond boy, with Kieran's pillowy pouty lips, sat there and sneered.

"Okay," I said again.

"Two, we have the problem of Kyle's compulsion to cheat." Krieger looked sharply at me. "He's been threatening Dora. Telling her harm will come to her if she doesn't write his essays for him. Aidan's been trying to help her."

My chest constricted. I turned to my son. "Is this true?"

No response.

"Why are we here, then?" Amy blew a strand of blonde away from her forehead. Her streaks had to be fake. No Midwest girl looked like that by default. "This is between you two."

She gestured to Kyle and Dora, who shrank from the table.

"Your son isn't innocent," I said.

Amy turned to Patrick. "Are you going to let her talk to me that way?"

"Now wait," Krieger said. "We're not assigning culpability. We need to fix the behavior going forward. The idea is to clear the air among all of you."

Did Patrick's wife know we'd dated? Trying not to stare at her, I caught his gaze instead, and he held it. I thought I saw pleading in his eyes, like *Get me out of here.* I felt that too.

Then I landed on Dora. She chewed her nails with intention, never looking up. Like Hannah—the way she was after the *Titanic* party. She was never the same after that night. My insides twisted. Guilt upon guilt. Meta-guilt. A guilt sandwich, made with two slices of guilt and a chewy guilt filling.

I regrouped, switched to lawyer mode. "Alright. The goal is to end the problematic behavior. Let's create some actionable items to meet that goal."

Amy rolled her eyes. "Easy. Kyle doesn't talk to my son anymore, and you keep him out of wrestling."

Kyle glared daggers at her, his eyes off the table for the first time. "You're not my mother."

"If you're cheating, you deserve to be punished." Amy snapped her head back, long hair flying. "He punched my son, too. Did you know that? At a party Friday night. Where were you then, Mrs. Cannon?"

"For the last time." I ground my teeth. "It's Ms. Cross."

"Oh, excuse me. Ms. Cross." She bit down hard on my name. "Where were you that night? I didn't see you when I went to pick Aidan up from Mallory's house. You act all holier-than-thou, but it looks to me like you're basically absent from Kyle's life."

Anger burned, low and slow, in my gut.

"Why don't you ask your husband where I was?" I asked.

My words had the desired effect. Krieger recoiled, and the kids looked like they wanted to jump into a portal to another dimension. Amy's fury drove her to her feet. Luckily, the giant table protected me. She'd have to climb across it to get me.

"That incident didn't happen on school grounds," Krieger said. "It's an aggravating factor, certainly, but it's also a distraction from our ultimate purpose."

"My ultimate purpose is to never see any of you assholes again." Amy grabbed Patrick's hand. "I'm taking Aidan out of this school. You deal with this other shit yourself. Come on, Aidan."

She locked her other hand around her son's wrist. Patrick cast a glance at me, and I flinched.

Tropical Storm Reed eddied outside and into the parking lot. Amy threw open her van door—of course she drove a van—as tiny, icy flakes trickled from the sky.

The teacher turned back to us.

"So." She cleared her throat. "No more cheating, then, right?"

35

Caroline

After Patrick's wife stormed out, her son and husband slunk out behind her. I stared at him as he passed, willing him to look at me—why? So we could communicate telepathically? But he didn't.

I turned back to the table. "What do we need to do? If Aidan isn't here, then Kyle can wrestle?"

Yes, I'd changed my mind, but I had the right to. If Patrick's terrible wife said my son couldn't wrestle, then I'd say he could.

Krieger shook her head.

"I'm afraid not. He'll be on academic probation. I suggest a tutor through the winter and spring, and if his grades improve, he can return to sports in the fall." She side-eyed Kyle as if she were pretending he wasn't there. "I've heard he's talented. It'll help for him to focus on football."

I looked at my son. He stared at the floor, kicking his sneaker at the faded green carpet.

"Kyle," I said. "Thoughts?" Like we were in a corporate meeting. I'd read that treating one's child as an adult can boost self-esteem.

"Can we go home?"

"I'm also recommending a three-day suspension," Krieger said.

"What?" Kyle and I chorused.

Dora fidgeted beside us, and for the first time, I was conscious of her movements. I felt fear on her, so like her mother. It was unnerving.

"Kyle's actions are classified as academic misconduct. And frankly, Dora's at risk here."

"At risk? Are you saying my son could hurt her?" My voice jumped an octave. "That's so unfair. She did the work for him. Isn't there a consequence for that?"

It was the wrong thing to say. Krieger stiffened and made a note on the paper in front of her. I leaned over to read the green-ink scrawl, and she moved her elbow to block it so I couldn't see.

"Dora isn't to blame here, Ms. Cross. Kyle coerced her." I heard the knife in her words, and my chest filled with shame.

I stood, roughly, kicking back my chair. I scrabbled at Kyle's elbow, my fingers brushing over his tough, hairy skin. He jerked to his feet, a puppet on strings.

"Fine. So, he returns to school Monday?"

"Correct." Krieger snapped her notebook shut.

We walked out into the empty hallway: me gathering my emotions, Kyle trailing.

When we were far enough from the office, I rounded on him.

"You're a freshman. This is how you start things off? You continue down this road and I might start thinking about military school." I paused. "I don't even know if those exist anymore, but by God, I'll find out and consider them seriously."

His skin pinked around his collar. Shouts came from down the hall, sneakers skidding on gym floors. Basketball maybe? People could hear me. I flushed, too.

"Let's just go," he said.

"Don't you dare tell me what to do." I turned around and headed toward the school's outside doors. "I hope you like cleaning and laundry, son, because that's what you'll be doing for the next three days. Help me get caught up from all your dad's laziness. I might even rent you out to the neighbors."

"Um, Mrs., um, Ms. Cross?"

Dora stood awkwardly between Kyle and me, her knobby knees encased in leggings, a faded hoodie around her slim shoulders. She appeared nerdier than Hannah was. Hannah had been the most mainstream of all of us, at least until she got sick. I had to remember that Dora wasn't entirely her mother.

"I need a ride home. I was wondering..."

"Oh, of course." My guilt returned, never gone too long. "I'll take you."

I heard a throat clearing. Krieger was beside us, her coat on, her bag slung over her shoulder. She looked tired, as if she'd used up all her energy yelling at me and Kyle. A little bit of schadenfreude bubbled up inside me, but I tamped it down.

"Dora, are you sure you don't need a ride?" Krieger's voice was saccharine, laced with sanctimonious sugar. "I can take you."

Dora pushed back her bangs. "I'm okay, Ms. Krieger. If you remember, I know Kyle's mom. We're working on the same project."

I liked the low, professional tone. The girl sounded so much older than fourteen—or was she fifteen? So mature. She could probably run circles around the college interns at my firm. And then I remembered the project she was talking about. *Jude.* The money. I laced my hands together to keep them from trembling.

Krieger frowned. "You're sure?"

Dora turned to me, holding her moon face up. I was a few inches taller than her—my heels helped—but she seemed even smaller, a little child. "I need to talk to Ms. Cross. I've broken through the last code."

36

Dora

Kyle's mom instructed him to sit in the back seat, and I felt a frisson of satisfaction.

The Cross/Cannon family lived in a development, a little bit outside of town. I leaned back in the front seat and watched the fields roll by. Corn, grass, cows. That was Chesterfield. The houses in this section of town were new construction. My grandmother said that people were buying houses here because the land was cheaper, and then they'd commute into Cleveland. I could see her in my mind's eye, shaking her head.

"Long way to drive to save some money," she'd say. "We're out here because we're part of this town. Born into it."

Native or not, I couldn't wait to leave.

We idled in their driveway.

"Did you want to talk here?" Kyle's mom asked mildly.

"It depends." I willed my heart to slow. "We need to find a Braille alphabet. We could do that here, or you could look it up on your phone..."

I'd planned to go to the library, but most normal people had Internet access at home.

"We should get something to eat. I'll order a pizza." Kyle's mom acted like this was nothing, like we weren't on the verge of a major breakthrough. "You found Braille? Where was it? I didn't know what to do next after escaping from the storage unit."

As soon as Kyle's mom turned off the car, he leaped out and raced into the house. I followed Ms. Cross, tentatively, but I could still hear his pounding steps on the stairs, the slamming of his room door.

We headed for the dining room table. I blocked out the world around me, pretending I wasn't in Kyle's house. My singular focus was on the code, on cracking it. I dug in my bookbag, pulled the game box out, and put it on the table, running my fingers over its top cover.

"See the bumps? We need to look up the Braille alphabet and find out what these letters say."

"Were you really in danger? I mean—do you feel like Kyle threatened you?"

The non sequitur threw me. Kyle's mom held her phone in her hand, but she wasn't tapping it. I didn't say anything, just stared down at the game box, running my hands over the raised surface.

"Okay. We won't talk about that now." Her screen lit with blue and red from the pizza app. With the sun going down behind her, light played over her face. "I'll have to get gluten-free crust for Kieran."

She typed on the phone, and I held my breath. Would she get to the Braille now? What were we even doing here?

But then she said, "I've got the site up. Do you think you could write out what you're feeling?"

For a minute I thought she was talking about me and Kyle again, but as she handed me a legal pad, I realized she wanted me to write the letters out as if they were dot patterns we could see. A fat Sharpie marker sat on the table. I grabbed it and scribbled on the yellow paper, breathing in the marker's tangy scent as I wrote.

I handed the pad to Kyle's mom, along with the marker. She inked in the English alphabet letters.

Actually—the first five were numbers. *1534 Chester-Simon Road.*

"That's not far from here. A little out of town but not too far." Kyle's mom pulled up the maps app on her phone and entered the address. She turned the screen to show me. "We could get there tonight. What do you think? Do you want to go?"

Her eyes glittered, and her breath hitched. She was excited.

I had been. But now, I wasn't sure.

"Where do you think we're going?" I studied the board game, its title, its summary. **Back to the Castle,** it was called. A sequel to one of the earlier games. *In the heart-pounding sequel to* **Castle Falls,** *players must discover a multi-million-dollar fortune—before the multi-millionaire finds and kills them. Here is the game of the century, heralded as "thrilling" by the Ohio Boardgamers Association.*

Ms. Cross—Caroline—saw it at the same time I did. "Some of the letters aren't italicized. Did you see that before?"

I hadn't, but I should have. I didn't know this Jude, or why he was important, but he had meant something to my mother. And to Caroline.

Her Sharpie flicked out to circle the special letters. **He lives here.**

37

Patrick

The shit hit the fan at home.

We piled out of the van and thundered into the kitchen while Aidan screamed at Amy.

"You're taking me out of school? I didn't even do anything! Where are you going to send me? It's not like there are a ton of options here in buttfuck nowhere."

"Watch your language!" She smacked her hands on the surface of the kitchen island. "I don't want you anywhere near that kid."

"You're the one who said he'd stay out of wrestling." Aidan crossed his arms, leaning in over the island. "That's what should happen. I'm not the one who should be punished."

Amy twisted her lips. "You got in a fight with him. His bitchy mother was right about that."

I didn't like hearing her call Caroline a bitch, but I kept my mouth shut. My turn to be blasted was coming.

"I fought with him because he was teasing Mallory and Dora. Jeez.

A guy can't even be a good person anymore." Aidan stood back, looking more like a man than I'd ever seen him, despite his short stature.

Amy's mouth quirked. "You don't care about those girls. You were just trying to get him kicked off the team."

Aidan went silent after that one.

Liam, meanwhile, perched on the couch, enjoying cartoons in the family room. Thank God I'd collected him from the neighbor outside before anyone could witness our epic family smackdown. I slipped out of the kitchen and sat next to my little boy, and he leaned his small-child body against my chest. I closed my eyes and pretended everything was normal, that I was in control.

The fight died away, and Aidan retreated to his room. I watched *Peppa Pig* with Liam as he cooed and laughed. Those pink pigs, they knew nothing but happiness, a simple life. Nothing but muddy puddles and sunshine for them. The rabbit lady ran every business in town, and everyone else reaped the benefits.

I wondered how Miss Rabbit must feel, always being the one other people relied on. Maybe she felt like me. Always stressed, always lonely, always seeking comfort and safety.

Amy came down the stairs and held out her hands for Liam. "I'm putting him to bed."

"You mean you're going to bed with him." *Good.* Maybe she'd let everything drop.

"I'm certainly not going to bed with you," Amy said.

Liam jumped into her arms, and she held him tight.

I felt his absence, conspicuous, the lack of his heat against me.

"It's not what you think." I needed to explain myself, even if she didn't want me to.

"I don't think anything." She rocked our son, bouncing on her heels. "You were with her when you should have been with us."

I opened my mouth to say something, but no words came out. Amy took Liam upstairs, leaving me on the couch, the TV xylophone ringing out the *Peppa* theme with no one to hear it but me.

I changed the channel, turning on History. Nazi armies marched across the screen, but I wasn't paying attention. The show's sound filled the void surrounding me. All I could think about was how royally I'd messed up.

Amy never returned.

I stared at the flickering TV. I was also unable to stop thinking, to stop crucifying myself for my own worthlessness. I wasn't making enough money to keep this lifestyle afloat. Our credit card balances still ballooned, as I charged stuff I couldn't afford, because I poured all my cash into this ridiculous mortgage.

I had to do something. I had to change this life.

My phone rattled on the couch beside me. I picked it up, eyed the text. Caroline.

I clicked on it.

Big news. You have to come. Bring Aidan.

I glanced at the digital clock on the cable box. 7:03 p.m. Not super late, but Amy and Liam were already asleep, and Aidan would be winding down soon. *It's a school night.*

You have to. It's Jude. We've figured it out.

My heart sped to a clip. Who else had she brought into our alliance?

$333,333.33 and counting, threes repeating to infinity. Even that money would be better than what we had now.

I stole upstairs, slipped into my son's room. He was curled up in bed, playing a video game on his phone. I shook his shoulder.

"Aidan, c'mon," I said. "We have to go."

He stirred. "What is it? Dad, what's wrong?"

Of course, he would think something was wrong. But something was going right. At least one question in my mess of a life was being answered. "Nothing. We have to go. But don't worry. Everything is fine. Better than fine."

He rubbed a hand over his face, creasing the sleep out of his skin. "Are you sure?"

I wasn't, entirely, but I cared enough to find out.

AFTER THE TEXTS, Caroline called me. A blank face blinked at me from my buzzing screen—the number brand-new to my contacts list.

I didn't know if Amy could hear. She'd be on her phone or her Kindle, playing around, letting her brain go empty. I felt for her. I really did. Those few days I'd spent unemployed had made me antsy. So much crying and drama. Kids were exhausting.

But I wasn't hiding anything from my wife. I didn't regret anything I had done in the past week, didn't regret going to the storage unit with Caroline. It wasn't my fault Jude chose this moment to come back into our lives, in the most dramatic way. Amy didn't understand. To her, it was all high school politics, both then and now. She hadn't been there. She couldn't know what growing up in Chesterfield had been like. Jude was a magnet, the pull that drew us all together, and then the bomb that blew us apart. Amy may have thought our story was about Caroline, but it was always about Jude.

When I answered, Caroline drew breath and it all came out in a rush. "Dora has the last clue. She found him."

In theory, none of us knew what we'd find at the end of this madcap scavenger hunt. But, instinctively, we knew. What else—who else—could we be searching for?

"Where is he?" I held my reaction close, standing in Aidan's bedroom, knowing he was watching.

"She has the address. It's not far. We can get there in twenty."

"Done. I'll pick you up." I punched the phone off before she could say any more. "Come on, Aidan."

"You still haven't said where we're going."

"We have to stop at Ms. Cross's house to get her."

Aidan's forehead creased. "I don't want anything to do with that family."

At first, I'd planned to give Aidan the option of staying home, but then I realized this was an opportunity to make peace with Caroline and her son. I didn't like the animosity between us. True, our boys hadn't known our pasts when they became rivals. They couldn't help it. They were both talented, and it was a small school. Not everyone could be the starter, especially when there were sophomores, juniors, and seniors to contend with. But Aidan needed to learn that life wasn't always about winning.

In fact, this was about collaboration. Once we found Jude, the three of us would split his money, and life would be better for all of us. Maybe my son hated Kyle and didn't want Caroline to get her share, but we'd still have ours, and I hoped that would be enough.

"Come on. It won't take long."

He shook his head.

"You're not the one who got suspended. School tomorrow," I said.

"All the more reason I shouldn't go with you."

I tamped down the anger rising in my chest. "All right. You're going. I want you to make things right with Caroline."

"Seriously, Dad? You want me to be friends with your girlfriend?"

"She's not my girlfriend." I tapped my phone. "We have to go. It's getting late already."

"Mom doesn't like her, so what's the deal?"

"I'll tell you in the car."

There was one thing about my son—he cared about people. About their stories, their hearts. That was why he wanted to help Dora, why he went to that other girl's house with her that night and got in that fight. Yes, the rivalry simmered between him and Kyle, but he could have ignored it, chosen not to engage. I knew Aidan would follow me when I teased him with that story.

We exited quietly through the front door, so Amy wouldn't hear the garage door rising. Luckily, I'd parked in the driveway.

"Sit in the back," I said to him as we approached the SUV.

"So she can sit up front?" He placed himself on the second seat, hovering behind the center console. I started the car. We only lived a few streets away from Caroline. Both of our families lived in these outer-ring developments, the homes of Cleveland commuters.

"She's the adult, you know. Put on your seat belt."

"You're going to order me around the rest of the night?" Aidan grumbled and stretched the belt across his chest. "Who is this woman to you? Kyle's mom?"

"You're right. She was my girlfriend." I kept my voice even as I pulled onto the main road that ran between our two neighborhoods. "We dated all through high school. She and her family just came back to Chesterfield."

Aidan leaned forward. "Why did you break up?"

I saw him move in the rearview as I focused on the drive. Snow dappled my windshield, and I turned on the wipers.

"She wanted to go to California. I didn't." That was the short version.

"So you went to OSU, and she went to California?"

"Are you going to be okay with this if Kyle comes?" I didn't know if the boy would be there, but after the dustup a few hours ago, I wasn't sure Caroline would leave him at home.

Aidan glowered. "I don't want to see his face. Back to the story. Mom came after her? You ever had other girlfriends?"

Not as such. "I dated a handful of other girls. OSU was a big place. It's practically a city in itself."

"But Ms. Cross—you loved her?"

I swallowed as I turned into her development. "I did, yeah, buddy."

38

"Let's go!" Caroline called up the stairs. "Kyle! I'm not leaving you!"

Muffled sounds from upstairs. I picked at my fingers, chewed on the skin of my thumbs. I didn't want Kyle to come with us, but I'd tolerate his presence to meet Jude.

There was still so much I didn't understand. These three—Mr. Reed, Ms. Cross, and Jude—they were friends, and friends with my mother. And Jude was this famous mysterious presence. But besides my mother, what connection did they all have? And what did it have to do with me?

"Your dad's not home." Caroline thumped up the staircase, her voice getting quieter as she reached the top. But she was loud enough that I could still hear her end of the conversation. "Do you think I'm going to leave you to your own devices after what you did? You owe it to Hannah. I mean, to Dora."

I flinched at the mistake.

"Do I have to get out that leash I used to use when you were a toddler? I bet it's still around here. In a box."

Thirty seconds later, Kyle tromped down the stairs behind his mother, a hangdog look on his face.

It'll just be for an hour or two. Maybe not even that long. I'd already been in the car with him to get to his house, after all. I could handle things for a little longer.

Caroline stopped to text, her thumbs flying across the screen. Kyle leaned against the wall next to the stove. He inched his back along it, scratching.

"Patrick's coming," Caroline said. "We can all go together."

"Are you fucking kidding me?" Kyle muttered.

"Shut your mouth," Caroline said.

"This is all bullshit anyway." He reached into his pocket, but Caroline clip-clopped across the kitchen and snatched his phone from his hand. "Come on!"

"You should apologize to Dora. While we're waiting."

Kyle stepped away from the wall and slumped into a chair. Their dining table was in a nook, looking outside a big, open window. It was dark now, storm clouds rolling across the sky, and the early night would be coming soon. But I could picture this being a beautiful space, a light-filled one, a place where a family could sit together and be close to one another. My body burned with embarrassment just thinking about it. It wasn't a place for me. I wasn't supposed to be here.

"I should go," I said hastily. "Ms. Cross, would you mind taking me home? You and Mr. Reed could go."

We'd have to split the money, I realized, thinking about it for the first time. I'd been so focused on the codes that I hadn't remembered the prize we sought. But that would still be more than three hundred thousand dollars... if I could trust her.

"Nonsense." She smiled—the first time I'd seen that kind of expression on her face. It was a warm smile, the kind a mother should have. "I was wrong to be competing with you before. We should have worked together from the beginning. You deserve to be here."

"My grandmother... She won't like this."

Caroline checked her phone. "Patrick doesn't live far. His development's just the next one over. We won't be gone long."

"Yeah, but..." I sighed.

"Oh, honey." Caroline went to me, put her hand on my shoulder. It felt wrong. This woman who once hated me was now pretending she was my best friend, a surrogate mother even. "I'll take you home when we get back, and we'll talk to her together. Your mother was my friend, you know. When we were kids? Your grandma might like to see me."

Car noise in the driveway. Caroline rushed to the door and flung it open. Mr. Reed didn't even get out of the car. I didn't see him behind those flaring headlights.

"Come on." She waved at us. "No time to waste."

We scrambled into Mr. Reed's SUV. Snow was spitting down. I put my hoodie up, shivering and wishing I'd brought a heavier coat.

I stumbled into Aidan, a shadow against the back window.

"Oh, sorry," I mumbled.

"Are you shitting me?" Kyle yelled. "You expect me to go on some wild-goose chase with this asshole and his asshole dad?"

"Kyle. Stop it," Caroline said through gritted teeth. "I'm sorry, Patrick."

Mr. Reed guided the car out of the driveway and into the road. "They'll figure this all out by the time we get home."

If I'd thought the afternoon in the office was awkward, this was supremely worse. I sat between them, avoiding Aidan's splayed-out legs. Kyle was beside me, wedged into the corner, hoodie up. I couldn't see either of their faces. Patrick and Caroline sat in front, like they were our parents and we were the messed-up family that had resulted.

What did I want from all this? I looked out the window, at the snow spilling down from the sky. What did I expect to find at the end of all these codes and trails? What would Jude be like? What would he tell me? I shivered again, hugged myself behind the stretch of the seat belt. The nylon dug into the side of my neck, against my sweatshirt.

Ten, fifteen minutes passed. The woods around us grew thicker.

We turned onto a dirt road, and Mr. Reed slowed as we bumped over rocky terrain. I'd known there were dirt roads out in the country part of Chesterfield, getting deeper into rural territory. Amish families lived here, and some reclusive rich people. People who didn't want to be found.

"This is it," Patrick said.

He eased the SUV left. We started up a hill with a driveway cut into its side, then dipped into a ravine before climbing again. A creek, frozen over, sputtered a little at the top. The weather had been so mercurial the last week, the river didn't know if it wanted to be ice or water. Our tires ground against the rocks as we crested into the paved courtyard of a huge mansion.

I looked up. And up and up. The building was like something out of a movie—a sprawling estate. There was no way anyone in Chesterfield could have built this a hundred years ago. Some architect built this house new and made it look old. This was most definitely the house of a rich person.

My heart knocked inside my chest. I didn't know what, but something was about to happen.

Patrick turned off the car, and we piled out. The two adults moved fast, on their way to the front door, and I stayed as close to them as I could, drawing my hoodie closer. The boys remained inside the van, and I was glad I wasn't in there with them. Maybe they were even duking it out now.

But I didn't care. I wanted to know what would happen here, what we would find. The house loomed above us, its lit-up towers and turrets stark against the dark sky. I wanted to go inside, to touch the furniture, to explore these hallways. I wanted to live here.

Caroline rang the bell.

The huge, heavy door moved backwards, and a person stood behind it. Was this Jude? I studied the man. He was lean, cheekbones cut tight to his face. His hair was gray and cropped short. He looked hollow, spent. His face didn't match the picture on the game boxes, but I still wanted to step inside and hear his story.

But Patrick and Caroline didn't seem to know him.

"Where's Jude?" Caroline asked. "Who are you?"

"I'm Greg," the man said. "He's been expecting you. Come in."

We tromped in, shaking the wetness off our shoes. I bent to remove mine, then stopped. That was something you did in your friend's house because her mom didn't want dirt tracked all over the carpet. People didn't need to take their shoes off in a mansion. There were probably maids and stuff who would clean the floor later.

The boys appeared behind us. I guessed they didn't want to sit outside in the cold, especially since Kyle was only wearing a hoodie, like me.

Greg reached forward and clasped each of our hands. "There's not much time now. Follow me."

Part Two

From "The Great Genius of Edward Elgar," a high school paper by Jude Lassiter

It could have been that Elgar was really worried about his own death. Here is a quote that he said about the Enigma Variations:

The Enigma I will not explain – its "dark saying" must be left unguessed, and I warn you that the connexion between the Variations and the Theme is often of the slightest texture; further, through and over the whole set another and larger theme "goes", but is not played . . . . So the principal Theme never appears, even as in some late dramas – eg Maeterlinck's L'Intruse and Les sept Princesses – the chief character is never on the stage.

Some people think that the "dark saying" is referring to Elgar's own death. And, sadly, that day did come, in 1934 at the age of seventy-six. He died from colon cancer.

1

Caroline

Of course this is Jude's house. I stared into the flying ceiling.
New construction—it had to be. Amish people of the
past two centuries didn't build Victorian mansions. And
the place wasn't completely Victorian, either. I was no student of architecture, but the interior didn't scream Downton Abbey estate, despite
its look from the outside. The interior front hall was large and open, but
where I would've expected a wide staircase with heavy wooden banis-
ters was a tall, thin set of stairs leading to a long upper hallway. The
stair rails were sleek and black, contrasting with the slick brown hard-
wood steps.

I looked down, around, behind us. Along the cream-colored wall,
where there would have been pictures of dead relatives in a nineteenth-
century English home, were paintings of cartoony peacocks and sloths.
Definitely not a manse of old. Jude had designed this house to be tricky
—an anachronism. Two centuries from now, people would still be
confused.

Greg beckoned for us to keep following him. The sights, the smells, all of it was so overwhelming. The thought of our prize, the money, zapped me in the gut as we climbed the stairs. I hadn't remembered it again until that moment. Where were we going? Maybe at the top of the stairs, we'd find Jude. He'd hand us his bags of cash and finally tell us why he'd sent us on this chase.

Greg had said *it won't be long now.* Was Jude dying? That would make sense. That would be a good reason to give away his money. I imagined him sitting on top of a stack of it, like Scrooge McDuck rubbing his feathers together. Jude would never be so generous otherwise.

At the top of the stairs, we found another cartoony painting. Edward Elgar, that obscure composer of graduation songs, that British code-loving knight Jude obsessed over. But here, Elgar didn't appear the way he did in music history books. He sported a longish, tousled haircut, and he wore small, round glasses reminiscent of hipsters and Harry Potter. This Elgar was impish. The tiny placard below the painting, hung where Elgar's nipple would have been under his green T-shirt, explained as much.

"Gregory Collins." I read the name of the artist. "Is that you?"

Greg nodded. The man who'd opened the door for us—the man we followed now—he'd painted Elgar.

The second-floor hall ribboned out before us, long and lonely. As we'd climbed, I'd almost forgotten the troupe behind me. I turned to check on them. Patrick zoned out, shell-shocked. The three teenagers' faces reflected the others—expressionless.

Dora had to be thinking hard, her mind working behind her curious expression. She was quick, sharp-witted. That girl was made of my friends, of my childhood. She was born from my past. This house represented her history, maybe her future.

Since I'd met Dora, I hadn't contemplated the matter of her father. I assumed Hannah had gone away to college to get knocked up. And Dora looked so much like her mother, her father could have been anyone. But as I stood there—I'd stopped walking for a moment, arrested by the Elgar painting—I remembered Dorabella Penny, a woman Jude had raved on about when we were kids. Elgar's friend. The composer had written her a coded message, and no codebreaker had ever broken it. At least, since the nineties, when we were in high school.

The girl passed me, her willowy hips scooting by. She put her finger in her mouth.

Maybe Hannah's daughter was a coded message. Maybe the answer was in her DNA.

The problem was, I still didn't know the question.

GREG LED us down the long hall to a heavy black door. More style confusion. He twisted a wrought-iron knob, and we filed inside.

The room was dark except for soft orange lamplight. A window lined the far wall, but a velvet curtain covered it. Below another painting—this one a furious storm of color—a hospital bed sat. An outlined human in the bed. Quiet beeps emitted from machines connected to the human. This was a sick person. Someone who should be at Bright Flower.

Not my mother. I pushed that thought from my mind, shoved it to the far recesses. I had to make room for the realization that this was Jude.

I'd been right. He was dying. But I didn't think he'd be this far gone.

I swiveled my shoulders, took a step toward him. When I looked back, Patrick's face was a mask. The color had drained from his cheeks, and he appeared sallow in the wan light. We heard our friend's breath rattling.

Dora stood by the door. Aidan's hand gripped her shoulder. Kyle slunk into a wooden chair just inside the entryway.

"We'd hoped the disease wouldn't progress this quickly." Greg's voice seemed odd in the space, too unfamiliar, when all I wanted to do was sink into my thoughts.

I needed to puzzle this out, to make sense of this mess. We'd been on a mission, it seemed, to find something great. This ending was too flat. This couldn't be our final treasure.

"I don't get it." Patrick opened his mouth to continue but couldn't finish the sentence.

"When he got sick, he told me he wanted to play one last game with you all." Greg twisted his fingers. "We thought... We set everything up. We thought we had more time."

"So, it was you the whole time? Bribing everyone. Sending the emails?" I asked.

The man nodded.

"Was... is there... " Patrick began to stammer, but I shushed him.

A game indeed. This was a sick one. I thought back to Lena at the library, to the storage unit owner. They'd known the truth. They could have exposed Greg at any time, but they didn't.

I looked from my dying friend to the faker.

Why get our hopes up, make us think we'd all be together again and that we'd finally be forgiven? That the slate would be wiped clean? A joyful reunion, complete with cash?

We should've known that was impossible.

2

Dora

So, this was Jude Lassiter.

Not a man at all anymore. Just... a thing. A smelly thing, hooked up to tubes and wires. A husk.

I stood near the door in the gloomy room, hiding however I could. The smell overwhelmed me. On the surface, I sensed a whiff of antiseptic, reminding me of the alcohol Grandma would pour on my scraped knees. I assumed that was from the medical stuff. The bandages, or whatever. But there was this other smell, a musty one, as if this guy had been dying in this house for a hundred years. It was a dirty smell, like an old book with yellow pages, dust bunnies clinging to the top spine.

I'd never seen a dying person, not even a dying pet. Sure, I'd seen roadkill. And Mallory had wailed when her gerbil died. His name was Simon, after the vampire from the *Mortal Instruments* series. I guess she figured that moniker would make him immune to the ravages of death.

I hadn't seen my mother die. She'd disappeared along with the wreckage of her car, her body consumed by flames. Nothing left of her but ash.

My heart fluttered as Aidan's hand snaked onto my shoulder.

"Are you all right?" he whispered.

"Yeah. You?"

"I don't know what to think."

That was a fair reaction. The whole thing was just... weird.

Caroline started to cry, softly, as if she wanted us to hear but didn't want to make a scene. Aidan's dad patted her on the shoulder, like Aidan had to me. But then she sank backward so that his arms would catch her. I didn't do that, and Aidan's hand fell away.

I stepped closer to the bed.

"What's the prognosis?" I asked, using the word I'd heard from TV medical dramas. Nights waiting up for my mother to come home from her bartending shifts, curled against the nubby couch, watching shows I probably shouldn't have been allowed to see.

Greg shook his head. "He went downhill fast, about a week ago. We have a doctor coming in daily, and he has nurses on staff 24/7. There's been no change over the last three days or so."

"He's been unconscious." Caroline moaned and hid her face in her hands.

"In and out. You may still get to talk with him." Greg ran a hand up and down Jude's pale arm, so white, even against the crisp clean sheets. "We think he's been waiting for you all. Hanging on."

"Too damn young," Patrick said.

It was the first time I'd heard him speak since we got there. His voice was hoarse. I realized that Caroline and Patrick were the same age as my mother, and Jude couldn't have been much older. Hannah had been thirty-eight. It seemed old to me, but probably not to them. I swallowed.

"Cancer. The great equalizer," Greg said.

"And, of course, he has the best doctors." Caroline's voice gained strength.

I was reminded of earlier that day, at school. It felt like such a long time ago now. Her strident insistence, in that room, when we were all together before.

"Of course," Greg said. "The colorectal unit at Cleveland Clinic."

I didn't have anything to contribute to the discussion. So, I studied his face, his features. Jude's jaw was slack. Eyes closed. His hair was gone, presumably from chemo. I knew this look from TV, but those cancer patients had been created with makeup, healthy actors' hearts beating in those healthy chests. This man wasted away, living in the barest sense of the word.

I couldn't explain it, but I felt a weird connection to him. Had felt it since the first time I saw his face on that game box at Mallory's. I thought back to the photo in my mother's room. Could have Jude have been my father? I couldn't see any trace of myself in him, and I had no proof either way.

Except... there was proof.

Racing in his blood. In his dying cells. His genetic code, twisting and turning up the ladder of his DNA. No hair... But there had to be another way. I closed my eyes, thinking of health class, when we'd learned about the follicles, the skin cells. Maybe I could slough some off from his arm? Or tell someone that I needed a sample?

My jaw clenched as I stared down at him. It could be so simple. I could just ask. But no one wanted to tell me the truth. The only truth ran in my veins and his.

Or someone else's, I supposed. But if he wasn't my father, then why was I even here?

Greg stopped the silence. "We should let him rest."

"Then what are we supposed to do now?" Caroline went to the window and heaved aside the curtains, lifting them away from the glass.

The snow came down hard and fast, as it did where we lived—the Ohio Snow Belt, far enough south of the lake to get the dense white stuff. It coated the trees, sheets of it spinning through the air, a violent cycling. The sky burned with night clouds, lit by the white in the air and the ghost of the moon.

"Why don't you stay for dinner and see if it clears up?" Greg gestured to the door. "Our kitchen is fully stocked. I keep some fine local wines in the cellar. Do you prefer red or white, Miss Caroline?"

He put his hand on her back, sliding her out of Patrick's arms, and directed her away from Jude.

The boys shuffled out of their way and into the hall. The adults filed out behind them. I lingered by the bed, still searching for some common ground between me and this almost-corpse.

3

Caroline

I couldn't stand seeing him.

I moved away quickly, bustling past the children and back into the long hallway, where I could breathe again. Took a few gasps—I didn't want to look panicked or overwhelmed, though my frantic insides were churning.

There were moments in my life when I'd hated Jude, and moments when I'd loved him. There were times when I'd loved him more than anything, wanted him even, but I had banished that thought to the spidery-web corner of my mind. Jude didn't want me. Any thought of being with him was futile, unwarranted. We didn't belong together. We didn't fit.

But there had been enough flares of emotion between us, hits of pure connection. The time he'd put his arm around me in bio, the heat of his body radiating off him onto me. The time he'd reached out to touch my long hair, his big pancake hand flat on my head. We mattered to each other. I hated those years we missed, the gap in between now and the last time I saw him. And I hated this house, this game. The artifice of it, the grandeur. I wanted to go back to when we were young, when we had all our lives before us.

I took the stairs as quickly as I could. Only Jude would build these slippery steps. He was asking for an accident. When I reached the bottom, I flew to the window, peering out. Still snowing.

Patrick, behind me, looked gray. Like he might vomit.

"Are you okay?" Before I could stop myself, I threw my body against his, as if he were a wall or a gigantic stuffed bear. Something firm and unmoving, something that would hold me up with no judgment.

"I could ask the same of you." He squeezed my forearms.

"He's dying." My voice was muffled beside his chest. "All this shit and he's dying."

"Now, now." A gentle interruption as Greg glided down behind us. "You had fun getting here, didn't you? That was all he wanted. You know how much he loved... loves games."

"I'm not sure that I would call it fun." I stepped away from Patrick, my face flushing, reminding myself I wasn't back in 1997. On the contrary. Today was the furthest from then I could possibly get.

"He didn't intend to be this sick when you got here. He wanted to break the news to you gently. It was never our intention for me to take over the game," Greg said.

I scoffed. As if he could control the trajectory of his illness.

"He could've reached out to us before he got sick." I swiveled my head to look at Patrick, who glowered.

"Well. I can't speak for that." Greg folded his arms. "Why don't we get something to eat? I'm sure Moira is already at work in the kitchen."

Patrick cleared his throat. "Sure. Before we get back on the road."

The thought of going home filled me with dread, even though Jude's house was only fifteen minutes from our development. We could get in an accident or stuck on that long hilly driveway. And I dreaded returning to Kieran, explaining to him where we'd been and what had happened. Who knew what he was doing, especially after his career-development revelation earlier? He felt like an insect to me, a fly I had to keep swatting away.

And then there was Kyle. Sullen Kyle, who haunted me, his frown so sharp and permanent. I was sure he was pissed because his phone didn't work and because he couldn't wear out his thumbs texting his friends.

If I got to pick, I'd either go back to high school, those halcyon moments with Patrick. I'd go back and try again, see what might lie in an alternate universe for us. Or, I'd go back to Bright Flower, climb in bed beside my mother, curl up with her and let the world fall away as I pretended to be a child again.

I shook my head, distracted. I'd wanted to pull Patrick back so we could talk about the money, but he had already gone ahead of me, following Greg. The two boys still lagged, and I wandered somewhere in the middle.

We entered a huge, light-filled dining room. Like the rest of the house, it made no sense. Its long wooden table in the center was classic, old-school: dark, aged wood, lined with ornate chairs on either side. The ceiling flew high here, too. But then, along the right half of the room, a large stage rose from the floor, curtains drawn across its front. Jude always loved the theater. Did he plan to host productions? The room was large enough that, without the table, it could serve as a mini-auditorium.

As if reading my mind, Greg spoke. "Jude hoped to host concerts, down the road. When he passes... I'd still like to do that. This town could benefit from some culture."

"We have culture." Patrick sounded a little defensive. "Chesterfield's not horrible. I've been here all my life. It's cool that Jude came back." He looked at the gray tile floor. "I just wish we'd known about it sooner."

"No use thinking we can change the past." Greg gestured to the table. "Sit, and we'll talk more. The staff will bring our dinners out."

Only then, as my son plunked himself down beside me, did I realize Dora wasn't with us.

4

Patrick

I didn't notice it at first—the Heckel bassoon, shining on a stand, in the far corner of Jude's platform stage. I was too busy taking in the sights around me, feeling like I was in some crazy movie, or even a video game. *Who has a house like this?* I scanned over every little detail—the patterned rugs covering the gray floors, the gold tassels on the heavy curtains. *Only Jude.*

I kept thinking about how much money all this must have cost, and my initial twinge of jealousy turned into a tidal wave.

We hadn't asked Greg yet, but now I knew. The prize was a lie. A lure to get us here.

Jude could've helped us before. Not only me, or Caroline, but Dora. He owed Dora more than anyone. And instead of giving back, of helping someone, he built this castle, this mishmosh of culture in the middle of Godforsaken nowhere. He was so selfish. Dying or not, that hadn't changed.

And then I saw the instrument, glinting off the light from the huge chandelier that hung over the long table.

As Aidan and Kyle sat across from each other, not meeting each other's eyes, and Caroline slumped over her place setting, I moved as if pulled by an invisible string. I'd never seen a Heckel in the wild. I'd never seen a Heckel at all. Of course Jude would've spent his money on one of these. I'd called it, after all, when I first heard the recording attached to my e-mail. The man was talented—the boy had been talented in school. But I'd wondered if part of the reason the recording had sounded so fresh, so full, was because of the instrument that made it.

I hadn't played my instrument of choice for a long time. Bassoons cost a lot of dough. I'd hoped to save up for one when I was at OSU, but then I changed my major to business accounting, and that goal fell by the wayside. I still had the clarinet I started on, and we'd played around with it when Aidan was young. Amy had also played clarinet, and she occasionally liked to noodle around on it as well. But it wasn't the bassoon.

There was something magical about the bassoon—the way it brought the brooms to life in *Fantasia*, the *Sorcerer's Apprentice*. The way it marched those men to the scaffold in Berlioz's masterpiece. It could sound so uncouth, yet also sonorous. It could be light and playful, teasing the listener, or it could bring you to tears. The best players could make you forget the instrument was so large and unwieldy.

I was never one of the best players, but I loved the way the long column came alive in my hands, my left thumb flicking across the span of keys from whisper to... whatever the top one was. My right thumb didn't move as much. It held me down, grounded me, in those low notes. I wanted to touch this Heckel now, even though it was so expensive that I probably needed a special insurance policy just to look at it.

"You can play it," Greg said. "He'd want you to."

I turned. "I don't have a reed."

Patrick Reed, you always have one. You are one. A stupid joke. I never had a reed. Bassoon players typically made their own, at least once they advanced past a certain skill level. But I never got that far, and I was forever breaking the expensive ones I bought from the music store. Jude had sworn by the ones his teacher made, and she'd taught him to make his own. But my parents couldn't afford for me to take lessons from her, let alone drive me downtown every week.

"Oh. Right." Greg nodded. "Well, maybe after dinner. I'm sure I could scrounge one up."

I looked longingly at the Heckel as I took my seat beside Caroline.

WINE FILLED MY GLASS, as if I'd conjured it. I looked up to see the person stepping away from me with a bottle. A muscular, athletic woman with a shock of orange and blue hair.

"I hope you like red," she said, a hint of an accent behind her words.

"I'm Patrick." I stood again, intending to shake her hand, but she kept moving.

Greg, across from us, folded his hands. Something about the way the man moved reminded me of Jude—his long, languid motions, exact and fluid at the same time. Did I only feel that way because we were in Jude's realm now? Because even though he slept upstairs, he was here in the room, etched into every groove of this table, hiding in the walls? I shivered.

"Moira's not much for pleasantries," Greg said, jolting me back to the moment.

Caroline tilted her head.

More people filtered in, the room filling with strangers. I counted eight. They moved to their places with a practiced ease. I realized that Caroline and I—and our children—were the actual strangers. These people lived here, worked here. They chatted with each other and smiled awkwardly at us.

"So, with whom do we have the pleasure of dining?" Caroline asked. Probably trying to be formal, but her words came out stilted.

I coughed. Aidan and Kyle looked like they were in purgatory. This was punishment enough for them. When we got back, I'd let

Aidan do whatever he wanted as long as he didn't speak to Kyle ever again.

Greg gestured around. "This is the team."

He pointed people out, gave us names.

"Everyone has house jobs as well as think-jobs. Jude doesn't want anyone to see each other as menial. Everyone's equal. We all work with our hands and our minds."

Moira scowled at us as she bustled about.

"Moira handles the kitchen, but she's also lead game designer. Our brains need time to slow down, you know."

That did seem nice. Idealistic.

"How long have you been here?" I asked. I wouldn't remember all the names, and we wouldn't be here long enough for that to matter.

"The house is new," Greg said breezily. "We'd already started production when Jude's diagnosis came in. At the time, it didn't seem as dire... and at first, it wasn't."

He nodded at a young man, who brought Greg a glass of white wine. I was a little peeved that I hadn't been asked for my preference.

"Initially, he responded well to the treatment, and most young people pull through. We thought he'd have more time to enjoy this place."

It all seemed surreal, the people moving as if choreographed. I smelled dinner, and my mouth watered. Fragrant nutmeg and fall spices, appropriate for the season.

"Chicken with pumpkin sauce," Greg said, as if hearing my thoughts. "One of his favorite dishes."

"You provide food and lodging for the team as well? Everyone lives here?" Caroline leaned forward. I could almost see her lawyer brain working. "It's in their contracts?"

"Absolutely." Greg sat back and took a long drag from his glass.

"I have a question." My son piped up, and I raised my eyebrows.

Even Kyle glanced at him.

"Yes?"

"How the hell did you get these people to move to Chesterfield?"

5

Caroline

I ate—well, picked at my food—but my thoughts wouldn't stop churning.

I kept thinking of Jude upstairs, his breathing rattling. Were those machines keeping him alive? Or was he refusing to die? If I knew Jude, the latter made more sense. And Dora couldn't have gotten far, was probably still upstairs somewhere, but I worried about her too. We never had ordered that pizza. She had to be hungry. And scared.

When I'd finished the main course, I got up, knocking my chair back. The others, absorbed in their food, didn't notice. Not even my son —which showed how important I was to anyone in that room. I found my way through the halls, back to the staircase. The halls were drafty, and I shivered in my thin sweater. I wasn't responsible for the girl, but she was still a child. All of us owed it to Hannah to protect her daughter.

Dora seemed to have a good head on her shoulders, though. She'd solved the puzzles to get here as fast as any of us. Patrick wouldn't have gotten here if I hadn't helped him.

I started my search in Jude's wing, since we'd already explored it, and I knew my way a little. The walls, decorated with their abstract art, were punctuated by heavy doors. I hesitated in front of the first one, which was open a crack, practically begging for me to go in. I wedged myself between the wall and the door.

A huge bed dominated the room, a California king. Four posters reached to the ceiling, and a canopy draped over the mattress. Sumptuous purple covered the surface: duvet, sheets, pillows. I inspected the side tables, which were topped by ornate lamps. The room was lit by them alone, a warm, dim light filling the space. My fingers rested on the gold handle of the top drawer. I jerked it, but it didn't budge.

Jude had lived here. I could feel his presence. This room—he'd planned it for himself, in all its simplicity and decadence. I was trespassing.

He hadn't invited anyone here. Maybe he hadn't even gotten the chance to stay here since he fell ill. The bedclothes smelled new.

I wanted to fall onto the bed, to let the cloth swallow me. But that would be unfair to Dora. I had to keep going.

Back in the hallway, I peeked into a few of the other rooms. They appeared to belong to staff. I didn't want to pry, so I slipped past them and finally ducked into Jude's room.

6

Dora

I hadn't meant to stay in the room with him.

It felt good to be separated from them, this random motley crew I now associated with. The mental work of dealing with Kyle and Aidan drained me, and now there was so much else to think about too.

Even here, in this enormous house, I felt claustrophobic. So different and foreign, and yet I hadn't moved an inch. I still stood in the township limits.

Why would Jude come back here?

For me?

His breathing was slow, regular, even. I slumped into a chair beside him, watching the glowing monitors. Thin tubes snaked into his nostrils.

The game couldn't be over. I wasn't ready. This wasn't enough. My whole future was tangled here. I couldn't bear the thought of going home, not after everything. I couldn't go back to school and sit in boring classes and listen to Mallory talk about stupid shit all day, every day.

My life, never very good in the first place, had cracked to pieces, and a new one shivered in its place.

Solving the puzzles brought my brain alive in new ways. Like when I practiced, either bassoon or trombone. I blocked out the rest of the world, felt the power of my wrists and arms as I drew the music from the instrument. If anything was off, I'd know. But if all the stars were in alignment, I could get caught up, lost in the way it all made me feel. Those experiences kept me going, the only parts of the world that seemed worthy anymore.

Those were the parts of the world I needed to chase.

And that was what Jude had done.

I looked down at him, and I felt something new—admiration. I didn't know him, didn't know any of the stories he'd spun with my mom or the others, but I knew his mind. He'd brought us here, all of us, with his machinations. He'd built this place from dead ground. He made even Chesterfield seem cool. Because who knew that this house existed? Granted, it hadn't been here long, but when people found out, they were bound to be interested. Something new and secret is a sure bet for gossip and intrigue. I was back to my original question—why would a multimillionaire choose this place? Maybe because here, he was the big fish. I pictured the headline: *Local boy makes good.*

I could make good too. When I returned to school, I could ask Ms. Krieger about other options. Could I go post-secondary, start attending college classes? I was only a freshman, but maybe the principal would make an exception.

Feeling a little more settled, I decided to see where everyone else had gone, but then I heard a cough and a gasp.

I jumped. My heart bounced in my chest.

Jude's lids fluttered. I took his hand. His skin was cold under mine, and I wondered if this was the end.

No. Too soon.

"Mr. Lassiter?" I asked, afraid to refer to him by any other name—being respectful. "I'm Dora. Hannah's daughter. I... I found your code. The one you sent to the house."

The eyes stayed closed, but they continued to flutter. I squeezed.

"If you're there... maybe we could talk?" My breath caught. "There's so much I want to know. I mean... I don't know if you knew about me, if you just wanted my mom here. But she's not..."

I felt the tiniest squeeze back.

"Please don't go," I said. "I have so many questions."

Another slight squeeze, the smallest pressure. Then, the lids fell all the way shut. The breathing regulated again. Smooth, easy.

Sighing, I slumped back into the chair beside the bed.

I LOST TRACK OF TIME, sitting there with him. Wondered if I could absorb his genius, if it circulated in the air here. But as I grew tired, my body slumping lower and lower, it became clear I wouldn't get any more answers today.

Maybe he needed to hear my voice again.

"I'm sorry," I whispered. "You're probably bored. And... I don't know what's going on."

I got up and drifted toward the large picture window. As I gripped the curtain, remembering how Caroline had struggled with it, I maneuvered my body so I could see without disrupting the curtain's path across the glass. Wedged between the fabric and the outside pane, I felt the wicked air howl beyond the barrier. I could make nothing out past the trees and the white.

"I guess we're not going home tonight." I returned to the chair. "I'll have to get a message to Grandma... that I won't be home. Do you think your friend could help me?"

I reached for Jude's hand again, but it was limp. He only breathed in response.

"You're right. I should ask him. I guess Grandma doesn't really care if I don't show up, though. As long as I wear the right clothes and makeup, I can do whatever I want."

"I'm sure she cares," Caroline said from behind me.

At her voice, I jumped so hard I almost fell off the chair. When I'd recovered, I said, "So we're sleeping here tonight?"

Caroline nodded. "We had dinner downstairs. It was... interesting. Aren't you hungry?"

My stomach did feel empty. I hung my head a little.

"Moira could make you a plate." Caroline frowned. "You don't have to stay with him."

"What if..." I didn't have to finish my sentence for Caroline to know what I meant. I was getting used to being with him, with his impending death. Over the past hour, I'd imagined his last breaths, how they would feel when he took them. How I would feel.

"Greg said he's been stable for a few days. I think we'll know if something changes." Caroline approached me.

I smelled perfume on her skin. A mother was supposed to smell like that—flowers and lavender. Hannah always reeked of drink or smoke or both.

I almost choked on a sob but bit it back. No one needed to know I was upset.

Caroline put her hand on my arm, guiding me up and out of the chair. "Let's get you some food and to a room. Greg's calling your grandmother. Everything will be fine, and you'll be home in the morning."

But as she walked with me into the hallway, I couldn't help thinking I would rather stay here.

From "The Great Genius of Edward Elgar," a high school paper by Jude Lassiter

Elgar wrote *The Enigma Variations* in 1899. This was his great achievement—an enigma, after all, is something hidden. In the piece, there are fourteen variations on an original theme, but no one knows what the theme is. Elgar said it was something everyone knew, so some scholars have speculated that it might be "God Save the Queen" or a theme from one of Beethoven's works. But others think that it might be something else, possibly a coded version of Elgar's own name.

Each of the fourteen variations are about one of Elgar's friends or family members. Their names and characteristics about them are evident. For example, Dora Penny's variation includes sixteenth notes that sound like stuttering. Apparently, Dora Penny stuttered.

7

Patrick

At dinner, I gorged myself.

Amy was always getting on my case for not paying attention to my food. "All you do is wolf it down," she'd say, with a roll of her eyes. "I spend all this time making it, and you don't even taste it."

Some nights, that might be true—if I came home exhausted from the commute, or if I was caught up in thought about something stupid Matt had said. But other nights, I was just grateful for the appearance of a hot meal on my plate. At the long table, with candles flickering in the centerpieces, none of us could really see our food. We could smell it, taste it, butter and spices on our tongues filling the roofs of our mouths.

Dinner went by far too quickly. Caroline disappeared early on, but I stayed, savoring each course as it appeared. When Moira brought out trays of tiramisu, my tight belt told me I should pass. But then, I thought—when else was I going to get a dessert cooked by my high school arch-frenemy's personal chef? Or anyone's personal chef, for that matter? I made a conscious effort to taste every bite. I was no longer hungry. Now I was only eating for the sheer pleasure of it.

As I enjoyed a final glass of wine, feeling a little dizzy, Aidan elbowed me.

"Are we staying here tonight?" he asked softly. My son was incapable of being discreet, but I appreciated that he was trying.

I nodded. "Don't want to drive home in this."

"Are you going to call Mom? She'll be worried."

"I've already texted her. Not much of a signal out here, so I hope she'll get it."

The signal part was true, at least. I could easily pretend I'd tried to get in touch with Amy.

I didn't want to keep her in the dark. But something held me back from trying too hard. She didn't belong here, didn't belong on this mission. Lately I'd been wondering—why was I thinking of her so negatively? Besides the fact that she froze me out most of the time. There was a reason we fell in love. I'd be willing to unearth that if she would let me.

Aidan hadn't finished all his dessert, and I wondered if it would be gauche of me to polish off his plate.

My son frowned. "My phone's dead. Otherwise, I'd try to call Mom. They don't have any other way to get a hold of her?"

I glanced down the table at Greg. He sat silent, fingers tented. He looked like a Buddhist monk in contemplation.

"I'll ask if they have a landline," I told Aidan. "But let's go find a place to sleep first."

JUDE HAD BUILT an entire wing for guests. Greg told us that, before the cancer, Jude had been planning to host interactive game nights here —where paying customers could stay in the house and participate in activities throughout the weekend.

"We might still do it," Greg said, as he led us up the stairs and into our corridor. "Once everything has settled down. I think he would like it."

I didn't love how they were talking about him as if he had already passed away. Jude deserved a fair sendoff. I hated thinking of him up in that room, hooked to those wires. The Jude I knew had been alive, vibrant, with a head full of stars and promise. People were drawn to him, like he was the flame and they were the moths.

My son and I traveled the long, carpeted hallway, ducking our heads into rooms. I found one decked out in black and white, a chess table tucked into a corner. When I stepped past the threshold, I caught sight of a few moves written backwards on the wall so I could see them in the mirror. *Black Pawn to C3. White Queen to B4.*

I couldn't help myself. I moved the pieces as directed.

Aidan jumped as "One Night in Bangkok" poured out through hidden speakers. I grinned.

"It's an Easter egg," I told him. "I wonder if those are in all the rooms."

"I don't get it."

"It's an old song. From a musical called *Chess*. Get it? It's a chess-themed room."

The song stopped, and we backed out into the hallway.

"Your friend is really obsessed with games," Aidan said.

"Yeah. And codes."

"Right."

Aidan pulled open another door. Behind it, we found a room festooned with dark purple and gold, complete with a suit of armor in the corner and coats of arms hanging over the beds.

"A King Arthur room. Right, Dad?" My son's eyes glimmered. "Can we stay in this one?"

"Sure," I said, without hesitation. I couldn't remember the last time I'd seen him so happy. Despite Kyle, despite everything, Aidan seemed excited. This was an adventure for us, something new to spice up our otherwise dull existences. And Aidan had his whole life ahead of him, so much more like this to explore, but I...

I flopped on the bed and stared at the ceiling. Whorls of plaster spun above me. Maybe I'd had too much to drink.

"I wonder what the clue is in here." Aidan sat on the other bed. Each suite was done up like a hotel room, with two queen beds. The chess room and the room we were in both had royalty themes. Maybe that had something to do with... something. Jude never did anything without intention.

"I'm sure we'll find it," I said.

"Man. I guess you have to give people something to do, with no phone and no TV." Aidan kicked off his shoes. "You going to talk to that Greg guy? About calling Mom?"

"That was my plan. But what are you going to do?"

He shrugged. "Might wander around a little, do some exploring."

When I didn't reply, he rolled his eyes.

"Come on, Dad. There's nothing to do here, and it's only eight. You really think I'm going to bed?"

"You just took your shoes off."

His words were laced with the self-importance of a fourteen-year-old. "We're inside. I might as well be comfortable."

There was no point in trying to make Aidan stay put. He couldn't get into any trouble here. With staff in every corner, and a raging snowstorm outside, he wouldn't get far if he tried to leave the house.

He ambled into the corridor. I followed and watched him as he approached the window at the end of the hall. He stood in silhouette, scratching his head, the snow careening down past the glass.

No, Aidan wouldn't get much further than the hallway. He'd be back in the room by nine-thirty. His school schedule meant he had to get up early, and his body would crash. I looked forward to the soft, cushy bed, the sheets Jude had chosen for his woodsy retreat—at least one thousand thread count. I wondered how much they'd planned on charging guests.

The lie about calling my wife still fresh on my lips, I went downstairs to the main sitting room.

Greg stood there, staring into the fire.

"There's a perfectly good couch right here." I gestured. "And this is called the sitting room."

He waved a hand. "I like to stand. Builds character."

"Well, I'm beat." I picked a spot on the couch. All that wine had lulled me into a hazy state. "What's your story, Greg?"

He inclined his head. I could make out the outline of his face, lit by the flickering of the fire.

"What do you mean?"

"You know what I'm talking about." A wine glass sat on an end table, half-filled with white, and part of me wanted to ask for my own pour. I liked the idea of continuing my tipsy swoon into the evening, everything around me taking on a rosy, wavy character. "No one gets to Jude without a story."

He laughed, then turned forward and linked his hands behind his back. "You're right about that."

"Come on." Even though I knew he couldn't see, I patted the couch cushion beside me. "Relax for a minute. Tell me about your life."

Maybe he had eyes in the back of his head, because he turned again, then glided across the room toward the wine glass.

"This isn't just a strategy to get more wine, is it?" he murmured. "Because if it is, all you had to do was ask."

"I wouldn't mind another glass. But I don't want to impose." My face flushed. I was sure the heat of the fire was tinting my cheeks a dark pink.

"Never. Not in our house." Greg produced a bottle, as if from nowhere, and filled an empty glass. He handed it to me, then seated himself, although he chose the couch opposite me instead of next to me. Maybe he only pretended he had eyes in the back of his head. I sipped the white gratefully.

We sat in silence until I summoned the courage to speak.

"Was there ever money?"

Every one of his movements was calculated, pronounced. He turned his head toward me with that perfect, smooth motion. "Do you mean the million-dollar prize?"

I nodded, heart thumping. My face flushed with the alcohol and embarrassment. "The clues said the game would be over when we found him."

Greg shrugged, gracefully. "Have you found him?"

I didn't respond. We had, hadn't we?

I didn't ask him about Jude again, although I was still dying to know. I closed my eyes and listened to the crackle of the fire, my thoughts spinning through my head. Of course, there was no money. Of course, the whole thing was a lie. A lie designed to get us here.

"Did you want to call your wife?" Greg asked. "I heard you discussing it at dinner. We have a landline. You should be able to reach her."

"That's okay."

"Or if you prefer, I could give you the wi-fi password?" Greg wrinkled his nose. "I'm not sure if it's up, but you could try e-mailing her."

I breathed out. "Yes. That's great. I can connect with my phone."

I pulled out the device and punched in the letters and digits as Greg recited them. Then I pocketed it again and returned to my wine, feeling the coolness of the rim against my lips.

"You're not going to e-mail her, are you?" Greg studied me across the few feet between us.

"Maybe I'll tell you that, if you'll tell me your story."

He guffawed. "You drive a dumb bargain, Counselor."

"Hey, I'm no lawyer." I crossed my ankle over my knee. "That's Caroline. You're already mixing us up."

"I'm just saying, I don't care if you call your wife or not, although I do find it interesting that you're choosing not to." Greg peered at me. "My story is the same as all of yours. I entered Jude's orbit and became pulled in by his gravity."

8

Caroline

When Dora and I returned to the dining area, the overhead lights were on. In the stark, bare light, the long table's artifice was clear. We couldn't pretend this was an ancient hall for knights or barons. It was just another room.

Moira shuffled between place settings, gathering the china.

"You're too late," she said. "I'm cleaned up."

"I'm not hungry," Dora said.

"You need a snack at least. String cheese? Peanuts?" I dragged her into the kitchen and surveyed the space. It was huge. Appliances and prep tables, gleaming silver surfaces. I could smell the remainder of dinner, notably the dessert I'd missed. Coffee and ladyfingers, a moist tiramisu. I didn't need the calories, but my mouth watered all the same.

"There's plenty of food in the rooms," Moira said. "You don't need to be in my way."

"Okay." I put up my hands. I didn't have the energy to argue. "What rooms do you mean?"

"Guest rooms. South wing." She pointed, stiff like a sentinel.

Dora and I followed Moira's directions, heading out through the sitting room and up to the south wing, into another long, lonely hallway. The wind howled past the windows.

My body ached with emotion and confusion. The feeling of being done and not done at the same time. We'd solved the mystery, but we hadn't claimed our treasure.

Dora opened the first door on the right. We stepped into a room decorated in all shades of green: forest, lime, olive. On the wall, a man stared broodingly at us from a glossy poster.

"It's Stephen Amell," Dora said. "The actor. From *Arrow*."

"Do you watch that show?" I didn't have much time for TV, what with the working and taking care of everyone else at home. My thoughts strayed to Kieran, and I bristled.

She flopped onto one of the beds. The living quarters in this hallway were nothing like the ones we'd seen on the other side of the house. This one resembled a hotel room, with two beds and an adjoining bathroom.

Dora stared at the ceiling. "I've seen it a few times. But it's hard to follow if you don't start from the beginning."

"Seems like all TV shows are like that these days." I opened the cupboards below the poster, revealing a refrigerator packed with snacks. I found a packet of crackers and Brie. "Dora, are you sure you don't want something to eat?"

"I'm really not hungry." She sat up. "I think I want to sleep."

"Are you worried about your mom?"

The girl didn't respond. I cursed myself internally. I'd gone too far.

Dora inspected her hands, avoided my eyes. "My mom's dead, Ms. Cross."

9

Dora

Kyle's mom asked if I wanted her to stay with me.

She seemed totally shocked about my mother. Like she hadn't known. Okay, she'd just moved back. Maybe she hadn't read the story. But it was all over the papers, all over social media, and I didn't like to talk about it.

As she kept rambling on about my mother and high school, I wanted to punch her in her pink lips. Maybe then she'd stop fussing over me. The worst part was that I should've appreciated it. But I was so used to taking care of myself. I wasn't about to stop now.

"Okay, then." She inched backwards. "I'll only be down the hall. Tell you what. I'll stay in the room just across from you here." She giggled, though I could tell she was forcing it. "Hope I get a guy just as cute as Arrow on my wall."

"It's Oliver Queen," I muttered as she shut the door.

When she was finally gone, I sagged against the green comforter, all the air leaving my body.

I hated everything. Despite the soft bed, the snacks and drinks, more luxury than I'd ever seen...it was all so overwhelming. I felt like a stranger in my own life.

The codes and the hunt had given me such a sense of purpose. I'd felt alive, like the solution might bring me out of the drudgery of Chesterfield, school, writing two papers for every English assignment. At least I wouldn't have to worry about that last thing anymore. If Kyle tried anything with me, I could just call his mom. Her new weird obsession with taking care of me would do the trick.

Even if I got money—which wasn't looking promising now—I still had to live with Grandma until I turned eighteen. Three and a half more years. Seemed like a lifetime.

When I thought of my mother, how she'd never truly made it out, a fault line inside me cracked.

I rolled onto my side. I needed to turn off the light, needed to sleep. But that sense of pursuit still filled me. This couldn't be the end. I couldn't lie here, surrounded by the scents of lavender and jasmine from an oil candle sitting below Stephen. It was calm, and pleasant, and soothing, and not for me. I grew up in a world without those things.

I waited ten minutes, timing with the digital clock on the nightstand.

Then I left the bed and tiptoed into the hallway, my Converse-covered footsteps muffled by the carpet.

My best bet was to leave the wing with the guest rooms. All the others would be there: Kyle, Aidan, Aidan's dad. If I wanted to be alone, I needed to explore.

The south wing emptied into the main foyer of the house. A fire blazed in the center of the largest room. Aidan's dad sat there, talking to Greg, and I rushed past. They were deep into their conversation, and neither one seemed to have noticed me. I exhaled as I ran up the steps to the north wing, where Jude was.

I poked my head into his room for a moment, to make sure he was okay. His chest still rose and fell. I sighed and scurried off. The staff would be going to bed soon too, and I needed to figure out where I could hide.

The hall ended there, but there were more rooms in the building. The house stretched further back to the west. The dining room was located there, on the first floor. The ceiling went up high in that room, so maybe there wasn't a second floor? Architecture wasn't my strong suit. Neither was geometry. I wasn't good at picturing spaces and the way they were laid out. I could barely figure out where I needed to step for marching band.

I squeezed my eyes shut and chose a door on the left, across from Jude. When I opened it, I found myself in yet another dark hallway.

Moving slowly, I felt along the wall. I kept flinching, as if a bogeyman might leap out of the shadows and get me. I inched along, sneakers flush with the wall, moving west, until my fingers met a door-frame, then the knob.

Inside the room, I explored the inner wall, searching for a light switch but found a lamp first. Once I pressed it on, I could see dimly.

This was a library. It extended down the hall, back towards the main part of the house. My breath caught as I traveled the shelves, looked up and down at all the books lining the walls. Each shelf held a hollow with an awning and an object. There was a stuffed raven, probably signifying Edgar Allan Poe, and there was also a deerstalker hat. That was for Sherlock Holmes. These were all symbols of mystery.

I hadn't read many mysteries, besides the Poe and Holmes stuff we studied in school. As I scanned the spines on the books, I didn't recognize any of the authors' names—Ellen Raskin, Carolyn Keene, Sara Paretsky, Michael Connelly. I felt like I shouldn't be there, but I also felt the excitement sizzling in the room, the promise of stories waiting to be consumed.

And I didn't know where to start.

I ran my hands along a shelf and pulled out the first book they landed on. A slim paperback, musty with age. *Encyclopedia Brown: Boy Detective.*

Clutching the book, I sank into an armchair by the fireplace. The fire wasn't lit, of course, and I felt cold and tired. A plaid blanket lay over the top of the armchair, so I drew it over me, huddling into the knit. I rested my head on the back of the chair and settled in to read.

❧

When I woke up, what felt like hours later, the wind roared outside.

I blinked into the darkness. Then I wrapped the blanket around me and went to the window, wishing for a pair of warm, fuzzy socks.

The snow pounded against the glass, unrelenting. Big floodlights shone on the courtyard in front of the house, and the snow had buried Patrick's car and covered the turnaround driveway. No one would get out of here tonight. Maybe not even tomorrow morning.

I needed to go back to the room, the one where I was supposed to sleep tonight. My neck hurt from dozing off in the chair. The house was quiet, but it breathed. This library was scary.

Clutching the *Encyclopedia Brown* book like a talisman, I crept out towards the door.

And then something heavy, fleshy, fell on me and knocked the breath out of my chest.

10

Caroline

Hannah was dead. This girl was all we had left of her.

Dora hadn't wanted to give many specifics. She said it was a car accident, that it was all over the news. I hadn't been in town when it happened, six months ago, and this was the first I'd heard of it. I could Google it later, once we had signal again or when I could get on wi-fi. But it wouldn't matter. She'd still be dead.

Swallowing my grief, I told Dora I'd leave, that I wouldn't go far. I opened the door across the hallway.

I found myself in a Queen-themed room. The poster on my wall showed Freddie Mercury, in his signature pose, holding the mic like a lover. Above the bed, a single copy of the album *Hot Space* hung in a frame. This room had only one bed—maybe for more intimate gatherings.

Exhausted, I fell on the mattress, like I'd wanted to do in Jude's room.

Jude loved Queen. We were a shade too young to be alive when they were popular, but the songs were always on the radio, especially when we listened to the classic rock stations. I remember Jude talking about "Bohemian Rhapsody," dissecting it. He made everything an academic assignment. "I've read many theories about the song," he'd tell us, his ever-present joint flaring between his lips. "But my interpretation is of a cry for a help. From a man who hid everything until it was too late." He'd throw out his arms, puff out his skinny chest. "Let me go!"

"I will not let you go," one of us would say—it didn't matter who—but we'd grin as we said it, knowing the next line would come.

So, in a way, this room brought me closer to Jude. Even if he slept across the house, I could feel better knowing his work had brought this space to life. I liked that thought.

But I couldn't sleep. I turned off the light, and all I could see was the blinding snow outside. It didn't feel like night, but it didn't feel like day either. We were stuck in some awful in-between.

I couldn't relax, as I turned everything over and over in my head. Hannah, dead. Jude, on the verge of it.

What would happen in the morning? Would we say our goodbyes to our corpse-like friend, then turn away as if we'd never been here? I couldn't fathom that idea—not now, not when he was clinging to life. Not when we'd gone through so much to get here.

Not when we'd been promised so much.

But I missed my mother, and I wanted to see her. Tell her about all of it. She'd know what to do—about Kieran, about everything. I needed her.

I sighed, buried my head in the pillow.

Then I heard a murmur in the corridor outside. Men's voices. One mid-range, a baritone—the other a higher timbre. Patrick and Greg.

I didn't want to pry, but I also wanted to hear what they were talking about. I slid out of the bed and inched to the wall, crouching low.

"Thank you for walking me up," Patrick said.

I thought I heard sorrow in his voice. He sniffed. Yes, he'd been crying.

"It's no trouble," Greg said.

"It is, to have all of us show up like this? And especially to stay the night."

"We knew you were coming," Greg said. "We just didn't know when."

Silence for a second. I imagined Patrick swiping at his face. I wanted to tell him it was okay to cry, like I told Kyle, when he was five and scraped his knee at the park.

"I don't understand why he would do this," Patrick said. "I mean, he could have texted me. It's not like I live far from here."

"Oh, honey," Greg said, in barely a whisper. "You know Jude never does anything by halves."

Not even death.

When they said their goodbyes, a door opened. Footsteps pattered back the other way, down the hall.

I could find Patrick. Our cell phones didn't work, but there weren't that many rooms in this wing. I could simply knock until I found him. Then I wouldn't be alone anymore, no longer forced to confront my wild mind on my own. We could at least talk, maybe watch a movie if we could get the satellite TV to work. I wasn't sure if it would in this weather. But I'd try anything to distract myself.

Finally, I gave up and flicked the light back on.

I looked around the room again, searching for amusement, something to occupy me. The far wall held a bookshelf, and I inspected the titles, wondering if one might spike my interest.

My hand traveled along the spines of the books. I plucked one off and opened it, but the letters swam across the page. Suddenly, I felt punched with sorrow, that I couldn't relax enough to enjoy a book. My life was falling apart, crumbling as I scrambled to find the pieces.

With anger now, I spun toward the shelves, diving my head towards the wood. I wanted pain. I wanted a wound. Anything to make me feel something other than sadness.

My body careened into the books. I hit them hard enough that I expected to be buried in a waterfall of pages and covers. Maybe I'd die of a thousand paper cuts.

But I stumbled, kicked, and turned, as the floor slid out from under me. I couldn't see, and I scrabbled for a place to put my hands, hair flying in my face.

One second, I saw the shelves. The next, darkness.

A squeak. I realized it came from my throat.

The walls closed in. I gasped for breath. *This is how I go. Like a mouse trapped in a wall. Starved to death.* My heart squeezed into bursting.

It's all too much.

"Caroline?"

I forced myself to inhale, to exhale, to stay in this world. I wouldn't let it all overtake me. I had to get through this.

The voice belonged to Patrick.

I plunged forward, pushed myself through the veil. Spun out of the wall and stumbled into another room.

My face met the carpet. Burns streaked the inside of my arms, the backs of my calves.

"Caroline. Jesus."

I felt his hands on my elbows, rocking me clumsily.

I leaned on him to hoist myself up, the skin all over stinging. Then I surveyed my surroundings: a chess-themed space, all black and white.

"The rooms connect," Patrick said.

"Great observation. I'll nominate you for the Nobel when we get back."

He scowled. The shelf rotated back into place.

I sighed and crawled toward the bed. I wasn't about to move again.

"I wonder why." Patrick sat beside me, leaving a few inches between us.

I shrugged, burying my face in my hands.

"Jude," I muttered through my fingers. "Some trick for his guests. For all those mystery nights he'll never get to have."

We fell silent. I could almost hear Patrick in my head. If Jude could die, any one of us could. We weren't immortal.

I sat up. Light filled the room, from an overhead fixture plus a lamp near the bed. This space felt impossible to betray, with Aidan's Axe cologne on the sheets. We weren't criminals. I could touch Patrick.

I scooted towards him, laid a hand on his thigh. He bristled.

"Where's Aidan?" I whispered.

Patrick's breath hitched. "Don't know. He said he was looking around."

Patrick relaxed, enough to relax me by proxy. I melted into his side, the warm soft muscle tingling where he touched it.

"Dora's staying in my room." I traced a wandering circle on his jeans. "There's nowhere to go. We're in limbo."

Patrick reached for me, hoisted me onto his lap. A hard length pressed into my leg, and my body responded. We smashed together, our lips and breath finding each other, and it felt like coming home.

11

Patrick

My fingertips on fire, I felt my way along the inches of Caroline. Her body both familiar and alien, she lit every synapse in my brain. I found my path on her bare skin, traveling roads I hazily remembered. And the map had changed—presumably with pregnancy or time.

I stopped short below her bra line, her breath in my ear. Felt the sag there, and thought of Amy, how she became less perfect after each boy, and yet she was all the more alluring, a treasure I could no longer reach.

Would I unravel Amy by opening Caroline?

I sat back. Caroline did, too, her lips parted and bitten, cheeks flushed.

"God!" she yelled, falling backwards on the bed again. "This is so unfair."

"You're telling me," I mumbled, the pain in my groin a hot needle.

"I didn't mean..."

I adjusted my pants. I could still feel the raw pressure of her lips, the taste of honey. "I know."

Caroline got up and moved toward the spinning bookcase. "I should go back."

We'd already gone too far. I imagined taking her through that middle passage. I could press her against the wall inside, take her where no one else would ever find us, the secret safe. I longed to do that, to dwell in the satisfaction that would come from that. But then the guilt would come, which already surrounded me like smog. It would grow thicker, impossible to see through.

"I don't expect you to upend your life," she said when I didn't reply. "I don't need another husband. This isn't about that."

"I love Amy. And my kids."

"Right." She hesitated. "Did you know she was dead?"

Electricity ran through my body, a pure shot of adrenaline.

"Who?" Even though I knew exactly whom she was talking about.

"Hannah."

"I saw the article in the paper."

Caroline swiped at her eyes as she backed farther away from me, toward the spinning wall. "I just found out, Patrick. Dora told me just now. I don't even know what to say... I don't know why you didn't tell me. Why Dora didn't tell me before."

"It's not our fault."

"That's the first thing you go to?" Sobs spluttered out of her. She seemed incredulous, unreal. "Absolution?"

I folded my arms. "Isn't that the first thing you went to?"

She shook her black bob, mussed from my hands, then retreated like she had never been there at all.

I LAY AWAKE, sparking with lust but refusing to do anything about it. My punishment.

I'd turned off the light, and the shadows made everything that much more surreal. Knowing she was so close. Not knowing where

Aidan was—but I wasn't too worried, because he couldn't get far. He could sleep in another room.

The snow slanted across the window, eerie beyond the cold glass. Floodlights illuminated the front of the house—the mansion, if we were getting technical. My room would never be completely dark.

A chill passed through me. I hoped Aidan hadn't stumbled into a romantic liaison of his own. There wasn't a single individual here appropriate for him. I'd have more than hell to pay if that kind of relationship surfaced. But my son didn't seem that into girls yet—or boys, for that matter. He cared about football and being a leader in school.

He was a good kid. Amy's doing, of course. I'd done nothing to contribute to the cause, beyond working to support him and starting the occasional game of ball. Amy taught that boy to be a man, and it should have been my job.

I rolled onto my stomach, then on my back, trying to find a comfortable position. No such luck.

As I stared into the ceiling, I noticed something I hadn't before, when it spun in circles amid my drunkenness.

A small, red light blinked. A pinhole camera.

12

Dora

"**W**hat the fuck!" I yelled, or tried to yell, as my face was muffled by boy-limbs.

"Shit, Dora." Aidan scrambled away and leapt across the room.

I didn't see where he went because I was too busy trying to get my breath back.

When I could finally feel my lungs, Kyle lunged toward Aidan.

"You bastard, you stupid, asshole bastard," Kyle chanted, almost like a mantra. Rawness scraped in his throat.

"What's your guys' problem!" I yelled. Someone in this big stupid house would have to hear me, come help. I was just a little person. I wouldn't be able to break the two of them apart. "Stop!"

They kept punching. Pummeling each other. Kyle was big yet lithe and Aidan was small and fast. They darted and jabbed, blows landing with fleshy, painful sounds.

I had to think. No one was coming. They would both be blooming with bruises and blood if I didn't intervene.

I glanced around the room. Lamp—no, that would hurt them. Chair? Too big. Then my eyes landed on a couch with a set of throw pillows piled atop it. I rushed to the pile and gathered the pillows in my arms, then threw them wildly, awkwardly at the fight.

"Stop!" I screamed again, as if that would make them stop. As if they'd listen this time.

Kyle took a pillow to the face. He stumbled backwards. I ran in front of Aidan, seized his wrists. Blocked him.

"I'm done with this," Aidan said from behind me, his rough breath in my ear. "This is freaking bullshit. I'm done."

Kyle crouched on the floor, legs akimbo like a spider. He didn't speak.

"Are you done?" I asked him.

"I want to leave." He spit on the new carpet. "This place smells."

My gaze landed on the window behind Kyle. The glass was still covered with snow, a blanket of it, blocking the outside world.

"I don't think leaving is an option," I said.

"I didn't ask to come here." Kyle found his feet and stared at both of us as if we'd killed his pet goldfish. "None of this makes any fucking sense. You," he pointed at me, "were supposed to get me through school so I could go to a college with a good football program. And you," he pointed at Aidan, "were supposed to sit down and shut up and let me be the quarterback."

"Fuck," Aidan said. "You think things are always going to go your way? People exist for you to use them?"

Kyle balled his fists, as if getting ready to wheel another punch. "My mom is fucking your dad."

"Wait, what?" Aidan spun toward Kyle.

I moved with him, the human shield between them.

"I went back to the room, and my mom was kissing your dad." Kyle made a face. "She told him she's leaving my dad. After we moved all the way out here from California. I should have stayed there."

"Did you have someone writing your papers there, too?" I asked.

Who cared if I agitated him further. I was sick of this nonsense, the way these jerks were treating me. I was tired of letting them get the upper hand.

"None of your goddamn business." Kyle folded his arms across his broad chest. "Besides, Dora. I know you only did it because you want me. Admit it."

"Gross." I stuck out my tongue, but shame washed over me all the same. Yes, I'd had a little crush on Kyle, but he didn't have to rub it in. Besides, that crush was the furthest thing from my mind, as I'd just painted myself into the spot of human shield between two selfish boys. In a giant mansion in the middle of nowhere with my mom's dying friend.

"My dad's not leaving my mom," Aidan said.

"Just wait." Kyle stalked out of the library.

I stepped into the hallway and watched him go, heart thumping against my chest.

When I returned, Aidan was slumped on the couch, which was newly bereft of its pillows. His face was red and lined, his eyes closed. I realized I didn't know what color they were—that when he opened them, I'd have to look and find out. That was the kind of detail I thought I'd want to remember, when inevitably he'd drift away from me, just like everyone else did.

"He should go back to California," Aidan mumbled. "He belongs there."

I sat beside my friend, careful not to get too close. "I'm not going to write papers for him anymore."

"Good for you."

I couldn't tell if he was being sarcastic or not, so I let the comment pass. The clock on the mantel ticked. Aidan's breathing grew shallow.

"Are you okay?" I prodded his shoulder. If he was going to have internal bleeding or something, I couldn't let him fall asleep in this place.

"Fine," he murmured.

"I'm not sure you're fine. We need to get you to your dad."

"He was kissing Kyle's mom. Seriously. I don't want to see that assface." Aidan sounded wounded, like he never thought his father would betray him that way.

But I didn't know what that kind of trust breach was like. I'd never trusted my mother to begin with.

13

Caroline

My heart still pounded, and my eyes overfilled with tears. I fell onto the bed in my room, burying my face into the billion-thread-count pillow. The room whirled. I wondered about pressing my lips so far into the fabric that the pillow would choke me, cut off my breath.

No. You're literally the worst human ever. Living on this planet is your punishment.

I rubbed my eyes, streaking moisture across my cheekbones, then got up and lifted a water out of the fridge. It was cold, and I sucked it down too quickly, my belly cramping with the flood. Then I sat in the dark, still swiping at my face.

It wasn't even ten o'clock. Patrick—a living, breathing source of comfort—was so close and so off-limits. And my son? Who knew what depths of the house he skulked through? I could almost feel my arms around him, that taut little baby-body, his blond curls, his face violent red as he fought bedtime. But then he'd relent and sag, and I could kiss him a hundred times, that soft skin.

God. The memories crushed my chest.

I had to go to bed. Kyle, Patrick, Dora be damned. *Hannah,* whispered a little voice, and I ignored that too. I had to sleep, had to erase this wretched day and start over.

A sharp rap on my door. I groaned. It was probably Kyle, finally finding me. I got up and trudged over to grant him entry.

Only it wasn't Kyle. It was the orange-and-blue-haired woman from the kitchen.

"Got an alert you drank all the water." She thrust another water bottle at me. "Brought it in case you wanted more."

"You're too kind." I took the bottle, and she turned to go, but I stopped her. "What do you mean, you got an alert?"

She thumbed toward the end of the hall. "Guest accommodation. Jude conjured it up. Predictive tech. You keep bringing them water, they drink more of it, they pay more for it."

"Um." I bit my lip. "We're paying for this?"

She rolled her eyes. "Whatever."

"I just..." I swallowed. "Wasn't sure why you'd listen to the alert otherwise."

Her name was Moira, I remembered, as she arched an eyebrow. "I guess, I figured you might need more water for the night. I was thinking about you. Maybe you're not used to that?"

I looked down. The carpet carried a zigzag pattern into my room. "I'm kind of not."

"You're one of those." Moira lifted a finger. "Be right back."

She disappeared down the corridor. I sank back to where I'd been, stared up at the bed's canopy until she returned with two glasses of red wine. I reached eagerly for one. She raked a hand through her hair and took a deep drink of hers.

"Thank you." I wrapped my palms around the glass.

"There are some things only a human can see." Moira plunked onto an armchair beside the bed. "And I can see you're among the Jude-scarred."

I tensed.

"It's okay. We can talk about it." A line of dark red bloomed on her top lip. Her skin was oh-so-pale, and her accent sizzled as she relaxed. "We're all in that company together."

My mouth went dry. I took a gentle sip. The wine was earthy, fertile, as if it had been made from soil instead of grapes. "I haven't seen him in years."

"But you loved him."

I started to shake my head, but Moira chortled, holding up a hand. "You can't lie! Not here, not in his house. Everyone who comes near him loves him. It's a fact."

What did I love? I felt like a cardboard cutout of a human, no substance past the outline of my body, the illusion of a face, a smile. I never should have come back to Ohio, where all things return to die.

"I might have," I said casually. "It's been so long. What about you? You must be... close."

Moira leaned forward, brushed away a frizzy curl. "Are you wondering if he's banged everyone in this house?"

"Meh." Jude and I had never been a thing. I didn't care.

"Well, he has. Yes, including me." She took another long swallow. "You're probably wondering if I'm a dyke, too. People usually do, when they see my hair. My clothes."

I stared at her. I wasn't the kind of person to make assumptions like that, but I wanted to know where she was going with this. After all, no one would know by looking at me that I'd dated both women and men pre-Kieran.

"I like 'em all. Aw, hell, though. I'm not here to hit on you."

I swallowed. "It's okay."

It was no big deal if she was hitting on me. But I'd had enough of sex for the evening, and for the moment, I was still married.

"I can just tell... When two people are the same." Moira sat back, her glass already empty. "Maybe he didn't fuck you, but he hurt you. He's good at that. Jude Lassiter, not exactly number one in the empathy department."

I saw him then, in my mind's eye. Sauntering across the snow in

Patrick's backyard. Tossing his joint down, snuffing it with his boot. He would have let the world burn if it meant he had to admit his guilt about Hannah.

I finished my wine and set the glass on my nightstand. "He hurt so many people. When he dies... do you think people here will be happy about it?"

Moira got up. She looked at me askance.

"Hell, no. He's gotta hang on. He's bankrolling us." She pointed at me as she went for the door. "Enjoy that water."

"Moira!" I raised my hand to stop her. "Was there ever money for us? That million dollars he talked about?"

She frowned. "I don't know what you're talking about." Then she was gone.

I sighed, all hope gone from my body. The wine spiraled through my system, and my eyelids finally drooped. I sank into sleep.

14

Dora

I walked Aidan down the stairs to find his room and his father.

But I wasn't about to stick around. After Aidan's dad opened the door, and Aidan launched himself inside, yelling, I snuck away.

I found my way back upstairs to the library, winding the path I'd taken the first time. The house was so weird. It felt like an old mansion, but the carpets and fixtures were all new, smelling like they'd just come from Home Depot. I crashed into the chair where I'd fallen asleep earlier. The room was cold, so I wrapped myself in a plaid blanket.

Snuggling down into the warm, plush fabric, I chewed on a fingernail. I didn't know what secrets this room held, but it was special. It was the last place I'd felt anything at all.

Why was I here?

I felt a connection with Jude, and I wondered, kept wondering, if he was my father. I knew that my mother, Aidan's dad, and Kyle's mom had all been friends in high school. Kyle's mom was so weird, acting all obsessed with me. I had the feeling something had happened back then, something they didn't want to talk about. Something that involved my mother. And Kyle's mom felt guilty.

The realization punched me in the face. I buried myself deep in the plaid blanket, only my nose sticking out.

School, and my teachers, felt so far away. The room surrounded me like a living entity, a time warp I'd fallen into. The clock ticked, but its two hands stayed fixed on the twelve. Permanent midnight.

I could let myself slip back into sleep. Maybe, when I woke up, the world would be bright again and we could leave, plowing a path out of this bizarre place. But if I did that, what would I be missing? What mystery would I never solve?

Slowly, carefully, I removed the blanket from my shoulders and stepped into the shivering dark.

I approached the bookshelf, ran my hands along it as I'd done before. I didn't know what my fingers were looking for, but if there was something here, I'd find it.

Without a light, the titles faded into their spines, melting into meaningless objects. And there were objects mixed in with the books, although I couldn't identify them. One looked like a huge, bulky computer, but there was no screen. And there was something paddle-shaped, which hung from a peg built into the shelf.

Finally, I found a switch—above the fireplace. When I flicked it, the fireplace came to life. Fake flames brightened the room. Even that was an illusion.

I could see now. I peered more closely at the book titles.

I recognized some of them from school: Jack London, *White Fang*— S.E. Hinton, *The Outsiders*. Golding's *Lord of the Flies*. Apparently, the assignments at Chesterfield High hadn't changed much over the years. But there were other titles I didn't know—Patrick Rothfuss, *The Name of the Wind*. Ellen Raskin, *The Westing Game*. A big stretch of books by Christopher Pike, whom I'd never heard of. I pulled one battered, baby-blue paperback from the shelf—*Remember Me*. Its pages were torn and worn. Well-loved.

My mother was never much of a reader, but she liked that I brought books home. She always took me to the library when I wanted to. At least, if she wasn't working or passed out, and then my grandmother would step in. Other than Mrs. Caldwell's domain, I'd never seen so many books in one place. I pulled spines loose, not sure what I was hoping to find.

Then my traveling gaze landed on Salman Rushdie's *Midnight's Children.*

Rushdie... the name sounded familiar. I vaguely remembered my World Civ class and *The Satanic Verses.* That was it. The Ayatollah Khomeini had issued a *fatwa* against the author in the eighties. Rushdie could have been killed on sight for breaking the rules of Islam. I couldn't believe someone could be persecuted simply for writing a book, and that was a long time ago. But our teacher said it still happened all the time—in art, and in life. That lesson only taught me how sheltered I was, how much more I needed to learn.

I grabbed the book and opened it, but instead of pages fluttering, I heard a metallic thunk.

Between the covers, I saw a hollow crevice—a hidden compartment. Something had fallen loose.

I dropped the book to the carpet. The fresh smell wafted up from the floor as I felt around. *Something gold, copper, silver...*

I brushed against a small object. Then I palmed it, its grooves digging into the skin inside my fist. A key.

"Midnight's Children," I said out loud. That was what we were— me, Aidan, Kyle—right now.

And the stopped clock on the mantel had led me straight to this.

15

Patrick

My son barreled into my room just as I was finally falling asleep.

I sat up and blinked. "What were you doing? Where were you?"

"I should be asking you that question." Aidan flicked on the light beside the other bed, and a yellow glow bathed his cheeks. Bruises blossomed under his eyes.

"What the hell happened?" I reached toward him, but he flinched away. "Aidan—come on."

"I don't want to talk to you." He turned, fluffing a pillow on the bed. "I'm tired."

"You're hurt." I jumped up. "I'll go find Greg. There must be a first aid kit here somewhere."

"I don't need anything." Aidan's voice was muffled. Within moments, his snores filled the room.

But now I was awake again. I paced back and forth between the chess set and the giant picture of a queen piece on the wall. Moments ago, I'd been tossing in the luxurious sheets, comfortable yet also wishing for this night to end. I wanted to be home. Sure, I could barely afford our house, was pulling money from my ass to keep us all alive. My wife didn't want to sleep with me, and I wanted nothing else but to kiss my high school girlfriend, who hovered just out of reach. But being home would be better than staying here, in this strange place, haunted by the ghosts of my past.

I opened the door and emerged into the hallway. I needed to find some medicine for my son, something to put on his face to ease the pain, to sanitize the wounds from... what?

Kyle.

I approached the kitchen. The fire died in the main room, no longer tended, letting itself go out.

Greg and Moira were still awake, talking in there. I was about to open the door, but I paused. "...the money," was the end of Greg's sentence.

I slid to the wall on the side and held my breath.

"None of them will find it," Moira said. "They'll leave at first light. Or whenever I can get the truck to come."

"I'll shovel the whole driveway if I have to," Greg said. "I don't know what the hell Jude was thinking."

"He was supposed to be awake when all this happened," Moira said mournfully.

"Yeah."

They didn't speak for a few moments, and I considered opening the door then, if they weren't going to continue their previous line of conversation.

"Regardless, I think he wants the girl to have it," Moira said.

"It doesn't matter what he wants, does it?" Greg's voice softened. "He's going to die, Mo. We have to come to terms with that."

At the words, tears pricked my eyes. I couldn't help it. I hadn't gotten to say goodbye to him, not properly. Why hadn't he just called me? Instead of playing this ridiculous game, not knowing when we'd show up? *Because he was afraid.* I wondered if Jude was telling me telepathically, beaming his own thoughts down the stairs from his sickbed.

I wiped my eyes, feeling tiny wrinkles growing at their edges. We were so old now.

"The will says whichever one of them finds it will inherit it," Moira said. "He won't be around to take care of us anymore."

"Well, what happens if none of them find it?" Greg asked. "Is there a provision in his will for that?"

Money. Find it. Which one of them finds it.

She didn't reply. I slid down the wall, my legs bending.

The money was still in play. That cash would change my life. Seriously. I could pay everything off, quit my stupid job. Tell Matt where he could shove it. Travel the world with my wife and maybe even make her love me again. I could send my boys to good colleges and sit on the back porch during our hot summers, drinking a sweating beer and pursuing my passion, whatever that might be. I could start playing again—clarinet and bassoon. I could join a community band and play Jude's Heckel. I could do... anything.

Jude's money was hidden somewhere in this house?

The door swung open and hit me in the face.

16

Dora

I clutched the key and stood in the center of the library, turning in a slow circle.

I was exhausted, but now adrenaline rushed through my legs. I felt like a deer, newborn and trembling, ready to gallop in any and all directions but still unsteady on her feet.

Where could this key fit? I examined the objects on the bookshelf first. The large box-thing with all the keyboards— maybe it was connected, but I was too tired to figure out how. Maybe there was another clue in a book—a book with "lock" in the title? I scanned up and down, squinting and reading, but nothing sparked.

There were cupboards below the shelves. Creamy and white, built into the walls. Storage for more stuff.

"The best hiding place is sometimes in plain sight," I muttered, running my hands over the latches.

I opened all the cupboard doors. Nothing underneath was locked. Everything opened easily. Under the first row of shelves, I found a box of cords and a bunch of old video game stuff. If there was ever a time I wanted my mom—now was it. These were all the old systems she used to play on. I blew the dust off one of them, a nondescript gray box—*Nintendo Entertainment System,* it read. I knew that brand, from the Wii and Switch. This must be one of those old-school systems. There was also one that read *Super Nintendo,* with the same gray exterior but with purple toggles and buttons.

I could bet the cords went with the systems, but there was no TV to play them on, and I didn't know how they hooked up. So I left those and moved on to the next cabinet.

More old tech. In this one, there was a long black box with a spot to plug in... a tape? I vaguely remembered those, from when my mom used to put on *Star Wars* for me when I was little. We didn't have a DVD player until I was maybe ten. The VCR was expensive, but we liked watching movies, so we splurged on it. I had no idea where the tape player had gone or where any of those tapes were now. Maybe Grandma had gotten rid of them when she cleaned out my mom's room. She'd sold so many of my mom's things. I had no idea how to hook up this device either, so I kept going.

I sighed as I hit the last cabinet. Looked like this was the place where Jude stored all his old crap. He certainly had plenty of choices. But I supposed the library made sense. It was a place for old things, an archive. I fought my drooping lids as I opened the final set of cabinet doors.

17

Patrick

My nose exploded with pain. I bit my tongue, tasted the blood seeping through my lips, and held still.

The door creaked back to its previous position. Greg and Moira were already gone. The sharpness in my face subsided to a dull throb, but my head felt like it might burst. I got to my feet.

My joints ached from crouching. God, I was getting so old. We took those days for granted, the ones where we used to run around like crazy fiends in my backyard or Caroline's, chasing each other for the sheer pleasure of moving our bodies. Now, I was like an ancient mechanical puppet, needing oil to grease the grinding in my gears.

I shuffled around the side of the open door and darted, as fast as my sore ass could dart, into the kitchen.

Aidan. That was why I'd been down here in the first place. He needed ice and painkillers. And I needed painkillers, too. I was sure a good bruise would show up on my face, compounding with the one that still stung from Matt's punch.

My thoughts spun as I searched the cabinets. Baking powder, flour, pasta noodles. Spices and salt. I had to speak to Kyle, tell him he needed to step off my son. Caroline and I had to work this out. I pushed aside flashes of her soft skin, her lips, her hips buckling under my hands. I wasn't allowed to want her.

I had to think about this from a rational perspective. Painkillers. Ice. Get Kyle sorted.

Then whatever this thing about the money was...

Whoever finds it, they kept saying. Well, not that exactly. They mentioned his will. What was "it?" I thought we were supposed to find him, find Jude. And we had.

Secrets still hid in this house.

Medicine wouldn't be in these food cabinets. I had to refocus. My initial thought was that the kitchen would have a first aid kit, for possible burns, cuts, or accidents that might happen. I scanned the walls, searching for a box that could hold those kinds of supplies.

Accidents. Greg and Moira. What would they do if we found it, whatever it was? *You have to come to terms with it. He won't be around to support us anymore.* The staff here relied on Jude for their livelihood. They'd all come here, helped him to build this monstrosity of a home/game park/potential resort, even when they knew he was sick. And they knew someone else might inherit his money.

All of it? More than a million dollars?

One of us... brought here for this game.

My stomach churned. I had to go up and see Jude. But first, I had to find that kit. Make sure my son was okay.

I found it, hanging on the far wall near the window. I rushed over and opened it, and bandages tumbled out. I grabbed what I needed, snatched ice from the freezer, and hightailed it back to our room.

When I returned, Aidan was snoring softly.

I rooted around in the room's minifridge, and my fingers found the edges of a cold, plastic water bottle. I wrenched off the top to guzzle it. Then I ripped open the tiny blister packs of ibuprofen, pushed the pills down my throat. My entire head pounded.

I didn't know what time it was. And I didn't want to wake Aidan.

But I didn't want his bruising to get worse. So, I found a washcloth in the bathroom and wrapped ice in it. It was already melting, wet against my skin.

I went to Aidan's side and laid the cloth gently on his cheekbone. He stirred a little but didn't wake.

If he took the medicine, it would help with the swelling. But as I watched my boy—so big now, gangly and limber—I thought back to when he was small, when we would syringe the berry-flavored liquid painkiller into his mouth while he slept. I couldn't do that now. He would have to decide on his own when he needed relief.

He sighed and rolled over. My arm stretched to hold the ice in place, but the farther he got from me, the farther it fell.

I walked around the side of the bed and grabbed the washcloth. Then I set up a little first-aid spot on the nightstand: ibuprofen, water bottle, cloth. I scribbled a note: *Ice in freezer. If I'm not here, be back soon. Get some rest.*

Then I left the room to find Jude.

18

Patrick

It took me some time to find Jude's room. I kept getting lost in this cavernous house, with its rabbit warrens and wings. Places like this, games like this, existed in Jude's head, and he wasn't content with keeping them there. He had to be the one to build them.

Once I found the correct staircase, I almost thought it might move as I climbed it, like the ones in *Labyrinth.* Jude loved David Bowie—no surprise there. But I had no need to cling to the railing, and the steps seemed more familiar by the time I reached the landing.

The smell of sweat and sickness blew out of the room as I moved the door out of the way. A woman stood up from Jude's bedside, popping up like a mouse out of a hole. She was pale and thin, and—was it—"Hannah?"

The woman winced. "You must've mistaken me for someone else."

I felt heat in my cheeks. "Oh, shoot. I'm sorry."

Hannah was dead. For a split second, I'd thought she was back from the grave, or maybe never really dead at all.

The woman danced toward me, on light feet. "It's okay. I'm Erica.

I'd shake your hand, but I'm becoming a little worried about contaminants with all these new people in the house."

"You're Jude's nurse, then?" *And probably also his marketing manager or something.*

Erica ducked her head. "You're one of his friends."

"Yeah."

I looked beyond her at his still form, his chest barely rising and falling. It was too late to spit out any other words. Exhaustion lived in my bones.

"I'm glad you all made it here," she said. "He doesn't have much time left."

"You weren't here when Greg brought us up before."

"I do night shift. He has another nurse for daytime." Erica rubbed her eyes. "I'm used to being awake. I need to check his vitals, make sure his medicine is working..." She fingered one of the lines running between the IV pole and Jude's body. "I barely know the man, but he seemed like such a nice person. You knew him well?"

She must have been hired from a nurse service. She wasn't like the rest of the house staff. She had just been brought in. I licked my lips and nodded again. This little bird of a woman didn't have to know I hadn't seen him for almost twenty years. That our relationship was frozen in time, older than my children. For all she knew, I'd been talking to him regularly, before all this happened.

"It's been a long time." I dropped into a chair beside him.

She found another chair, made eye contact with me, firm and gentle. Like a nurse should be. "I'm not used to having visitors in the middle of the night."

"Yeah, well. Hard to sleep in your best friend's random mansion that you didn't know existed." *Shit.* I was spilling my guts to her. Didn't take long.

Erica tilted her head, questioning.

I sighed, spread my legs. Put my hands in my hair. Studied the ceiling, its whorls and patterns—new construction, new patterns? Did Jude cipher a code into the walls of this place? "I don't even know where to start."

~

I STAYED up with Jude and his nurse until the sun rose. It was hard to tell—the thick-draped windows shut out most light—but I could feel it. My circadian rhythms signaled it, telling me how much of an idiot I was for pulling an all-nighter. I couldn't exactly argue.

Erica yawned. "I must say, that's quite the story you've got there. Patrick, is it?"

I flushed. My stomach had started to feel a little queasy, as if I'd spent the night on a cruise ship instead of in this dark, hot room. "Yeah."

"Do you make a habit of narrating your biography to women you've just met?"

I thought of Amy. We'd been at an OSU party, and she was so beautiful, and I kept racking my brain trying to think of something about myself that would impress her... so I told her about Jude. All his codes, his mysteries. He was the story I told people when I met them. My story wasn't interesting enough.

I shrugged. "Thanks for listening."

Erica shot me a little grin as she exited, and I wondered if I had made a mistake.

I staggered back to Jude's bedside and flopped into the chair beside him. Not much about him had changed. Oxygen tubes snaked into his nostrils, but he was still breathing on his own. The breaths came slow, ragged, but silent.

He wasn't that close to death yet. He wasn't rattling. I thought of my dad, the cancer that ate him from the inside, and of the way he'd clung to every breath with an unholy sound.

Did we know if he could understand us or not? Had Jude heard everything I'd said, or was he in some pre-death dream state, out of it? I'd assumed that from the beginning, but now I wondered how lucid he was. Had he known about the time I'd spent with Hannah when Amy was studying abroad, the quarter before we got married?

For all I knew, my secret wasn't so secret to Jude. Maybe he and Hannah had been in contact all along. Amy got pregnant only months after our wedding, and I hadn't had time to even think about my friends from high school. Caroline had gone to California. They were part of my practice life, the one where I thought I was grown up and in charge. When my real life began, I realized how completely stupid I'd been. I didn't want any of those reminders sticking around.

"Jude?" I didn't know I was going to say it until I did.

I expected him to open his eyes, to sit up, like he'd been playing this whole time.

Instead, I heard a rumbling, deep in Jude's throat.

"Well, shit," I said. Every time I blinked, the room spun. Sweat beaded on my forehead. "You heard it all, you clever asshole."

That same rumbling sound, and I could swear a smile tugged at his mouth. His eyes stayed closed, his bony frame still.

Suddenly, I felt as if my insides were going to explode. I scanned the floor for a trash can, anything to contain my vomit. But I couldn't find a thing, and then I was throwing up all over the brand-new carpet.

19

Caroline

Dreams are supposed to be the way the brain consolidates memories. Or at least, that was what I remembered from my long-ago Berkeley psych class. So, it was no surprise that my dreams consisted of Patrick, darkness, and confusion. Gray spirits rising from unknown places, hot lips on my skin, anger driving through my fisted hands. Images and colors. Hannah's face, contorted in misery.

I woke with a gasp, legs tangled in the sheets.

Light spilled through the window—day. I blinked the pictures from my mind, the sensations I'd been feeling in my subconscious. The room around me came into focus. The wine glasses from the night before. Empty plastic water bottles. Pile of blankets. Not how I liked to keep the environment around me when I was away from home.

I immediately sprang into action, picking up the detritus and smoothing the sheets back into place. We'd be home soon.

I drew the shade all the way up. The window looked out on the back lot of the house, a place where a garden might grow if it wasn't so cold. Snow blanketed the grass and piled up on stone fixtures—an angel, a tall water bowl.

At least the snow had stopped coming down. But it would be hard to get out of that long, twisting driveway. I estimated a fall of at least six inches overnight. They'd need to call a plow service, and those guys would be backed up with work most of the morning. I hoped someone had a phone that worked.

Even though I still only had my same clothes, I wanted to take a shower. I felt disgusting, with the moss of sleep on my tongue and dirt in my hair. I had to wash away Patrick's touch, the memories of the night before. The thought of Hannah destroyed. I closed myself in the bathroom, turned on the water, stripped down. I drew the soft linen curtain across and lost myself in the pouring warmth.

I always felt better when I had a plan, so I began to devise one as I stood under the stream. Luxury soap and shampoo bottles were built into the shower wall, and I squeezed some of the sweet-smelling floral shampoo into my hands. The scent helped me think. It was a new day, and there would be a new to-do list.

I wanted to make sure I saw Jude as much as possible before he passed. I'd return to this house, as strange as it was. But I wouldn't stay here again. I'd have an escape plan, a way out. I'd gather my son and Dora, get back to Chesterfield proper. I needed to see my mother, too, and talk to Kieran.

I rinsed my shampoo and worked conditioner into my hair. Butterflies spun under my skin as I considered that conversation, predicted how it would go. He would be angry at first, but he'd come to terms with it. He'd return to California, meet some surfer girl. It would be better for him.

Kyle would want to go with Kieran. My son hated it here, hated Ohio and its crappy weather and stupid small school. I never should've made him move here when he was so happy in the sunshine state. His place of origin.

It was my fault Kyle acted up, that he'd been harassing that girl, Dora's friend. That he was making Dora cheat for him.

I rinsed the conditioner out. Tears welled in my chest. I liked that no one could hear me under the spray as I sobbed.

20

Dora

My head ached. My throat was dry.

I sat up, blinking in the sudden sunlight. When I ran my hand along the side of my face, I found grooves, imprinted from the carpet. I could smell its offensive newness.

I moaned, the sound coming from deep in my belly.

It took me a few moments to get my bearings, to figure out that I hadn't just dreamed a bizarre set of dreams. The kink in my neck roared, and I drew back my shoulders to pop it out. I stretched my legs and feet, which had been as asleep as I was, pins and needles arched through them.

The little key had fallen from my hand. I saw it there, winking in the sun. Yelling at me, like, *how could you forget?*

I pushed my hair back and took a breath. Then I opened the last set of doors.

And the safe sat there. It stared back at me from behind the cabinet doors, small and gray and squat. It yelled at me, too, like the key had. *Come at me, bro,* it taunted.

I cursed myself for falling asleep as I shoved the key into the lock. The sun was out, and the snow had stopped. They'd be coming for me soon. But I couldn't leave without learning Jude's secret.

The lock fell free in my palm. I cast it aside. Another squat box was inside the safe. *God, please, not another lock.* When I removed it, I found only two VHS tapes, nested together in a box set.

I removed the tapes and inspected the labels. They read *Titanic* and *Titanic: Part II.*

This had to be a clue. Why would someone—Jude or anyone else—conceal these tapes in a locked safe if they weren't important? And what did *Titanic* even mean? I knew it was an old movie with Leonardo diCaprio, and it had come out when my mom was in high school.

I had to figure out how this tape thing worked.

I crawled back to the first cabinet, where I'd found the VCR. I'd been too tired to put those cords together then, but now I had a mission. I pulled the player from its home and blew off the dust that had gathered on top, then pulled its cords free as well. I coughed. How could this thing have collected so much grime when the house itself was so new? The machine must have been old before it got moved in here.

I studied the cords, looped them around my arm. All these different ends, different colors—blue, yellow, red. If I had a TV to plug this thing into, I might be able to tell where they went.

Ugh. My breath felt stale and gross. My hair kept falling in my face. I pushed it back again, wondering if I could wrangle it into a ponytail with these stupid tape cords. Despite all the mysteries in this room, I was sure there was no hair tie hidden in one of these books. Why did I keep it so long and stringy, anyway? No wonder guys didn't notice me... no wonder I faded into the background. I would get it cut as soon as I got back to civilization.

I abandoned the VCR to the floor, stood, and stretched my neck and back. I tiptoed to the door and listened for a few moments. I could hear rustling below, murmurings, voices. But they didn't have to know I was here. I hoped I wouldn't have to leave the room to find a TV.

I scanned the room from my new vantage point. Perhaps there was something I was missing, something I could see in the daylight that would've been obscured last night. The shelves, the open cabinets, the furniture... my gaze drifted over everything, wondering about hidden compartments, hiding spots for a screen...

Then my gaze landed on it.

21

Caroline

A s I was toweling off, the phone beside my bed rang. At least that meant some forms of communication were working. I answered.

"It's me," Moira said. "Do you want some clothes?"

The thought of Moira seeing me with my clothes off made my face burn. I drew my towel closer to my skin.

She chuckled. "Relax, I'm not watchin' ya. The sensor goes off when a guest uses up the towels."

I blew out a long breath. "You're freaking me out."

"It is sort of freaky," she said. "But anyway, I could tell you had a shower, so…"

I didn't want to get back into my gross clothes again. "Sure. I'll put on the robe until you get here."

When Moira arrived, she pushed a package of yoga pants and a soft cotton shirt into my hands. There was a bra and underwear too, and socks. "You have all this stuff for your guests?"

She half-smiled, shook her head. "Nah. This is my stuff. We're

275

about the same size. And if I'm right, you're not the kind of woman who likes to be dirty."

I flushed, took a step back. In the light of day, I could tell—she really was flirting with me. *Come on now, Caroline. You're still married. You crossed the line with Patrick. That doesn't mean you can cross it again just because she's a woman.* Yet, I still felt it. A shimmer of something between us.

"Thank you," I said. "You're right."

She grinned as I shut the door.

CLAD in my new comfy duds, I descended the long staircase from the guest wing into the main lobby. The fireplace was out, and sun shone through every window. The house looked different in the daylight, as if some of its magic had been stripped away. It was only a structure, mismatched by Jude's crazy sense of style.

No one was in the lobby, so I stepped into the kitchen and dining area. Maple-syrup smells propelled me through the kitchen.

Greg stood by a skillet, spatula in hand, but hissed when he saw me. "I'm making the magic happen! Don't distract me!"

I rolled my eyes and entered the huge room where we'd had dinner. Without the candles, it too seemed like a less intimidating space. I tried to picture guests waking up to this. Even if Jude had lived, the place wasn't ready.

And then I reminded myself—Jude was still alive.

In my mind, I'd already written him off. He was a person, still breathing, still existing, but I'd never talk to him again. I'd never see him ooze his way across a crowded room, moving toward me as if I were the magnet that attracted him, that liquid smile crossing his elastic face. So, he was gone.

All the chairs were empty. I'd expected to see at least one of our other guests down here. Kyle was probably asleep. I didn't know what time it was, but it was before noon. Aidan and Dora were teenagers, so it made sense that they'd be sleeping too. But Patrick was also missing.

I slid into the spot at the head of the table, looked down at the all the settings spread out in front of me. I felt like a queen with no kingdom to rule.

Greg finally burst out through the kitchen, plate in hand.

"I've got lots of pancakes and waffles," he crowed, swanning down before me. Then he did a double take.

"I know. Where's everyone?" I asked.

"Mo's coming, and some of the other house staff will be here. We need to get that snow moved so you all can get home."

I nodded. Through the big picture window that opened out to the courtyard, I could see one of the stone fixtures, an angel weeping toward the sky with her hands up. She wore a crown of white.

"But the people I came with." I got up to follow Greg as he bustled back toward the kitchen, grabbed the swinging door and held it so he could duck inside. "Don't you guys have this sensor thing that goes off when people use stuff in the rooms? That's how Moira..."

I didn't want to admit I'd seen her twice since the middle of the night.

"Yeah, we have that. I saw that Patrick drank one of the water bottles. That was at two in the morning, though, and I wasn't about to go traipsing down to ask him if he wanted something else to drink."

Greg spun to the kitchen counter and reached for a plate of bacon.

Patrick had been awake at two in the morning. That was why he hadn't come downstairs yet. I relaxed a little as I poured some coffee and helped myself to the masterpiece of breakfast. They'd be here, all of them, when they'd recovered from their night. By then, the road crews would be through, and we could go home.

The rest of the house staff trooped in, heaping their own plates, and I smiled a little as I sat back. I'd enjoy my meal with them before I left for good.

From "The Great Genius of Edward Elgar," a high school paper by Jude Lassiter

The Dorabella Cipher is Elgar's most famous code. Elgar was married to a woman eight years older than him, so he was interested in other women, too. Dora was one of the women he liked. He liked her a lot, enough to write her a code that no one has been able to break in the years since his death. It's a series of squiggly lines. It doesn't work as a simple substitution cipher, and Elgar had used the same squiggly lines in another code, but they don't match up with each other. A few people think they might have broken the code, but the solutions they have posed don't make a lot of sense. I think this code will stand the test of time as one no one will ever be able to solve.

This is a non sequitur. Just because someone is married to an older individual doesn't mean they will immediately fall for someone younger. I would appreciate some citations in this paragraph. -Mr. Peachtree

22

Dora

That big thing with the many keyboards.

It sat at the top of the highest bookshelf. It looked like an old typewriter, but it didn't have a keyboard like a computer did, and there were extra rotor wheels and electric-looking wire circuit things. It seemed vaguely familiar, like maybe it was the predecessor to the typewriter (that was an SAT word—I gave myself ten points).

But the most important thing about it was that there was a big space behind it. Plenty of room for a TV screen to hide.

I scanned the carpet for a makeshift footstool, something I could climb on. I pushed the plush ottoman to the shelves. When I stood on it, my feet sank into it, but I was eye-to-eye with the big thing. Cool.

A little card sat next to it. I read it. *The Enigma Machine.*

Enigma. We'd played that in band. The variations. Edward Elgar had written them. Same guy who wrote *Pomp and Circumstance,* with the world's most boring bassoon part. Quarter notes till death, and then you had to repeat over and over because of all the kids walking across the stage. The. Worst.

But this thing probably didn't have anything to do with band. I kept reading.

Machine used to encrypt and decrypt sensitive messages during World War II. Its cipher messages were eventually decoded by the Allies, leaving the Germans vulnerable.

Jude was the master of ciphers, and this machine was the master of ciphering.

I rubbed my fingers into my eyes, hard. The light that crept in from the windows had gotten brighter, more blinding. I had no idea what time it was. The clock, of course, still read midnight. I sat on my haunches on the ottoman, eyes closed, seeing stars on my mental screen.

Sure, I liked codes. I liked solving puzzles. But there was no way I could solve this. I had no idea how this machine even worked, if it worked at all. And if it was an artifact from an old-time war? Forget about it. Jude was already dying, but if I messed up his stuff, I was sure he'd find a way to smite me from the afterlife. I mean, I didn't really know the man, but if I was a collector of that kind of stuff, I'd probably smite someone from beyond the grave too.

He couldn't expect anyone to actually use the machine. That was impossible. There had to be another way.

And I was so close. So. Stinking. Close.

23

Patrick

I woke up in a pile of my own vomit.

The stink hit me first. Like a plow through my consciousness, pulling me out of my stupor. Then it was the nausea, a bolt of electric pain to the stomach. I threw up again, my insides revolting. Heat pounded through my joints.

I couldn't lay there, not with the mess all around. I army-crawled forward, leaning on my elbows, until I could get leverage enough to stand. By the time I'd gotten clear of it, I was nearly at the door.

"I'm sorry, man," I told Jude, if he could hear me, if he was awake. I could picture him laughing, mocking me from wherever he was, that space between alive and dead. The bardo, didn't some people call it. Purgatory.

Someone would have to come and help me clean this up. I couldn't do it, not in my state. My dinner lay in pieces all around the room. *Disgusting.* Heat spilled up the back of my neck. I thought of Erica—she'd be asleep all day—she wouldn't tell everyone in the house my story? Maybe I'd hallucinated her.

I was sick because of these people. Something in the dinner had made me ill. Or there had been something in the water I slugged, the stuff that was in the fridge in the room. I thought of the money as I swayed down the hall, down the steps, hugging the banister. If all of us were dead, Moira and Greg would get Jude's money. It would be so easy for them to poison us all, to trap us and kill us in fine fashion. Caroline and I, the kids—we were sitting ducks.

My face ached. My stomach lurched again. There couldn't be anything left in there by now. I'd lose my balance next. Lose consciousness. Liam would grow up without a father, and Amy would have to find another husband. Aidan might be sick by now too. I'd left the water for him to drink.

I paused at the edge of the stairs. Better not to let them know what I knew. I'd ask for help. They wouldn't be able to turn me away without looking suspicious.

The scents of maple syrup and bacon wafted through the main lobby, and my insides churned. Any other time, I'd be on top of that breakfast in a heartbeat. Today, I wanted to throw it all out a window, see it steam against the snow.

I found a seat by the empty fireplace. I couldn't go in there. People were walking around and talking in the other room, but I couldn't engage. Not yet. I had to rest first.

My mind spun as I rested my head on the leather couch behind me. I was down so low, my legs were out almost to the middle of the carpet, and the inside of my back crimped. Caroline could drive me to the hospital, but there was so much snow... and if Moira and Greg were trying to kill us, they certainly wouldn't bring in anyone to clear the driveway. We'd have to walk to the road. Uber wouldn't work—you had to schedule those ahead of time around here—but did I have the number of that guy who drove Amish people around? He'd taken me to the airport a few times.

My hand drifted to my pants pocket. No wallet. No phone. The stuff was in my room.

I needed to get Aidan anyway. My forehead burned. So did the inside of my ears. I looked into the hollow of the empty fireplace, picturing the flames that had danced there the night before. This place was a death trap. All I could see was death.

24

Caroline

Moira insisted on cleaning my place setting for me, even though I was the only guest at breakfast. She waved me away, saying, "Get your shit together. We're busy."

Greg had waved me away from the kitchen, too, but then he'd let me help him bring the food out. Maybe since the house wasn't open for guests yet, they weren't used to having us around. They didn't know what to do with us. We were wayward stragglers, a surprise of sorts. Although they'd known we were coming, they didn't know when, or if, we would solve Jude's clues.

It still felt wrong that all this was ending. Jude was gone, at least in my mind, and I'd started thinking about what would happen when I got back to Chesterfield. I'd put aside the hope of getting any money from him. My plan was in place, and I'd move forward. I wouldn't see Patrick again, at least not until things had cooled off between us. I'd check up on Dora, but I didn't have to do anything beyond making sure my son wasn't bothering her. I needed to build a new life for me and my son, a life that would lack a husband.

But the mystery was gone now. We'd found Jude, and this place, and I wouldn't be able to pretend he didn't exist anymore. He had lured us here, and we'd spent this weird night in this strange house. Jude had changed me yet again. Changed us.

I was musing on this when I drifted into the front living room, and I almost stumbled over Patrick's long legs.

He smelled rotten, stale. I grimaced. He was covered in vomit, his own from the looks of it. It was splashed across his shirt and tracked down the front of his pants.

"Patrick!" I bent to shake him but didn't want to touch his clothes, so I grabbed the flap of his cuff and wobbled it.

He didn't budge. Yeah, that wouldn't work. I tried a small shove, strategically placing the heel of my hand against his shoulder.

His eyelids fluttered. He moaned.

"What's wrong with you?" I whispered.

I didn't want the others to hear me—although, I couldn't put my finger on why. Maybe I didn't want them to see him so vulnerable. His forehead radiated heat. *Shit.* I'd kissed him last night. Any virus he had would be traveling through my system by now.

"Caroline?" he mumbled. He opened his eyes, and they flared when he caught sight of me. "We have to get to Aidan."

"Why? What's wrong?" A cold line of fear went up my spine. Patrick would have to get up and move himself. I wouldn't be able to do it, and I was sure as hell not going to get any of that grossness on me.

"They're poisoning us, Car." Patrick groaned and sat up.

I hopped back.

"The staff."

I scoffed. "We have to get you into bed. You're delirious."

"I heard them talking last night."

I glanced back into the kitchen. Waited.

"Moira and Greg," he said. "They were talking about a prize that Jude left for us to find. That if we found it, we'd inherit all his money."

He really was delirious.

"We're not getting the money. The million-dollar prize isn't real," I said. "It was a trick to get us here."

"No." Patrick was insistent, even in his fever. "*All* his money. The whole estate."

Adrenaline zapped through me. More than a million dollars. The promise of freedom, returning slowly, teasing me.

I couldn't help picturing it. Getting on a plane back to California. Buying a new house, near the water, in whatever part of the state I wanted. I could even afford San Francisco. Or one of the plum suburbs in the mountains. Kyle would go to an elite school, he'd get therapy, and I could send my mom to a pricey rehab. I wouldn't even look back at Ohio in my rearview.

My thoughts revved into gear. There was a prize in the house. The game wasn't over. Where would I find the next part of it? I tracked the paintings up the side of the staircase wall. Maybe there was a clue in one of those?

Patrick cleared his throat.

"I drank the water in the room," he rasped, coughing. "I left it for Aidan. We have to make sure he doesn't drink it."

My brow folded. "You think they poisoned us so we couldn't win the money?"

He nodded.

"Honey." I didn't think, just called him that. "I drank plenty of water from my room fridge, plus a bottle of wine that Moira brought to me. And we all ate dinner last night. You're the only one puking."

He processed that. "Oh."

I steeled myself and grabbed the inside of his elbow, using the couch for support as I dragged him up. "We need to get you to your room, though. Let's check on Aidan. It'll make you feel better."

He reached his feet, and I let him lean on me as we headed, painfully slowly, toward the guest wing.

From the journal of Jude Lassiter, 2002

There might have been one other person named Dora in Elgar's life. I've been studying Elgar for all these years, following the Elgar Society, getting deeper into those codes I started in school. It turns out that Elgar may have had a mistress, one Dora Nelson, who had a daughter named Pearl. Elgar's daughter? The thirteenth variation of Enigma has a mysterious dedication, one that has always been assumed to be a friend... but maybe this dreamy theme has a connection to Pearl, or Elgar's mistress?

25

Dora

I paced the carpet, trying to think.

Outside, I heard commotion. I went to the window, peered out. A bunch of people were in the driveway, tromping through the snow. From so far up, I couldn't identify them. Maybe a road crew, assessing how long it would take to dig us out. The driveway wound through the long forest, obscured by trees. I guessed that I had at least an hour or two until it was completely plowed, if I could stay up here without anyone finding me.

Could I simply stay here? If I didn't solve it?

I cringed, thinking of how pissed my grandmother would be already. I hadn't been able to call her from my phone, true. But I could've tried to contact her on one of the house phones. The storm hadn't knocked out our power, after all. It was simply unsafe to drive. For all I knew, she'd filed a missing person report by now.

A tear welled at my eye. I flicked it away. Being here had made me forget... being launched into this mystery, this... enigma. I chuckled a little at my own joke.

For lack of another thought, I sat with the tape machine and the *Titanic* box. Maybe there was a clue inside I had missed. I pulled the tape out and opened the plastic top, where I could see the long stretch of shiny film. I figured I'd better not touch that, or it might mess up the recording. I hadn't seen that many of these, but I knew they were fragile.

I ran my hand around the inside of the box. Nothing. I even peeked into the flap where the tape would go in the machine. Maybe there was another tape in there or some other clue. But it was empty. All of it was empty.

Damn, damn. Damn.

I wanted to run to the other wing of the house, to shake Jude and wake him, to make him tell me what he was hiding. And where.

Back to pacing. I walked the length of the bookshelf, then noticed a small CD player plugged into the wall, along with a stack of CDs. I plucked the top one off the stack. Maybe a melody would jar something loose. The first one on the pile was Elgar's *Enigma Variations*, as performed by the Redlands Symphony. I'd never heard of them, but they must be good, if they had their own CD. Another piece of old tech, thinking of the tapes back at Jude's little trap of a storage closet. I wondered how the generation after mine would consume media. What would replace streaming? We'd probably be piping audio and video through chips implanted in our heads.

I extracted the shiny disc and placed it gently in the top of the player. As the first melody filled the room—way better than "Pomp and Circumstance," at least—I tugged at the liner notes. *Enigma*, after all, could have something to do with that machine, the one that concealed the screen and my way to play the tapes. This was my last chance. If I didn't find something here, I'd have to leave the library to search for another TV. Maybe I could do that while all of them were outside, looking at the snow.

The shiny page of liner notes unfolded in my hands, and I gasped.

Delicate, handwritten scores of sheet music came along with it.

26

Caroline

Patrick swayed in the shower. I'd helped him strip off his pukey clothes, and then I threw them in the corner, although I wanted to burn them. At least, the smell of jasmine and elderflower from the shower gel filled the air. Getting him in the shower had been a feat. I averted my eyes as I pushed him behind the shower curtain and turned on the spray. I'd seen his equipment, obviously, had felt it, not too long ago. But all of that felt so improper.

I could see his shadow against the side of the curtain. He was barely on his feet.

"I feel like I'm going to barf again." He moaned.

"It's okay, honey," I said, still calling him that. I couldn't stop myself. "You can do this. Just get through this."

"Can you check on my son?"

I hesitated. I didn't know which room he was in, and the thought of knocking on all the doors, poking my head into every space...

Then I remembered the secret door.

"Sure," I said. "Patrick, hold on, okay?"

I stepped up to the bookshelf that I had fallen through only a few short hours before. With a tentative push, the shelf gave way. I turned through it, my hands stuck on the side of the wall, hanging on as I'd told Patrick to do.

And then I heard a yelp.

Patrick's son pulled the sheets up to his naked chest. He was awake, bleary-eyed.

"Oh, sorry," I said, as if I hadn't just walked through a wall. "Your dad asked me to check on you."

"Where did you come from?" He blinked at me.

"The rooms are connected. Mine is behind that rotating shelf." I thumbed back toward my room. "Your dad got sick. Are you okay?"

He nodded, his fingers clutching the top of the sheet. "Yeah. Fine. Just fine."

"Okay. Cool."

We stared at each other. My mind went through the possibilities for conversation. I had nothing to say to this child, other than to convey the information he needed as to the whereabouts of his father. But something else lingered between us, something that tugged at me.

"Do you know where Kyle is? Have you seen him?"

Aidan frowned.

"Not since he did this to me." He pointed at his eye.

There was a red ring around it, purpling and bruising at its edges.

Shit.

"I'm so sorry." I took a tentative step, examining the scratch from where I stood, not close enough.

"What's his problem, anyway?" Aidan closed his eyes. He looked tired, like we all were. "He's so angry all the time. I mean, if it were up to me, we could be friends. I don't want anyone to ever get hurt."

Neither did I.

"Okay, well, we'll find him," I said. "You rest. We'll get home soon."

I couldn't face the kid. So, I disappeared back into my room.

The shower still ran. I stuck my head into the fog. "You awake in there?"

Patrick moaned.

"Are you gonna get sick again?" I picked at my cuticles as one edge of a French-manicured nail began to bleed. I'd thought Kyle had ended up in another room, but I also thought he would've surfaced by now. It was nearly noon. Where else could he be? His phone was on the nightstand, useless, so I couldn't use it to track him. He had to be somewhere in the house.

No reply from Patrick. I braced myself, then stuck my head into the shower.

Patrick knelt on the tub floor. "I'm an idiot, Caroline."

"Did you get sick again?" I repeated.

"I cheated on my wife. I lost my job. I'm a fucking failure." He collapsed backward.

I whipped the curtain shut before I could see anything private. I needed to retain some of my dignity, even though I had contributed to his cheating.

"My best friend is upstairs dying, and instead of helping him, I bared my soul to some nurse I don't know and then puked my guts out all over his floor. He's dying, and I puked on his floor."

Patrick sounded so sad. My chest filled, and I swallowed tears. I couldn't cry, not with all the steam in my throat, not in front of him. Because I'd betrayed Jude, too. I was already pretending he was dead, already thinking about the next puzzle I needed to solve so I could get his money.

Which reminded me... I needed to find my son.

I wanted to stay with Patrick, to comfort him. But before this week, I hadn't seen him in seventeen years. My son could be in danger. That meant more than any game or duty I might still have to my long-ago friends.

"It's going to be okay. Someone would've cleaned up in Jude's room. I have to go," I said, gently. "Are you going to be okay in here?"

"Don't leave. Please."

"I have to find Kyle. Then I can come back."

Silence. And then I realized Patrick was breathing silently, after a series of heaving sobs.

But I couldn't stay to help him.

"Aidan is in the other room," I told him. "I'll be back as soon as I can."

27

Patrick

When I was done crying, I turned off the shower. Embarrassment surged in my gut along with the nausea.

She was going to find Kyle. Yes, okay. I could understand that. We needed to get our children together and leave as soon as the roads were clear. But I felt so weak, all I wanted to do was crumble on the bed. I wanted to sleep forever.

My clothes were balled up in the corner, and I wasn't about to put them back on. I could smell them from my place in the tub. I finally had to turn off the water, as my fingertips were getting pruney, and Caroline was gone anyway. She wasn't going to slide into the shower with me. I wouldn't have another chance to touch her. Instead, I'd let myself go, and now I was a shivering mess, hunkered cold against the slippery surface. My blood raged in my ears.

I had to find something to warm up with. I was so hot, the fever steaming my skin, but I still shook. My teeth chattered. A fresh towel sat on the toilet. Once it was around me, once I got dry, I felt somewhat better. I didn't have anything to wear, but I could at least wrap myself

299

in blankets. With everything I had in me, I lurched to the bed and nestled myself among Caroline's bedding.

Once my head hit the pillow, I relaxed a little. I had been up all night, and this virus, or whatever it was, had taken so much out of me.

This poisoning. I pushed away the thought.

Caroline was right. I was delirious. If Moira and Greg had truly wanted us to go down, everyone would have gotten sick. I'd probably gotten this virus from some snot-nosed kid in Liam's preschool class. For all I knew, Amy was languishing on the couch at home, too.

Amy. I hadn't thought of her in hours. I'd been so taken with Caroline, with Jude. With the bones of my past. My confession to Erica, the mousy nurse. My wife didn't know where I was, didn't know where Aidan was. She must be sick with worry.

I had to call her. Had to let her know where we were, had to tell her we were okay. That was where Caroline had gone—to make sure her son was okay.

I didn't know my son was okay, either.

I knew he was behind the spinning bookshelf. Caroline had checked on him, but that didn't feel like enough. I wanted to get up, to check on him myself, but I was weak. I couldn't accomplish any of the things I wanted to do. All I could do was succumb to the mastery of my fever.

I dreamed.

Caroline's touch scorched me. My desire was so great, it had its own gravity. It propelled me toward her. I kissed her with verve, with the intensity I'd always wanted to heap upon my wife. But I was tired of waiting, tired of pretending I didn't have needs. I needed someone. I needed Jude. I needed Caroline. I wanted all of them, all at once, together. I wanted them to sate me.

Even Hannah lingered, background noise in our tryst. I remembered her, too, remembered the way she'd clung to me in Columbus when Amy was in Spain. No twenty-something boy should be expected to stay alone without his fiancée, without some form of female companionship. Hannah had been so eager, so willing, and when she told me she'd been with Jude, there was no more delaying it. I had to be with her.

But Amy was always there. In the background, on the outside. She was adulthood when the rest of it was childhood. She was responsibility. She was the person who would make me give up my fun and bow to her whim. She was the honesty of reality. I owed her more than anyone, because she had made me who I was, and yet I couldn't let her be part of this. Not now. She didn't need to be there.

And yet, she was.

"What the fuck are you doing?" Amy's voice cut through my consciousness. Screeching, high-pitched, insistent.

I squeezed my eyes shut. This was a dream. This wasn't happening.

And yet, it was.

Amy stood at the end of my bed, in Caroline's room. At first, I thought I'd hallucinated her. She was a dream, like Caroline and Jude had been. She wasn't supposed to be here, in Jude's Barbie dream house. She was supposed to be at home, taking care of the baby and posting on her mommy blog forums and making kale smoothies.

But the more she screamed, the more I realized she was here and in the flesh.

And she was pissed.

"I'm sorry, babe." I groaned. "I'm really... sick."

"And that explains why you're in this woman's room—in her bed— naked?" Amy planted her hands on her hips, and even in my haze, I could see her jaw was set tight. She looked like a Valkyrie, intent on revenge. Whether she was going for me or for Caroline, or both of us—I wasn't sure.

"She helped me," I said. "She got me in the shower."

Amy scoffed. "Sure, she did. And then she helped you with other stuff, too."

"Nothing happened. I swear." I closed my eyes again. Things had been so much better when I was drifting in the ether of nowhere. "What are you doing here, anyway? I thought the driveway was blocked. By snow."

"It's plowed. It stopped snowing hours ago." Amy threw up her hands. "I tracked you from your phone's last known GPS setting."

"I couldn't call you!" I felt a sudden surge of energy, enough to sit up straight. But I could smell Caroline on the sheets, her lavender and roses. I steeled myself. "My phone doesn't work out here. I have no idea how you were able to get a GPS signal off it."

"Whatever." Amy pointed at me. "I'm leaving. As soon as Kieran is ready. We're done. Out of here."

I sagged back against the pillows. It didn't matter, anyway. I couldn't go anywhere, couldn't do anything. I was about to die here with Jude, about to let the sickness take me, whatever its origin.

"Wait," I said. "Kieran?"

Interlude

H annah's world was spinning.

"I have to get home," she moaned.

"Ugh!" Caroline jumped away from the board. They had all jumped away, in fact—scrambled away from the Ouija, where Hannah had emptied the contents of her stomach. "You're gross."

Hannah could smell her regurgitated Taco Bell, not nearly as seductive the second time around. In fact, she might never patronize the establishment again.

"I'm sorry," she mumbled, crab-walking backward into a corner. The wall butted up against her back, stopping her from falling even farther.

"You're always sorry. Why don't you do us a favor and clean this shit up?" Caroline looked down her nose at Hannah. She perched on Patrick's bed, as if it was her throne. As if she owned this space. "Patrick, get her some stuff. Spray or whatever."

Patrick peeled himself off the floor. "Spray?"

Hannah had covered her face with her hands. Now, she parted her fingers and looked out at him. He seemed trapped. Caroline ran the show.

"Paper towels." Caroline pointed at the door. Her pert nose wrinkled. "Jude, why did you invite her again?"

Hannah felt Jude crouching beside her. She turned her head before her gorge could rise.

"Are you all right?" He removed her hands from her cheeks.

Her skin was burning. Hannah shook her head. She wasn't all right.

"What are you waiting for, Patrick? I'm getting totally sick right now." Caroline coughed. "I might barf too, and that would just be tragic."

Hannah couldn't move. She was pinned up against the wall, thinking of how nice this evening had been going up until now. Maybe they had met the ghost Jude had wanted to meet. Maybe not. Maybe Dorabella's spirit was simply some air moving across the Ouija board, an electric illusion, strong enough to feel real.

Patrick moved to get up. "I'll get that clean-up stuff or whatever."

She liked his quiet voice, his presence, centering the four of them. He stepped between Hannah and the mess, then left the room.

"I'm sorry," she said again. It was all she could think to say. Hannah had ruined things again.

"You should be." Caroline folded her arms. She was always doing that, closing herself off from the rest of the world. How powerful could she be if she would only let other people in? Hannah couldn't imagine what holding that power must be like. She wanted to sink into the floorboards.

Patrick returned with a bleachy-smelling spray bottle and a roll of paper towels. He was kind, as he mopped her mess. He and Jude both. They had always watched out for her.

She was so fragile, like a china doll, always on the verge of shattering. Still queasy, too.

"Will you drive me home?" she asked Jude.

Caroline let out a long, dramatic sigh. "He's too high to drive."

"I'm so glad we met Dorabella." Tears glistened in Jude's eyes. "I'm so glad we did that."

Hannah felt suddenly claustrophobic. She looked around, trying to ground herself, observing the physical objects in the space. The walls were blue, a little border of baseballs and basketballs trailing behind the bed. At the sight of the bed, Hannah wondered if Caroline and Patrick had sex. Sex was still an abstract concept to her. Since Patrick and Caroline had paired up, it was only right that Jude should kiss her.

Sweat beaded on Hannah's brow. How could she think of romance at a time like this?

Caroline rolled her eyes. "You're all ridiculous."

"I want to go home," Hannah mumbled, talking through her hands. "I don't feel good."

"Jesus. You know how to mess up a party." Caroline leveled a finger at Jude. "You take her out to the back and shoot her. I'll stay here."

She winked at Patrick, who squirmed a little as he cleaned the floor.

Hannah was so hot, so dizzy, she wasn't sure if she had heard correctly. Just an hour ago, she'd been pleasant and calm, basking in her independence, pleased to be away from her mother. That was the only feeling she needed, right then. But now—

"What did you say?" she asked Caroline.

Hannah felt Jude's hand on her back. Her stressed belly cramped and fluttered. Caroline didn't know her, didn't know how she struggled. How her every day was a limp from sunrise past sunset. Hannah loved to fall asleep at night, loved to let the darkness take her. Loved to conjure new ways to let free her pain.

"You may as well kill yourself already." Caroline sounded like ice, like the coldest poison chilling its way down Hannah's spine. "We know you want to. And I don't think anyone here would be sad about it."

Hannah pulled her wrist to her mouth. Her lips found the crack where she had parted the skin with her razor. She'd been trying so hard to feel something—to escape from the numb dark of daily life here— that she had pressed her weapon into that most vulnerable place.

How dare this girl make assumptions about her.

Hannah wouldn't take her own life. But she wouldn't be a victim, either.

She pushed the Ouija board away. Its letters meant nothing. Jude had been pushing the planchette, making things seem the way he wants them to seem. He curated his own world. They all did. And she wouldn't be part of it.

Hannah found her feet, and then she took herself down the stairs. They might have followed her, but they didn't, and she went straight for the kitchen. Patrick's parents were nowhere to be seen. They were away somewhere, ignoring all of them, giving them autonomy or whatnot.

Hannah would show them. She'd show them what a woman could do when she had power. When she got to choose.

She opened each drawer, each cupboard. Patrick's parents were disorganized. At her house, each drawer had a function and a purpose. She knew exactly where to find the knives there. She could find the razors. She welcomed their bite.

Finally, in a bottom drawer, she located what she was searching for. Hannah withdrew a long, flat blade. It wasn't as sharp as it could be.

She fell to her knees, bounced on them. She gritted her teeth. Held the knife the way she imagined she'd hold a lover, or a baby.

Hannah drew the sharp edge across her wrist. At first, she gasped with the pain, at the sight of the bright line welling there. But then she admired it, marveled at the blood raining down, watching it pool in a shiny puddle on Patrick's parents' kitchen floor.

28

Caroline

The staff had cleaned the kitchen and the dining room. The place looked as if no one had been there that morning, all the settings back to the way they had been before breakfast. All the fixtures in the kitchen shone. Greg's skillet glistened, a little bit of remaining water left from its washing.

I wasn't sure where else they might be. Upstairs with Jude? Someone must have seen my son. Morning was fading into afternoon, and my skin itched beneath Moira's yoga clothes. I didn't want to go home. That house didn't really feel like home, after all. I wanted my mother. When all this was over, I'd drop Kyle off, avoiding Kieran, and go right to Bright Flower. Tell my mother about the new windfall.

But before anything else, I needed to find Kyle.

I pictured the house from the outside. I'd been in the guest wing, and I'd seen the staff bedrooms, where Jude lay. I'd seen the kitchen and dining room. But there were some rooms to the right of the big main lobby—an entire wing, in fact. I spotted a gray door leading out to the right.

And there were the staff workrooms. A key-card lock blocked my entrance, but I could see them past the open window on the top half of the door. Rows and rows of offices.

A doorbell was installed on the creamy white wall. I imagined this was set apart so guests wouldn't think it was a part of the whole-house experience. And the staff had probably retreated to their offices. They had to work, after all. This wasn't all play for them. I winced, thinking about the puzzle, about the treasure I was missing out on.

When I pressed the round yellow button, Moira's voice came over the intercom. "I can see you."

"Then let me in!"

The door buzzed, and I wrenched it open, then marched down the hall.

I found Moira surrounded by screens and wires and black boxes. The technology dwarfed her. Her eyes glowed, flicking from monitor to monitor.

"Have you seen Kyle?" I asked her.

"Didn't you ask me that at breakfast? I told ya no."

I couldn't remember. "But you can see everything in the house from here?"

"This is the surveillance room."

Images of the different rooms in the house lit her screens.

"I can't see inside the guest rooms. But this one..." She pointed to one of the monitors, filled with text only. "This one tells me if a guest is unhappy or upset. It tells me when you drink your water and when you're out of towels." She winked.

"It's like a giant game of *The Sims*." I wanted to sit down, to talk to her further, but I didn't have time. I scanned the camera images for any trace of Kyle. "Can you roll back in time? See if he might show up on your past footage?"

Moira raised her brows. "It's possible, but I'd have to know which camera. When was the last time you saw him?"

I thought back. He'd been in the guest room with me, but that was well before midnight. "Is there a camera in the main hall? Go back to last night?"

"There's one above the main door." She toggled it, then pulled a timeline onto her largest screen.

I leaned over her shoulder. I could smell her soap, a sweet and spicy mix of orange and ginger. I breathed it in. Maybe it would help me calm down.

"I've also got one at an angle."

We watched as Greg talked to Patrick. Greg put out the fire.

"Why'd you wait so long to look for him?" Moira asked.

"Kyle?" I fought to keep my breath even, but I could feel my hackles rising. "I don't know. He's fourteen. I figured he could take care of himself."

"No." Moira swiveled in her chair. I noticed her eyes for the first time—big and green, with long lashes. Soft eyes, a contrast to her sharp cheekbones. "I mean Jude."

My lips hung open. I had no response. I watched the footage rolling by.

"There's Kyle." I pointed. "Chasing—Aidan?"

"Must be." The two boys streaked across the main lobby and rushed up the stairs.

An image of Aidan's eye flashed in my mind. That vulnerable child. A young Patrick, overlaid with the blonde, compact filter of his wife. Maybe instead of worrying about Kyle, I should think about punishing him. How could he keep torturing this boy?

"So, they fought. Upstairs?"

The camera kept rolling.

Then Kyle returned, taking the stairs two at a time, his face bruised and broken. All I could see in that granulated image was my little boy, his cheeks so round and soft, innocent, sweet. I had to push aside that memory to fully see the hardened, set jaw, the clenched fists. He yanked his coat out of the foyer closet, shoved his feet into his shoes, and wrested the front door open.

I saw nothing after that.

"I have to go," I said, my feet already carrying me out of the offices.

"Wait. There's more footage..."

But the footage would still be there when I got back. If I got back. If I found him.

~

I BLUSTERED INTO THE SNOW, the sun blinding against the white. At least, it was no longer coming down.

He'd left in the middle of the night. He was somewhere on the grounds, cold, alone.

My ankles ached. The only shoes I had were the little booties I'd worn to work that day, and they covered my feet okay, but they were high, and they hurt. The snow wrapped around my legs, the wind flapping Moira's yoga pants. Chill seeped in between my skin and my clothes. I pulled my fluffy coat tighter around myself, trying, failing to block the cold.

I went around the back of the house, through the snow-covered courtyard. Someone had been by with a shovel, so I stayed on the path. My shoes would be ruined, but I didn't need more freezing water inside them. There was no place a teenage boy could hide, not out here, though.

I stepped off the path, cringing as I went, mincing my way past the stone statues. There was a sloping drop-off behind the house. Bare, icy trees scraped the sky.

I stared down at the hill, at the white mass dipping down into the valley. Pictured all the sticks and leaves buried beneath the accumulation. The animals hiding in burrows. My son tumbling down, thinking he might fly.

No. I whipped around, the wind whistling against my ear.

I stalked back toward the house, taking a detour onto the path. He could be inside. I hadn't looked hard enough.

But I stopped short. A new car sat in the driveway—a van. A mom-mobile.

A man stood beside it. From my vantage point, at first, I couldn't identify him. His white face blended with the sky, with the snow. He was washed out. Long blond hair, a surfer's style. A ragged flannel coat.

29

Patrick

"Where's Aidan?" Amy prowled around the room, pulling up pillows and sheets, as if she might find him hiding beneath them.

"Kieran's here? You mean Caroline's husband?" I gritted my teeth through a wave of nausea.

"I'm talking about our son." She glared at me, pausing in front of the bookshelf. Which our son was, in fact, behind.

I nodded at it. "Go ahead. Push it. But before you do—you came here with Kieran?"

I sat up straighter, reaching for my faculties. There was nothing left in my stomach. I had to be able to fight this, to push it away.

"Yes, I came here with Kieran." She said the name as if she were trying to spit out a swallow of poison. "I was on Facebook, trying to figure out where you were, and I posted in the Chesterfield town group. He messaged me and said Caroline wasn't back yet either. We put two and two together. It wasn't that hard."

"Amy." My jaw was so set that it ached. One more pain added to the growing list. "Do you think we would take our teenage children off to a rendezvous?"

"It's a great cover!" Her voice shot to the ceiling. I thought she might rattle the books off the shelves. "Great way to sneak around, using them as an excuse! What, did you think bringing them here would make them like each other?"

The bookshelf moved behind her.

She jumped back, her feet catching on the carpet, and she stumbled onto the bed. I groaned as she hit my ankles. Patrick, the Punching Bag.

Aidan emerged from the revolving entrance, his bruise angry and green. He looked like he'd survived a kind of teenage trial, like he'd been in the Hunger Games. He reached for his mother.

I watched them embrace, from my hot, sick, naked platform. Amy sighed as she pulled him close to her. I imagined her smell, the softness of her skin, and jealousy prickled in my chest.

"Baby, what happened?" she asked him.

I retreated to the position of observer. It was better than being the accused.

He murmured into her hair. I couldn't hear him, and I didn't know if he was trying to keep anything from me. I watched.

"Oh, honey." Amy smoothed her hand over his head, cupped his cheek. "We have to get you home."

She ushered him toward the door. I sat, incredulous.

They were almost gone when I finally managed speech. "What about me?"

Amy turned back, her eyebrow almost in her hairline. "What about you?"

Then I was alone again.

The feverish part of me wanted to go back to sleep.

But the rest of me wanted to leap after them, to pull them back into my room. To tell them how sorry I was, beg for their forgiveness. I could tell them everything, and there was no guarantee they'd forgive me.

Sleeping wouldn't require any effort on my part. But if I wanted to do anything else, I would need clothes.

I had the ibuprofen from the night before. And the water. If I took it, I'd be admitting that the staff hadn't poisoned me. That I'd gotten unlucky, somehow, with some sort of stomach bug. It was all bad timing. A coincidence.

I dragged myself forward on the bed and twisted the cap off the water. Downed the medicine. Then I laid back on the pillow, blew out a breath. I had to get some strength. I had to move forward.

All I wanted was to go home. To that big, beautiful house we couldn't afford. But it was home. The house I grew up in. We'd made it our own. I wanted to surround myself with the warm smells of Amy's cooking, to play on the floor with Liam. Where was Liam? I wanted us all to be in the same house together. I wanted to make hot chocolate and go sledding with the boys. Our family had broken, had splintered apart in pieces.

This was Jude. He was the stake, the dagger splitting me in two.

I loved him. I would've done anything for him.

But I wouldn't choose him over my family.

I surged forward and grabbed the phone on the bedside. Fumbled on the keypad and found the zero.

Someone answered. I didn't recognize the voice, didn't care. It was a someone, someone who could help me. "It's Patrick. I'm in the guest room. I don't have any clothes..."

Laughter from the other end of the line. "Happy to assist, Mr. Reed."

30

Dora

I smoothed my hands over the thin paper and read over the lines of music.

I didn't have an instrument in hand, but I could mimic the movements that I'd make, playing the notes. Bass clef was easy, in my muscle memory for two instruments. I was a bit rusty on treble clef, but I could still plink out invisible notes on a keyboard.

Four themes, written each in several lines of music. Each one with initials at the top of the line, just where the key and time were, and the tempo setting.

C.C. Allegro
P.R. Andante cantabile
H.M.M. Furioso
D.L.M. Dolce

I HUMMED the notes out loud as I air-played them, but the CD was also playing, and I couldn't think. I couldn't guess the pattern.

I stabbed the off button on the player, then hummed again.

This was a code. I could feel it vibrating inside me. What did the initials mean? The lines of music sounded vaguely similar, connected somehow.

Maybe there was another clue in the Elgar notes. I moved the delicate sheet music aside and laid out the shiny CD insert. A little bio of Elgar, some information about his British heritage—nothing more than an online encyclopedia entry, the kind I used for reports. Blah, blah.

Then I saw an image: Elgar's original score for *The Enigma Variations*, or as the liner called it, *Variations on an Original Theme, Opus 36*. The caption read that the papers were housed in the British Library. I leaned in closer. In Elgar's fluid hand, it read, "Dedicated to my friends pictured within."

I read down the page. Each variation was labeled with a set of initials.

My heart jumped. My hands felt like they were lit with sparklers, like everything I touched might flicker and catch fire. I jabbed the on button again, and the orchestra sawed away at whatever variation they had landed on.

C.C. Caroline Cross. She hadn't taken her husband's last name.

Patrick Reed. Hannah Marie Madison.

D.L.M. My initials.

Jude wrote these. They had to be the last clue.

I glanced back up at the Enigma machine. These were the Enigma variations. They had to be connected.

I braced myself as I tugged the ottoman back to where the machine rested on its perch. Then I studied the keyboard. The machine didn't look like it needed to be powered on. There were electrical wires crossing its top, but it didn't have a real plug.

I hesitated. I didn't want to touch the keyboard, for fear of messing things up. Did this thing even have a reset button? If I messed it up, would the code still work?

The initials, first. I could touch the buttons for those letters. I pressed the C button, and the machine thunked. Whatever gears were inside it turned and spun. I pressed the C again, and the machine responded again. Maybe I was in business.

I typed all the initials, then held my breath. The last rotor rolled into place.

I heard screaming from below me somewhere. Sounded like someone was getting murdered.

I leapt off the ottoman and hit the carpet. In case of gunshots. I expected something to happen with the machine, with my last press of the button.

The screaming continued. I crawled to the window, peered out. I could barely see the front door, and Caroline slamming herself against it, wailing. I had missed a lot.

I shrugged. I supposed I'd find out what was going on later. For now, I could keep moving. No one was dead... at least, as far as I knew.

Back up on the ottoman. Back against my nemesis. The machine stared back at me with no eyes, holding its secrets.

It wasn't the initials. What else?

Back on the floor, facing the music. Literally. Ha.

I had to think. I had to riff. Jude's friends, their initials. He'd written these for them. Their own Enigma variations, I realized as I hummed the tunes again.

Think, Dora.

I looked between the lines of music. The theme with my name on it was written in treble clef. *Of course,* because I was a girl—a woman— and my voice register was higher. A-D-A. E-D-A. Key of A. Didn't like that extra sharp.

A-D-A.

I might have shrieked "Eureka!" if I wasn't still unsure. But the flash of insight was enough to get me scrambling onto the ottoman and keying in those notes. Those note letter names.

I flew through the letters, each one grinding through the machine, and I held my breath.

Something creaked. Something spun. The Enigma shifted as if possessed by a spirit, rotating away to reveal an old TV.

I moved fast then.

Got the VCR. Found its cord, found the yellow and red plugs that matched the TV and the player. I fumbled with it a little. I had to change the TV to "source," but we had to do that at home with the smart TV, so it made sense. Then I slid the first tape inside and hit play.

The tape started in the middle of a scene. Leonardo diCaprio—I recognized him. He was still in movies, but he was a lot older now. I didn't recognize the woman he was with, but she was beautiful—long, curly red hair, almost the color of a purpley red marker. Her hair was the kind of curly I would have liked to have, the kind that would make me look like a woman in a painting, the kind of woman men might fall over for.

They were on the ship. The Titanic, I presumed. The lady at the front of the ship. Was it called the bow? The end part, where they usually put a fish or a mermaid. She stuck her hands out, and Leonardo stood behind her, holding her up.

I sagged back, almost ready to flop on the carpet again. It didn't make any sense. Why would this old movie be inside a safe, a safe where I had to find a key, if it didn't hold some significance?

I couldn't keep doing this. I needed to get home. My grandmother would be freaking out. Maybe she'd even called the police. I might end up in the blotter. I couldn't keep waiting for something to happen.

I sighed and let the tape play as I approached the library door.

Then I heard white noise from the machine. I turned back around, sighed again. The first tape over. Time to put in the next tape. Was there something on the next tape?

I didn't even care. I reached for the pause button. I'd leave it here, and someone else could deal with it.

"Dora."

I lifted my head.

A man faced the camera, looking straight at me. His skin like leather, a skeleton talking to me from the past.

31

Caroline

Kieran didn't see me at first. Maybe I could hide and go back around to the other side of the house. I darted forward. But my movement must have caught his eye, because he glanced over.

He crunched across the snow toward me. "Babe. What are you doing here?"

The endearment fell like a worm from his lips. It made me cringe.

"It's a long story. What about you?" I asked, clipped, businesslike.

"Looking for you." Kieran pushed his hands into the pockets of his flannel.

"Kyle's missing. Right now, our goal is to find him." I didn't have time to linger with Kieran. If he wasn't going to help me, I'd leave him.

"Um, okay." The wind blew through his hair, lifted it off the back of his neck.

I balled my hands into fists, squeezing them so tight my nails dug into my palms.

"You're not going to move?" I examined his eyes. They were milky-red, as always, the skin at his temples gray and wrinkling.

"It was hard enough to find you." He blinked into the sun. "I need a break."

"You need a break?" I advanced on him.

He stepped back, and I moved forward again. My rage propelled me. My hands ached to grab something, to rend the flesh.

"*You* need a break?"

"God!" Kieran put up a hand. "Caroline! Chill!"

"Stop telling me that!"

I tackled him.

My weight wasn't enough to bear him to the ground. But I punched him, fists flying at his smelly coat. He reeked. I couldn't land a punch, though, no matter how hard I tried. I pushed him up against the big door of the main house, pinning him as best as I could, my anemic blows unable to faze him.

I screamed, the primal force of my voice ripping from my throat. That was the best I could do, as I threw and kicked and wheeled, attempting over and over to bruise him like he'd bruised me.

The door gave way. Kieran toppled backward into the main hall-way. I pounced on him, still flailing, but in a moment, strong hands pulled me back. Kieran stared at me from the floor, a wild-animal look in his red eyes.

Moira held me. I recognized her scent, that spicy ginger. Her firm fingers put gentle pressure on my wrists.

Greg marched between Kieran and me, adding a human barrier in case I broke free.

"This is a civilized place." He bit off the words. "I don't want to have to call the police. My God."

"We saw you on the camera," Moira said, warm minty breath spilling against my ear. "I thought you were looking for Kyle?"

Sobs built in my chest. I choked on them, but then one of them burst out, strangled.

"I don't know what your problem is," Kieran said, more sober than I had heard him in a long time. "I was worried about you."

"I'm done with you."

Moira's fingers pushed against my pulse points. It was almost like she was giving me the strength, the energy to say it. My voice gained strength.

"I'm done."

"I saw Kyle on the camera," Moira said in my ear.

I froze. "Where is he?"

I PICKED my way down the driveway, which had finally been cleared. Little bits of rock and dirt bounced off my shoes, mixing with the snow.

When I got to the access road, I took a hard right. This road was pavement, and I moved faster, despite my improper footwear. At least, I had enough traction to run a little. My breath came harder as I sped up.

I reached the weight house and swiped the key card Moira had given me. I hadn't even known this place was here, but apparently, Kyle had found it, had found a way to get in. I flung the door open, panting.

Kyle lay on a bench, heaving a huge rack of weights into the air. The metal slammed down when he saw me. "Mom?"

I rushed to him. He sat up, and I snagged him around the neck, pulled him to me. Kyle groaned but consented to the hug.

As I released him, I studied his face, blooming with bruises of his own. The mirror to Aidan's, the opposite eye punched.

"Can we go home now?" he asked.

"I wish you would've told me you were coming here."

My heart fluttered as it slowed. I took him all in, this child I had made. His eyes as brown as mine. I couldn't see any of Kieran in him, not there. He was mine, and I'd keep him with me, at all costs.

"I'm sorry. I just got so mad." He fiddled with the weight on the end of the pole. "I hate Ohio, Mom. Do we have to stay here? Just because Grandma's here?"

I thought of the little house back in Chesterfield. How it wasn't yet unpacked.

"Why were you so mad, baby?"

His eyes filled.

"It's okay to cry," I told him.

"I'm not going to. It's fine. Are you and Dad getting divorced?"

I nodded.

He blew out a breath. "Okay. Yeah. It was shitty to find it out from Aidan. Are you sleeping with his dad?"

I recoiled. "Absolutely not."

We hadn't slept together. It wasn't a lie.

"Are you going to be?"

I lowered my head.

"I kissed him. That's all. He was my high school boyfriend." I licked my dry lips. "I'm not breaking up with your dad because I want to be with anyone else. I just want to... be."

Kyle didn't say anything. I could almost see the thoughts at war behind his flop of hair. I missed his baby curls. I used to let his hair grow out, but football had ended all that.

I extended my hand to my son. "Let's go, honey."

He stared up at me. "Where?"

"I don't know yet." I looked out the window at the access road, outside the weight house. I didn't know how far it went or how far it could take us. I knew that it could take us back, though. "We'll figure it out."

32

Patrick

I took careful steps down into the main lobby of the house.

I had all my stuff. My wallet and phone smelled terrible, but I had them with me. My coat was in the foyer closet.

When I'd peeked out from the guest room window, I saw Amy's van. The two women I'd slept with were both here... well, there was one other. But it seemed weird that the woman I lost my virginity to and the woman who'd borne my children had both come up this driveway.

I was going home with one of them.

I'd thought Amy and Aidan would leave without me, but they sat sullenly in front of the fireplace. Dusk had fallen, the sun creeping down into the horizon. It got dark so early now. A whole season of darkness ahead of us.

Greg came out of the kitchen. "I told them they couldn't leave until after dinner."

Dinner. I groaned.

"I don't need to eat." The ibuprofen had taken the edge off my fever, and I felt more like myself, but I still couldn't fathom the sight—or smell—of food. "Let's just go."

"Caroline isn't back yet," Greg said. "I'd like to make sure you're all back and accounted for, even if you don't plan to eat with us."

"Where is she?" I looked around, as if she might pop out from behind a piece of furniture.

"Wouldn't you like to know," Amy grumbled.

I ignored her.

"Kyle has been in the exercise building lifting weights." Greg tented his hands. "She went to retrieve him."

Amy perked up. "And where's Kieran, then?"

"With Moira. In the kitchen." Greg raised an eyebrow, his tone slipping into the realm of bitchy. "He told her he wants to go to culinary school. So, he's apprenticing."

I laughed.

"What's funny?" Greg asked, innocently.

And then the both of us burst into peals of laughter. It was almost like it used to be, with Jude. That tiny bit of snark.

Amy folded her arms.

"Don't be mean to him. He's the one who helped me find all of you." Then she looped one arm around the back of Aidan's shoulders. "No thanks to any of you."

I might be ignoring her for the rest of the week. Then we'd have to go to therapy. And I'd have to tell Matt where I had been. The thought of opening my phone and finding all his texts and emails made my stomach sink like a stone. My appetite would never return.

The door blew open, and Caroline strode in, hand in hand with Kyle. They dropped their hands as soon as they saw all of us. I imagined the teasing a fourteen-year-old might get if he was caught showing affection to his mother.

Moira poked her head out of the kitchen. "We're about done."

Her gaze traveled to meet Caroline's, but she said nothing else.

"Dinner?" Greg asked, stepping toward Caroline and Kyle.

He went to take their coats, and Caroline let hers drop into his hands. She stared at all of us sitting around the fire, as if the life had leached out of her during her time in the snow. Her porcelain cheeks flushed red.

"I think we should go," Caroline said.

My eyes flashed to hers. "But...the money."

Amy stood. I lurched toward a seat near the fireplace. Too hot, but it was a seat, and I could no longer stand. Caroline didn't have time to react to what I'd said.

On the staircase, a shadow moved down toward us. I gasped. Was it Jude? On closer inspection, it was only a small, skinny woman. *Erica.* I had to fight back my urge to vomit again. Guilt spilled through me. I was done here, but I wasn't done here.

Amy marched up to Caroline and poked her in the chest. "You slept with my husband."

Caroline shrugged. "So?"

Amy gasped, reeled back. "So, you admit it."

"Why wouldn't I?" Caroline looked back at her, blasé. "It was 1997. We were sixteen and horny."

My wife clucked. "That's not what I mean, and you know it."

"That's the only time we slept together. I mean, it was a bunch of times, but they weren't recent. Like I said, sixteen and horny." Caroline glanced over at Kyle. "If you do it, honey, make sure you use protection."

"Mom. Gross." Kyle put his hands over his ears. "I am over this place. Let's go."

Caroline looked around.

"Where's your dad? Probably off smoking something." She snorted.

"We've got some great shit." Erica sneaked into the circle of people around the fireplace. I saw the questioning looks on the others' faces as they tried to puzzle out who she was, and my belly tensed. *Please, God, don't let her do it. Don't let her ruin me.* Even though I supposed I was ruined anyway.

"Cannabis. Morphine, you know. For our guy up there." When no one said anything, she laughed. "Relax, people. I'm joking."

The joke fell flat, though. All I heard were the last four words. *Our guy up there.*

When I closed my eyes, I saw him dancing across that internal movie screen. He embodied life—that Cheshire grin, that monstrous intellect. So curious, always hungry for more—more sex, more love, more knowledge. Jude couldn't go, not now. I had missed so much of him. I had lost so much because... because why?

Caroline's face crumpled. Her legs gave out from beneath her, and she fell. She cried, burying her face into her hands. My wife stood, steps away from her, watching her like she was a theater act on display: The Crying Woman. But I knew what Caroline was feeling. What we were all feeling.

The money meant nothing. Our hearts would burst apart.

I thought of Hannah. Where was she? She was gone. We'd brought her daughter instead. Her surrogate. Her replacement. Her—

"Where's Dora?" Caroline asked.

33

Dora

Jude and I stared at each other across time.

"I knew you would get here." His voice was warm, if a bit weak. I pressed my hands together, twined them to keep them from shaking. "It wasn't an easy ride, was it? My dear. This is your victory."

My victory. I had solved it. There were no more clues left for me to untangle. This was the end.

I didn't love that, not as much as I'd thought I would. A part of me wanted more. Wanted Jude to send me on another wild trip into the unknown. I craved it, almost, the high that came from the inkling of an idea, and then the triumph that followed.

A smile teased at his lips. I felt sad for him. He didn't look at all like the man in the bed, but he was so thin. Probably at the very beginning of his disease. "Dora, I so hope you liked your variation."

He sounded so happy, so pleased with himself.

"Do you know the story of Elgar, my dear? How he wrote the variations for all his friends? You should read some of the books here, in the library. I've left them all to you." He chuckled. "Of course, it's very possible that you, Caroline, have made it here first. You've always been so driven. Only A-pluses for that gal." Jude winked at the camera. "But Dora still gets the books. She needs them, to grow her young mind."

He went serious. "Elgar talked about the dark saying that drove his Enigma theme. You, Dora, are named after one of those themes—the Dorabella theme. Miss Dora Penny was the young woman Elgar wrote his greatest codes for. And I wrote my greatest codes for you, my dear. My daughter."

I gasped again. Adrenaline shot through my twining hands, and my stomach fluttered. *Jude was my father.* I should've known it all along.

"Well, if Patrick isn't your father."

What?

Jude pouted.

"I'm not sure your mother even knows. But they've come such a long way with the genetic testing these days. I'm sure you could find out." He sighed. "My dear, if you've found this and I'm still alive, please seek me out. I would love to talk with you. My Dorabella, you may or may not be my biological child, but I've always considered you mine."

My throat tightened. I couldn't breathe. All these years without a father, now conveniently erased? *No.* Fuck that. He wasn't allowed to waltz in, even from the past, and claim his place in my life.

"Patrick, I suppose it could be you who sits before this tape. I did send you that extra clue." Jude grinned, as I tamped down my anger. "If it's you, just know I've always loved you."

Jude sat behind an oak desk. I wasn't sure where the camera had been recording. It looked just like an old-timey movie, wobbly footage and all.

"Now for the part you've been waiting for." Jude pulled open a drawer, slowly, and extracted a checkbook. "This is my gift to you, for making it this far."

Painstakingly, he took a pen to the check. I'd never seen a check before, other than on *The Price Is Right,* so I didn't have a clue what he was doing.

Jude held the check up to the light.

"Dora, you will be my beneficiary. You've made it this far, so I salute you. You've earned this." He paused, voice growing dark again. "Patrick, Caroline - you've disappointed me. Hannah's dead because of you. Because of the way you treated her, the way you tortured her. What the hell was in that drink you gave her that night? I can't say for sure. I was high off my ass. But when I saw that she had died, I knew. I never should have invited her to that party. Not because there was anything wrong with her." Jude stared into the camera, his glare icy. "Because there was something wrong with you."

Then he sat back, as if saying those things had exhausted him. I kept watching, my belly churning.

"I have made many mistakes in this life. I have done some great things. But you are both of those, Dora. And you deserve everything I have."

Blinking, as if I'd just come out of a dark movie theater, I left the library.

I walked, dazed, down the hall.

I was about to turn down the steps for the main lobby, when I hesitated. The night had just begun. The roads were clear now, and I had to get home as soon as possible.

But I had to say goodbye to him. I didn't know how much longer he'd be there.

I crept into his room and slipped into the seat beside my maybe-father. It smelled like carpet cleaner, overriding the medical, stale scent that had been present before.

"Hi," I said.

He didn't respond. As per usual.

I reached for his bony hand. The skin was gnarled underneath my palm. He wasn't that old, but the cancer had destroyed him. I found it hard to believe he had been so young and vibrant only a year or so ago, that the man on the TV and the man in the bed were the same person.

I cleared my throat. "Jude, I saw your video. I got to the end. It's Dora, by the way."

I expected a response. A crazy Lazarus moment, Jude rising from his almost-grave and embracing me.

But no. He kept breathing, the way he had been. Silently, gently.

"I don't know if you can hear me," I said, as if saying that would conjure an answer. "I'm a little mad, to be honest." More than mad, but the last thing I needed was to kill a dying man with my anger. "But I'm grateful. I'll be a good steward of your money."

The money felt like a dream. It wasn't real. But in my dream, I was already spending it on college. The thought of leaving Chesterfield made my heart light.

I clutched his hand, tears rolling down my cheeks. Waited there, hoping he might squeeze back.

Maybe he did. Maybe I imagined it.

After I left Jude, I resumed my trek down the stairs. Time to find someone to take me home.

As I descended into the lobby, I felt like a celebrity. All their eyes were on me, staring up from the lobby. Jude's friends—I didn't remember their names—the people who worked in the house. Were they all my employees now? Kyle and Aidan, standing apart from each other, both angry and sullen. A few women I didn't recognize, a man I didn't know. Patrick slumped in a chair by the fire, his skin nearly green. Caroline, her arms folded tight to her chest, pacing the front hallway.

When she saw me, she raced to me, wrapped me in a hug. "There you are! We were so worried."

Kyle grunted, across the room. "Hardly. You just now noticed she was gone."

Caroline smelled like a mom. My chest was so tight, as I thought about that. I'd never had that, not the way I wanted it. Caroline held me close, as if she never wanted to let me go. She could be an anchor. I was tired of being that for myself. I was ready to lean on someone else for a change.

My mom. What had Jude said? The memory was already hazy, growing dim. Caroline and Patrick had tortured my mother? Made her drink? Was it really their fault?

It was too much to unpack in that moment.

"I won the money," I said.

Caroline pulled back. "What?"

"I found the tape," I said.

Two of Jude's employees exchanged glances. Greg, was that the man's name? He approached me. Caroline's hand was still on the middle of my back. I liked having her there, like I had someone to advocate for me.

"Jude's recorded message?" he asked.

"Yes." I puffed out my chest. "It states that I'm his heir and that I'll inherit his estate."

No one moved. I sucked in air like it was coming from an oxygen tube.

"Well," Greg said.

Caroline rubbed her hand along my back.

"He's not dead yet," Greg said.

34

Caroline

Jude waited until after Christmas to die.

In the interim, we all visited him. I'd come after work to spend the evening with him. I'd tell him about my day, about the legal red tape I'd have to untangle daily. Not only at the firm, but in my personal life. I was working with Elaine to dissolve my marriage.

Jude was the best listener. He never had been before. He'd always flit away from you before you reached your point. He'd been maddening to talk to back then. But with his illness, he couldn't speak. A few times, he'd lift his head, and I knew he was there.

We didn't think he'd hang on that long. But his nurses knew. He wouldn't let go until he'd spent the time with us. We all owed it to each other, that time to heal. I'd spent so many years fighting it, denying that all of them still lived and breathed. And Jude had, too. He had traveled the world, accumulated his money, met so many people willing to stick with him to the end. He didn't need us. But he did.

In January, Erica noticed his breathing change. She called and told me to clear our calendars.

And on a Friday night, Patrick, Dora, and I wore heavy coats as we crunched up the long driveway to the house. Our breath puffed and fogged in the air.

Moira greeted us at the door. She embraced me first thing, helping me out of my coat. I sank into her shoulder, let her comfort me.

We could've made small talk. There was so much to catch up on. I had spent time with all of them, had seen Dora play in the band concert. But there wasn't enough time. There was never enough time.

All of us gathered around the bed. Dora held Jude's hand. I held hers. Patrick squeezed my hand, his long fingers draping around mine. Moira and Greg and Erica and all the other staff crowded into the room, too. He slipped away among friends, loved.

THE HEARSE CAME to retrieve the body and transport it to the mortuary.

Through all of it, Dora had stood, silent like one of the stone statues in the courtyard. But when the truck came, rolling up to the big front doors, she collapsed into me. She didn't cry, but her little body shook like a bird in a windstorm. I tightened her against me, hugging her close.

Once the truck was gone, Dora turned her face up to mine. "What does this mean? Will I inherit the money now?"

"Not right now. It'll go into a trust till you're eighteen. You'll have a trustee to take care of it until then."

Her cheeks drooped. "So, I won't be able to access it."

I wondered what it must be like to have a daughter. I'd never know that feeling. I smoothed her hair and let myself pretend Dora might be mine, even a sliver of her.

"Not necessarily. You may be able to receive distributions. But the will has to go through a lot of legal checking and paperwork. It'll be a while until you're assigned a trustee."

"Can you be my trustee?"

I hesitated. My life was in shreds. Kieran was planning to move back to California, although Kyle would be staying here with me, much to his dismay. I insisted he finish at least one year of school before deciding which parent to live with permanently. I'd be here in Chester-field with my mother, but I didn't know if I'd have time to help Dora.

"Maybe," I said. "I'll have to think about it."

She looked down, kicked the dirt. I let her go.

"You won't need the money till you're off to college though, right?" I couldn't think of why she would need it. A fifteen-year-old girl?

Dora's lips tightened. When she met my eyes, she seemed so much older. She didn't resemble Hannah as much anymore. Dora wasn't just a double of the frail teenager I'd known twenty years ago. She was a different woman.

"Jude told me about what happened," she said.

I blinked. "What?"

"He recorded it on the tape." Dora swallowed. "He said this entire game was set up to torture you. And to make sure I got the money. Because you hurt my mother."

I gaped, my lips open like a fish's. Thoughts of that night speared me, the guilt like a lance through my chest. Jude, teasing me with that prize. Bringing us back here, after all this time.

I DROVE Dora home that day. She brandished her key, and we stepped into the tiny, dark ranch house.

"Where's your grandmother?" I asked.

She flipped on the lights, even though it was the middle of the after-noon. "Who knows. Bridge club or something."

I swallowed. Fear flitted in my belly. I knew I should leave, but I felt responsible. Like I couldn't leave Dora here alone.

She turned to me. "I want to show you something."

How much did Dora really know about what had happened? I was a child. Hannah was, too. And it was so long ago. Jude couldn't possibly have told her the entire story. Not on video. Dora had explained to me how she'd found the extra codes in the library, how she'd uncovered the tape. He couldn't have remembered every detail, not so many years later.

I followed Dora down a long, dark hallway into a bedroom. It smelled dank, musty. To the right of the door, there was a wooden bureau littered with detritus: costume jewelry, credit cards, old receipts. Dora picked up a framed photo and held it up to me.

Graduation. I'd completely forgotten. Hannah had to stay back a year, so she didn't matriculate with our class. But in this photo, Jude, Patrick and I cheesed at the camera: me in my red cap and gown, them in their black ones. Cheap fabric that shone like plastic on the old film print.

"She kept this?" I studied the photo. If we'd tortured her like Jude said, if we'd done this to her, she wouldn't have remembered us as friends. She wouldn't have kept this front and center in her room, where she could always see it. My guilt flamed again, soured my stomach. I had been so cruel.

Dora shrugged. "I don't know why. I don't know... anything."

"I'm sorry." I pushed back the tears rising in my throat. "I'm so, so sorry."

35

Patrick

Amy and I sat on opposite ends of a long, gray couch.

The therapist faced us. Dr. Boone's beard was gray. Much like everything else in the room. Walls, carpet, too. I'd felt weird driving into the industrial complex. It didn't seem like the most comfortable place for couple's therapy. It looked a lot like the storage unit where I'd met Caroline that cold night to go back to our past. But there wasn't much office space in Chesterfield, and I was sure Dr. Boone's options had been limited.

"Tell me about yourselves." He had a long legal pad open on his lap, pen poised above it. We were a blank case, a new sheet of paper.

"Patrick cheated on me." Amy turned up her nose.

"I did not."

Amy crossed one long, thin leg over the other. "Did too."

"Okay, okay." Dr. Boone held up a flat palm. "Let's not be children."

I frowned at my wife. She was so far away from me, her bottom was

339

almost placed in the wedge between the couch arm and the cushion. For the past few months, I'd wondered if this marriage was even worth saving.

"It's a fact," Amy said.

Dr. Boone's gaze tracked across an invisible line from Amy to me.

I held up my hands. "You want the truth?"

Dr. Boone scratched some words onto his legal pad. *Both of them are insane. May need backup.* "I thought you could give me some background about why you're here in therapy and what you want to accomplish."

"The truth is—"

Amy stared off into the distance, focusing on a painting on the far wall.

So, I confessed to Dr. Boone. The twenty-first century priest. Although, I'd done it once already, in the dead of night, to a woman who may have forgotten my name by now. "The truth is that I cheated on Amy in 2002."

Her neck swiveled toward me. Her pink lips parted. "What?"

"I can pull up a couple's meditation if that would help," Dr. Boone said. "Deep breaths and all. Do you need a moment?"

"I need a moment to punch his brains out," Amy said, teeth clenched.

"And I deserve it." I felt lighter. I'd been carrying the secret my entire life, and that night I confessed it to Erica, I'd felt as if I'd unearthed it from a grave. Dusted off its bones. And I'd been wearing it around my neck ever since.

Now that I knew Dora, now that she was flesh and blood and not some conceptual girl, I couldn't ignore her. Each time I saw her—most recently at Jude's memorial, where we'd scattered his ashes off the back of the courtyard—I couldn't ignore the curve of her cheek, the strength of her jaw. She wasn't all Hannah, not Hannah's clone. She hadn't emerged from Hannah's head like an ancient deity.

As I'd watched Dora and Aidan that day. They stood together, huddled close. I worried they might start dating, and then I'd have to confront the uncertainty. She could be mine. She could be Jude's. When I asked Aidan later, he shook his head. He wasn't ready to go out, he'd said. But Dora was a friend, and a good one, and so that fear itched in the back of my brain.

Did I want her to be mine? I didn't know. If I was honest, I liked that she was one of ours. It was as if I shared something with Jude, and until the truth came out, the mystery would remain between us. Even with him gone, she was something we had both been a part of. Bringing that girl into the world.

Amy fisted her hands in her hair. "You've got to be kidding me, Patrick."

"I'm sorry. But I might have another child."

"Oh my God!" Amy shrieked.

Dr. Boone looked at the clock.

It took some time to recover from that. Although Liam had finally transitioned into a big-boy bed, I was still relegated to the guest bedroom. I'd slid back into bed one night, and she acted as if I wasn't there, but at least, she didn't kick me out. I resigned myself to my position, a man without affection, a man who earned his fate, and I let life slide by. We were together, and not together—somewhere in between.

One night, I was reading in the study. Caroline and I had been texting back and forth about Dora, and Caroline hoped I'd take over Dora's trust from Jude's estate. I wanted to, but I wasn't a lawyer, and I needed to learn the ropes. I'd get a small stipend from the estate for the job, which would help, since Matt had all but let me go from ForkFlavor. I ran payroll once every other week, but I rarely went into the office anymore. I was just waiting for him to revoke my access again.

Jude had left the business as a separate entity, which was confusing, but it would provide for the staff and run the big house until I figured out what to do. It occurred to me that in Dora's stead, I'd be in charge of Jude's games and the future of his company.

With the papers spread across my desk, I actually felt excited. I opened my laptop and pulled up some spreadsheets, running some scenarios to expand the mansion and the revenues we could bring in.

"What are you doing?" Amy stood on the landing, where the steps to my office met the kitchen. She wore a light swing dress, and her feet were bare.

"Liam in bed?"

She nodded. "Aidan went out with Kyle."

I raised my eyebrows. "You're kidding."

"I'm not. Kyle's going to therapy. He's supposed to forgive people he's hurt." Amy licked her lips. "Aidan wasn't sure about it, but he said Caroline told him that if Kyle tried anything again, she'd punch him in the face herself."

It was the first time Amy had said Caroline's name without wincing.

The long space stretched between us.

She drifted down the stairs and stood beside me. It was the closest she had been for weeks. I smelled her rose perfume, the intoxicating nearness of her, and resisted the urge to wrap her in my arms.

"These are the books for Jude's business," I said. "I told you about Dora's trust, right?"

"Yes." The word came out chilly.

"Well, I'm her trustee, and this is a big job. Potential income for us, too." I swept my arms around the office. "We can keep the old homestead, and I can leave ForkFlavor."

"About time," she muttered.

I reached for her hand, but she swatted me away. "Why did you do this, Patrick? I mean, it was one thing to have a little fling while I was overseas in college... but to keep this from me for so many years?"

I surveyed the sweep of papers across my desk. They suddenly looked more than interesting. "I've told you I'm sorry."

"I don't know if we can survive this. Honestly. I've been so angry at you." She wrapped a long hank of blonde hair around her wrist.

Amy was as beautiful as the day we'd met. Part of me hated the thought that I had hurt her. The other part of me knew it had been inevitable.

I turned my face up to her, forced myself to look at her. "What do you want, Amy? Tell me and I'll do it."

She kept twisting that hair. We were two people trying to meet, but we kept missing each other.

～

AFTER SOME BRAINSTORMING and some major group texts—me, Caroline, Greg, and Moira—I turned in my notice to ForkFlavor that night. Matt barely acknowledged it.

In the morning, my car wound up the long driveway to Jude's place. It was a gorgeous, sunny morning in May. I parked off to the side of the turnaround in front of the door, then rang the bell. My briefcase bumped gently against my thigh.

Greg greeted me with a grin, and Moira wasn't far behind.

"I'm telling you, you're brilliant." Greg clapped me on the shoulder. "I was so worried we wouldn't have a job after all this."

"Or a place to live." Moira winked. "And I was afraid I might never see your girl again."

"I don't think you need to worry about that." I winked back. "Shall we get to work?"

By lunchtime, I was happily ensconced in office life. Spreadsheets, dry-erase board charts and scribbles, scratched-out ideas on paper spread all over the conference table in the offices. Greg popped in, handed me my new ID badge. I'd be able to come and go from the house as I pleased.

And that did please me. Because there was a piece of Jude here.

On my way out that evening, I strode to my car, the warm breeze playing on my face. I felt happy for the first time in a while. I had work now that would fulfill me. I had my children to see when I got home. I'd play trains with Liam and talk to Aidan about his day, ask him how school was going, if things were better with Kyle now.

Amy had texted me. I clicked on it, not expecting much. But when I read the words, I paused for a moment, let them sink in. *I love you.*

36

Dora

I bumped off the bus with my bassoon and trombone for the last time.

Mallory had cried. Ms. Krieger had too, but I thought her tears were genuine. Mallory may as well have been a crocodile.

"What am I going to do without you?" she'd wailed as the buses pulled up to the front of the school. "I don't believe it!"

"I'm not going to the moon." I smiled. "I'll still be here for band. And next year, we'll be sixteen. We'll be able to drive. You can visit as much as you want."

"Whatever. It's like I'm Jekyll and I'm losing my Hyde." She paused. "Wait, that's not right at all."

I waved at her one last time before boarding the bus. I'd be going to a new STEM school in the fall. It was a few towns over, much closer to civilization, so I'd have an even more punishing ride. But I could listen to audiobooks, and I could do my homework. And my bus would bring me right back to Chesterfield High for marching band practice at 3:30 sharp every afternoon.

I knew it would be a lot of work, but I was excited. My first chance to stretch myself, to learn what I could really do. I didn't know what discipline would interest me most. I loved astronomy, and physics, and codes, of course. But I also loved English and reading. There was so much to explore.

And college—oh, I couldn't wait. The multitudes of them spread out in front of me like a buffet. So many to choose from. Could I go to a few of them, earn credits from each place? Cobble them together into the most epic of degrees? And study abroad. I couldn't wait to get my passport, couldn't wait to explore the possibilities for different trips.

Jude had made it all possible. I kept a picture of him inside my phone case now. It was from before I knew him, when he was young and vibrant. He mugged for the camera, his elastic face stretching to reveal his dazzling smile. He looked like the man he'd been when he was like me, when he had all possibilities ahead of him. And he'd known he would chase them all.

He had loved deeply, lived life the way all of us should live. At least, that was how I saw it. I'd learn my own lessons as I grew up. And I was still angry that he hadn't taken the time to find me when I was a child. When I could've given him even more love. My maybe-father hadn't been perfect, but he was still mine.

I banged through our front door and dumped my stuff on the floor.

"Last day," Grandma sighed. She sat at the table, hands wrapped around a mug of tea.

"Yeah." I rummaged through the fridge for a snack, settling on a cheese stick and a bottle of cherry limeade.

"Must be nice?" She hazarded a smile.

I peeled the wrapper off the stick and tossed it into the trash. "Yeah."

I planned to spend the summer online, at the library, taking place-ment tests and reading course material so I wouldn't be too far behind in my sophomore year at the STEM school. My other goal was to get up to Jude's house for some of the time to work with Patrick and the staff. It would be like a real business internship. Jude's games weren't part of my inheritance, but I wanted to make sure the company would remain successful and vibrant. Just another one of my diverse interests, I supposed.

But I was grateful that we wouldn't spend a boring summer locked inside.

Caroline had written me a check for twenty thousand dollars. She said she knew I would pay her back once I had access to the estate, but I got the impression that the money was her penance.

My crazy grandmother and I sat in companionable silence, because if she even made one comment about my hair or makeup or lack thereof, I'd tell her where to go. But instead, she reached across the table to squeeze my hand. "Your mom would be so proud of you."

I wasn't sure if Grandma was right about that. It was true that I thought about my mother every day. But those memories were fading with time, and I wasn't sure what to believe anymore. What Caroline and Patrick had done to my mother was in the past, but that photo still rested on her dresser. Jude had engineered that entire game to teach them a lesson, but had he also done it to teach himself a lesson? To atone for his own role in my mother's difficult life?

I didn't want to think of Hannah as a victim anymore. She was her own person, and she had made her own decisions. They shouldn't have hurt her like they did, but it wasn't their fault she died in that crash... was it?

And I didn't know if she'd be proud of me, because she'd never made an effort to know me.

College would be a great place for therapy. There was free help at all the campus health centers. I had a lot of my own shit to unpack.

"That reminds me." With one hand still in mine, Grandma sorted through a pile of mail that sat on the windowsill. "You got this today."

The DNA results.

I held the envelope, stared at it. My heart sped up. I traced the outline of the return address, with the name and logo of the DNA company imprinted in the left-hand corner.

"Are you hoping for a particular result?" Grandma asked.

My fingers trembled, and the envelope shook.
I put it down, on top of the stack of mail.
"No," I said.
The news could wait.

Epilogue

Before

What kind of cancer eats a man so young? he'd thought when he got the diagnosis.

Jude wondered what it would be like when it did happen. It was coming—it was coming for them all one day—but he had more to do.

He closed his eyes and drifted as his car wound through hills and valleys, heading for the freeway. Such a long way from Chesterfield to the airport.

He'd spent so many years building an empire. After college, he interned at Psych Games, and it didn't take him long to rise in the ranks there. Founded his own company by the time he turned twenty-six. Changed from Jude Lassiter to Jude the Game Master, created the world surrounding him from scratch. He'd done that in high school, with his friends. It had been easy enough to do so with colleagues, subordinates. He'd reinvented the world of gaming by turning real life into one.

It couldn't be over. He needed more time.

But he hadn't been able to stop thinking of Hannah. How he left her. How they all left her.

And all he could think about was how each one of them owed her.

Jude stepped carefully onto the curb. He ran a hand over his peach-fuzz head and shouldered his bag. His driver eased away from the departures drop-off into the sea of flowing traffic. Cars coming in and going from the airport, planes taking off in the distance. Roaring all around him, the sounds of the world.

When he got to the beach, he'd locate the cabana he'd rented. He'd set his stuff down, grab a folding chair and sit on the sand. He'd lie there, in the sun, letting the rays fall down on him. What was the harm now? And he'd eat. God, would he eat.

SHE MET him outside the airport, wearing a simple white tee and jean shorts. Not smiling, but not frowning. Her face held the most perfect neutral expression, like a doll's. Not giving away a thing about what lurked in her head. "You're doing it, then?"

He nodded. "All of it."

"Dora will get the money."

Dora. Her voice an echo of this woman's. He could still hear it, through the thin walls. That house, never built to last. A facade in so many ways. "It'll be in a trust, yes."

She breathed out a sigh. Her birdlike ribcage contracted.

"You're not going to reach out to her?" he asked.

People swarmed and streamed all around them, rushing to their destinations, but she didn't move.

"You're the last person to judge."

He arched an eyebrow, but it was a fair point.

"She's never needed me before. And I have so much work to do before I can go back to her."

Hannah's face changed then.

He remembered the moment he'd found out she was still alive. Her inexplicable voice, tones he thought he'd never hear again. Her variation spinning inside his head. His revenge story exploded from the inside. Yet he had to do it, had to continue with his mission. No longer avenging her death but simply doing penance.

On that curb outside the airport, Jude could almost feel her holding back tears. That hesitation hanging in the air between them: all the ways they'd messed up.

All the ways that little girl had suffered.

Hannah gritted her teeth. "It's the best ending we'll get."

"Are you going to join me in Costa Rica? I can get you a ticket."

She shook her head. "I don't know what I'm going to do."

He lifted his chin. "Take a good look, then, for this might be the last you see of me."

She laughed. "I'll never believe that."

"You never did say how you walked away from that crash."

"I never said I was in that crash."

"And you found me..."

"Your number hasn't changed in eighteen years."

"Sue me." It was his turn to laugh. "Actually, don't. I won't be alive to defend myself."

Jude was exhausted. He had wasted every surprise he could conjure. And he could no longer judge Hannah or even himself.

So, he walked away from her, leaving her in the crowd. And she was gone again, like she'd never been there at all

Afterword

This book explores issues related to bullying, depression, and culpability. While the gray areas in the book are fiction, they are much more serious in real life. If you or a child in your life is experiencing depression and/or bullying, I encourage you to reach out for help. Here are some resources to get you started.

Stop Bullying - https://www.stopbullying.gov/resources/external

National Alliance on Mental Illness - https://www.nami.org/Home

The Cybersmile Foundation - https://www.cybersmile.org/

Find a Psychologist - https://www.findapsychologist.org/category/healthcare-topics-issues/bullying/

Psychology Today - https://www.psychologytoday.com/us/therapists

Acknowledgments

This is the second novel I've written that I consider fully formed (after HOW TO REMEMBER). It was SO close to getting traditionally published. It came from a dream, and I've been passionate about it ever since I started it in 2017. I hope readers enjoy it. It brings me closure to have it out there after it lived so long in my head.

As I mentioned in the introduction, I had this novel on submission with my former agent, Lynnette Novak. I have to thank her for the edits she provided. I also am grateful that she introduced me to so many wonderful writers in the Seymour Crime Writers group (now the Coast to Coast Crime Writers). Thanks to everyone in the group, and specifically to Michelle Chouinard and Lisa Kaplan for their continued support.

Thanks also to my other wonderful writers' groups:

Ohio Writers on Facebook

Northeast Ohio Sisters in Crime

The Brain Trust: Julie Hatcher, Jane Ann Turzillo, L.A. McGinnis, Danielle Haas, Wendy Koile, Kathryn Long/Bailee Abbott. Look up their books!

To all the libraries and bookstores who have added my work to their collections and hosting me for speaking engagements—thank you so much. Black Cat Books in Medina deserves a special shout-out for their promotion of I LOVED THE MOTHMAN. I wouldn't be half as successful without them.

I cannot do any of this without the support of the Duskbound team: Kaytalin Platt, Mike X Welch, Aly Welch, and G.A. Finocchiaro. I am proud of the collaboration we have formed over the years. I am especially proud that we have created a robust storefront of items we can sell together. I've always wanted to found my own publishing house, and it's a hundred times better with friends—it's OUR publishing house.

My mother read HOW TO REMEMBER and actually liked it. Thanks, Mom!

Thanks to my coworkers for always putting up with my book nonsense.

Thank you to the readers who have supported I LOVED THE MOTHMAN and my other recent books. I have been bowled over by all the love. Don't worry, there will be more Mothman. He just didn't really fit in this story.

Thank you to my family—Ed, Oliver, and Henry Dubiel—and my sister, Jamie Stevenson.